HE WHO HAS AN EAR

By Norman Audi

PublishAmerica
Baltimore

First printing

At the specific preference of the author, PublishAmerica allowed this work to remain exactly as the author intended, verbatim, without editorial input.

ISBN: 1-4241-6415-X
PUBLISHED BY PUBLISHAMERICA, LLLP
www.publishamerica.com
Baltimore

Printed in the United States of America

DEDICATION

I would like to dedicate this book to my wonderful wife Suzie. She has been at my side for our forty years of marriage, has been a terrific wife and a great mother to our six children. She is a Proverbs 31 woman and I would extol her at the city gates if we had any.

ACKNOWLEDGEMENTS

I want to thank my wife Suzie, Greg and Carol Loss, and Paul and Susan Strand for editing this book. Carol has been instrumental in working with the publisher to get the book published. I would also like to thank Rob Livie, my son-in-law, for doing the front and back covers. May God bless them mightily.

FOREWORD

Norman Audi has written a very practical book that will be most helpful to many who want to understand how they can begin to hear God. *He Who Has An Ear* is one of the most practical books I have read on this subject. I believe many who read it will discover that they have already been hearing God speak to them, but they didn't know how to recognize His voice.

I found the biblical survey of God speaking and how He spoke to be very helpful. But, even more helpful was the section on how to discern His voice from other voices one could hear in his/her mind. The wisdom on how to act on the voice and how to apply the directions from God were also helpful. Norman Audi has worked to demystify "hearing the voice of God."

The strong emphasis upon the importance of knowing the Bible as a safeguard for discerning the voice of God will alleviate the fears of many Evangelicals. Norman Audi does not believe Jesus' words, "My sheep hear my voice." were meant only for a short period of time. He doesn't believe the followers of Jesus were to expect Him to speak to them only until the death of the Apostles or the canonization of the Bible. No, because of his commitment to the Bible, Norman believes Jesus meant what He said. Norman believes the Lord of the Church wants to speak to His Church by speaking to those within it who make it up. He believes that as Jesus continued his acts through His followers in the book of Acts, he still is continuing His acts today.

Norman and his wife Suzie have been with me on many of my International Ministry Trips through Global Awakening, where they have helped pray for the sick and cast out demons. I have watched them minister with integrity and compassion. He has led many people throughout his life to hear the voice of God. It is exciting that he will be able to teach thousands more the same practical steps that he personally has taught so many.

This is not a complicated book for scholars, but a book for everyone, especially the layperson. There is great power that comes from the ability to hear the voice of God because the rhema words of God creates faith, and faith releases the miraculous power of God. I discovered about 20 years ago when I first began to learn about God's speaking gifts today that they were powerful. The word of the Lord, whether it is perceived to be simply "knowing" that God has communicated something to you, or came as a gift of the Spirit is a powerful experience. Prophecy and Words of Knowledge are especially powerful in their ability to release faith and bring healing to either body or soul, and often both.

Prophecy has great power to bring good to a Christian or a church, but if mishandled it also has great power to hurt someone or even cause problems in the church. You have to decide to play it safe without the power of prophecy or face the possible release of power for good and for harm, if prophecy is mishandled. Believing that God speaks today is like handling nitroglycerin. Prophetic words have great power for good or bad if mishandled. I determined that I did not want to miss the power that they could bring, but I also didn't want to experience as a pastor the destruction of mishandling prophecies. I had a major conference each year for 5 years on prophecy and many other seminars and sermons on prophecy so we would know how to handle prophecies. Norm's new book serves this same purpose. But, it isn't limited to the gift of prophecy, or the gift of the word of knowledge. Its application is so broad that it also helps the non-charismatic or non-Pentecostal who has no language or titles for the "still small voice of God (") through which He leads His servants.

My grandmother knew the voice of God. She first heard it audibly when she was a rather new Christian. He told her to go into the bedroom and pray and he would heal her large goiter. She obeyed and He healed her. She told me it felt like a hot hand went down her throat causing the large goiter to instantly disappear. My grandmother was not a Charismatic, nor was she a

Pentecostal. She lived her entire Christian life as a General Baptist. This experience of hearing an audible voice was extremely rare for her. I actually don't know if she ever heard it audibly again. But, the internal voice of God she heard many times. When I was explaining to my grandmother what "words of knowledge" were and "prophecy" her eyes sparkled and she said, "So that is what it is called. I have had many experiences like that.' My grandmother was delighted to understand that she was moving in the gifts of the Spirit, was having words of knowledge and receiving prophecies. She knew she was hearing from God, and in the country Baptist Churches she attended it was just called, "the Lord showed me that…" or "the Lord led me to…" or "the Lord wants to…"

I believe our hymns are sometimes more biblical than our theology. For example, many Christians who attend churches who do not believe prophecy or other gifts are for today, still sing with full confidence the truth of the words of the hymn, *In The Garden,*

> I come to the garden alone
> While the dew is still on the roses
> And the voice I hear, falling on my ear
> The Son of God discloses
> And he walks with me
> And he talks with me
> And he tells me I am His own
> And the joy we share as we tarry there
> None other has ever known
> He speaks and the sound of His voice
> Is so sweet the birds hush their singing
> And the melody that He gave to me
> Within my heart is ringing
> And he walks with me
> And he talks with me
> And He tells me I am His own
> And the joy we share as we tarry there
> None other has ever known
> I'd stay in the garden with Him
> 'Tho the night around me be falling
> But He bids me go; through the voice of woe
> His voice to me is calling

And He walks with me
And He talks with me
And He tells me I am His own
And the joy we share as we tarry there
None other has ever known

Bottom line, Norman Audi helps us to understand that anytime we have felt led of God, we have heard him speak to us in one of his many ways of speaking. Perhaps it helps to understand that hearing and seeing in the Kingdom of God is actually perceiving that we have been communicated to by the Spirit of God. Norman's book will cause many to have the "aha" moment that my grandmother had as I shared with her what I was learning about the gifts of the Spirit. You too will perhaps hear yourself say, "So that is what that was."

"I knew it was God, I just didn't know what to call it." And, for many others, it will be an even more exciting revelation that will come by the understanding you will receive through *He Who Has An Ear* the revelation that you have been hearing from God, and didn't know it.

Don't set this book back down on the bookshelf or book table, and walk away without it. You need this book. It will help you. There are things to learn that will make your walk with Jesus more intimate. What could be more important and exciting than learning to better recognize the voice of the Good Shepherd that has been speaking to you? Isn't it time your reception became clearer so you could respond? He's waiting for your response.

Randy Clark
President and Founder
Global Awakening

ENDORSEMENTS

"Norm Audi's *He Who Has An Ear* reads like a textbook for discipleship. No matter where you are in your spiritual walk, you can put his principles to use immediately. This treatise includes a virtual who, what, when, where, and why of listening to the Divine. Norm's personal illustrations show how God works in the little things of life as well as major decisions. If every Christian operated in these truths, we would have a different world—imagine if all Christians actually said and did what they saw and heard the Father doing! Norm has lived the life, walked the walk-now he talks the talk! I highly recommend both Norm and his book."

Bishop Harry R. Jackson, Jr.
Senior Pastor Hope Christian Church
Founder High Impact Leadership Council

"I work at CBN News and love to bring people the news of what God is doing in the earth today. One thing in particular He's doing is calling His people to listen to him. And my good friend Norm Audi has done us a great service by writing this pithy and practical guide about listening to God. Now I don't have to just trust what Norm's saying in this book. Because you see, I've known Norm for years and I go to his house church, so I've been intently watching up close Norm walking out what he's talking about—that you can hear from God for all things both great and small in your life. Norm does and has taught the skill to all those around him who have ears to hear. Now you can learn, too, by reading these pages with an open heart. They're full of Bible, belief, and they're believable. Norm goes deep into the Word and completely covers the theory, but also gives plenty of practical, down-to-earth advice and lively, fun anecdotes. Listen up and you'll soon be listening to the Lord who loves you so."

Paul Strand
Senior Washington Correspondent
CBN News

"Because of his proven track record over many years Norm (Norman) is highly qualified to write *He Who Has An Ear.* I've been with him in ministry settings and have seen first-hand the amazing results of his hearing and then doing the will of God.

"I highly recommend this book because it takes the mystery out of hearing the voice of God. You will begin to hear God's voice with greater clarity, which I believe is critical in these days.

"This is an invaluable, practical handbook on the art of hearing God."

Garry Oates,
Author, *Open My Eyes, Lord*
International Conference Speaker

Contents

PROBLEMS IN LISTENING TO THE LORD

MORE LESSONS IN PUTTING LISTENING INTO PRACTICE

PREFACE

There was a time when I didn't know how to listen to the voice of the Lord. I would hear other Christians say, *"The Lord told me this or the Lord told me that,"* and I would wonder how do they know it's really God? I would hear Christian leaders telling how the Lord was leading them to do certain things and wonder how this could be possible. I had grown up with the misunderstanding that when people heard voices, they were ready for a mental institution. With this mindset I would pray to the Lord, not really expecting to *hear* His voice, instead just trusting He heard mine.

The first time I was aware of the Lord speaking to me was when I was in the hospital with a bad back. As I was lying there trying to get well, thoughts kept coming to my mind that weren't mine. What was going on here? Were they going to come take me away too?

Thoughts kept coming in a gentle, conversational tone and each time I would test the Spirit. It wasn't long before I knew without a doubt it was God's voice speaking to me. As our conversations progressed, I became more and more curious. I wanted to learn more about the *still small voice of the Lord.*

I had been correctly taught to test everything against the written Word of God, the Bible, and began to search the Scriptures on the subject of listening to the voice of the Lord. What really amazed me was how the Bible was filled with conversations between God and man. As I studied, I also found tapes, books and teachings on hearing God's voice. Years ago not much was written on this subject aside from the Bible, but now I discovered many such teachings. Tapes by Joy Dawson of Youth with a Mission were especially helpful. However, the majority of what I learned came from the Word of God.

My own personal experience, the experiences of others in listening and the results of teaching numerous others to listen to the Lord has played a major role in writing this book. I want to convey to you what I learned so you too can experience the joys of a closer walk with our Lord.

Christians for the most part want to listen to the Lord, but they don't know how. It is my prayer that this book will lead you step by step in learning to listen to God's voice. As I progressed in my search, a number of questions came to mind and I'm sure others have wondered the same thing as well.

> What is the will of God for my life? How will I know it?
> What are the different ways God can lead us?
> What is the most common way God leads us?
> How do I learn to listen to God?
> How do I know it is the Lord speaking and not Satan or my own voice?
> How do I know I am not being misled?
> How do I test the Spirit?
> What happens when I do not hear anything?
> How do I overcome my doubts that it is the Lord speaking to me?
> What should I do if I make mistakes in listening?
> What if other people are not hearing the same thing I am hearing?
> What part does confirmation play in the listening process?
> How do I get confirmation?
> What should I do when the direction I am receiving conflicts with authorities, such as my elders or pastor?
> What should I do when someone gives me a *word from the Lord* that I do not understand or relate to?

This book will attempt to answer these and other questions. As you progress, I pray you will gain insight into problems you may have already experienced in listening. When you are finished, you should be in a better position to understand the art of listening to God and understanding His ways.

If you are born again and have accepted Jesus Christ as your Lord and Savior, you have the Spirit of God. God is your Father and He wants to communicate with you. It doesn't matter what denominational background you are from, you can be hearing from God.

It is not my intent to push any particular religion or doctrine. Rather, I want to teach *Christians* how to listen to the voice of the Lord. There may be some parts of this book you disagree with because they don't fit into your doctrine. I simply ask that you keep an open mind and continue reading. Doctrinal differences pale in comparison to the need for all Christians to learn to listen to our Lord.

However, if you do not know what it is to be born again or saved, or if you're not sure you are born again, you *CAN* become a child of God. Romans 10:9 says:

> ***"If you confess with your mouth that Jesus Christ is Lord and believe in your heart that God has raised Him from the dead, you shall be saved."***

If you want to become a child of God and not just His creation, you can be born of God by saying from your heart the following:

> ***Father, I confess that I am a sinner, and I ask you to forgive me for all my sins. I repent (turn my back) from my sins and I renounce Satan and all that he stands for. I want to be a child of God, born again by the Holy Spirit. I believe that God raised Jesus Christ from the dead. Please cleanse me with the blood of Jesus Christ. Jesus, I ask you to come into my heart to be my Lord and Savior. I choose to turn my life over to you.***

If you prayed this prayer from your heart, you are born again. Congratulations! Rejoice and be glad, because now you are a *child of God!* God is now your Father and has saved you from your sins. In addition to being your Savior, He wants to be Lord of your life. He wants you to learn about Him, submit to His ways, follow Him and listen to His voice.

In order to get to know someone, you must spend time with him or her. In the same way, to get to know God, you must spend time reading the Bible and studying Scripture. Find a Bible-believing church and worship there as you begin to learn the ways of God. This is extremely important, for unless you are constantly in the Word and learning balance in a fellowship of believers, you can easily be deceived.

Now that you know for sure God is your Father, you have every right to hear from Him. As you apply the principles you learn in this book, you will begin a new and exciting Christian adventure. You are going to find out what it is to be led by the Spirit. And if you're a long-time believer, but all this talk of hearing from God is new to you, you'll finally have that fellowship with God for which you have yearned, but never gotten in your Christian walk. You are going to walk with God and talk with Him, not just sing songs about it. Your Christian walk will never be dull again! As you learn to be led by the Spirit, God will reveal Himself in new and exciting ways. Your life will never be the same.

Norman Audi

Chapter One

HOW DOES GOD SPEAK?

O ur wonderful God is a God of variety! He speaks to us in so many different ways that we don't always recognize them as being God. We have our own ideas as to how God should speak to us, and we limit Him to those ways. We decide *this is how God should lead me, and this is how I will be led.* God, knowing our frailties and tendency toward rigidity, will go along with our narrow finite view. But know for a certainty, we cannot limit God in His ways. Oh, how we try, but oh, how we fail.

I am going to tell you about some of the ways God speaks. I may not list them all, but at least you will have an appreciation for His variety and uniqueness. There is so much more I could say on each subject, but I'm limiting the discussion on each one in order to concentrate more fully on the last one, *the still small voice of the Lord.*

The Written Word

The principal way God speaks to us is through His written Word. He has revealed Himself to us in the Bible for a reason: that we may know Him more fully. The Old Testament is Jesus Christ concealed, and the New Testament is Jesus Christ revealed. In order for us to know our Lord and Master, Jesus Christ, and understand the ways of God, we must study the Word in both the Old and New Testaments.

The Bible says it best: ***"Do your best to present yourself to God as one approved, a workman who does not need to be ashamed and who correctly handles the word of truth." (2 Timothy 2:15)***

We cannot know God unless we are constantly in His Word. Sometimes we will seek revelation from God and what we are seeking is already found in the written Word if we would only look there. He has spoken through the Bible and will continue to speak to us through the written page. He wants us to use our *minds* as we learn of Him through the Scriptures. The greatest commandment is to **"...*love the Lord your God with all your heart and with all your soul and with all your mind....*" (Matthew 22:37)** God does not want us to be mindless robots.

The Bible has to be our constant source of Spiritual nourishment. Without a strong foundation in the written word and knowledge of God, we are only playing at being Christians. We must learn to feed on the Word, study the Word, memorize the Word, meditate on the Word and continually live in the Word. All revelation of God must begin and end with the written Word, the Bible.

Finally, and most importantly, any revelation that is contrary to the written Word is not from God, for God will not contradict Himself.

Witness of the Spirit as We Read the Bible

I'm sure there have been times for all of us while reading a particular verse, chapter or story that something will suddenly pop out and grab our attention. The Holy Spirit is personalizing that verse for us. He will make it clear that that particular written Word is meant for us for a situation in the past, present or future. One phrase that is used to explain this is, "*the Word was made alive to me.*" The written Word of God (the Greek word is *logos*) has now become the *Rhema* (Greek word for spoken Word of God) to us for a situation on our heart.

The problem with this is, more than any other method, many expect God to speak only in this way and will not accept any other way of hearing from Him. In doing this, we put limits on God by not allowing Him the freedom to lead us by other methods. Please do not misinterpret what I am saying here. The Bible is the living, revealed Word of God and I am not saying to stop seeking answers and confirmations in the Word.

I love the Bible and purposely use much in the Bible to prove the reality of the spoken Word in our lives. What I am saying is to be more receptive to receiving a Word from the Lord in any way He chooses to impart it. Be open to other ways we will be discussing, especially the still small voice.

Dreams

God used dreams to convey messages a number of times in the Bible. He gave Joseph several dreams indicating that his father, mother and brothers would bow down before him. (Genesis 37:5-10) As a lad of seventeen, he did not always handle his dreams very well. He was his father's favorite and, I imagine, was arrogant and full of pride. I suspect he even boasted to his family, especially his older brothers that they would bow down before him. You can guess how that went over.

If you have eleven big brothers and most of them want to kill you, there must be a good reason. They were probably fed up with their bratty younger brother's pompous attitude. The fact that their father favored Joseph above the others didn't help either. Joseph needed to be taught a lesson and it was God's plan to teach him. *"Pride goes before destruction, a haughty spirit before a fall." (Proverbs 16:18)* Because Joseph was prideful, God had to humble him before He could use him.

Joseph's hardships caused him to draw close to the Lord. He could have been angry and bitter and backed away from God for allowing these great misfortunes to occur, but he didn't. We too have to learn the same lesson. No matter what befalls us, God will never leave us nor forsake us. He will always be there for us.

Other examples of dreams and their interpretations involve the prisoners' dreams in Genesis, chapter forty and Pharaoh's dreams in chapter forty-one. In each case, Joseph interpreted those dreams correctly through revelation given by God. When Pharaoh told Joseph he heard that he could interpret his dream, Joseph said, *"I cannot do it, but God will give Pharaoh the answer he desires." (Genesis 41:16)*

In Daniel 2:27-28, Daniel interpreted King Nebuchadnezzar's dream and said, *"No wise man, enchanter, magician or diviner can explain to the king the mystery he has asked about, but there is a God in heaven who reveals mysteries. He has shown King Nebuchadnezzar what will happen in days to come..."*

The point I'm making regarding interpretations of dreams is that Joseph, like Daniel, had to hear from God in order to understand the meanings of the dreams.

Visions

While dreams are given when we sleep, visions are usually given while we are awake in the form of pictures or movies given by God to reveal something to us. The Scriptures are full of examples of visions, as in the book of Revelation where visions were given to John on the island of Patmos. Ezekiel had visions in the first and last chapters of his book. Daniel also had a number of visions. These are only some of the many visions in the Bible.

Many visions, like dreams, need interpretation from God. Visions can have symbolism that the natural man cannot understand. For example, a black figure could represent Satan, someone chasing us could also represent Satan and being rescued or saved often represents God's protection in our lives. God may give the interpretation immediately, but there will be times when the meaning will not be fully understood until some time in the future. For example, the church has been trying to interpret the end time visions for close to 2,000 years, yet the meaning still escapes us. When the time is right, the meaning will be fully revealed. Suffice it to say that visions are another of the myriad ways God has chosen to communicate with man.

God used visions, angels and the still small voice of the Lord one day in 1995 when our family was driving from our home in Cheverly, Maryland, a suburb of Washington, DC, to Clemson, SC, a drive that takes about nine hours. We were taking some items to our daughter Becky before we started our vacation at Myrtle Beach, SC. I noticed that the oil gauge was getting low as we were driving through southern Virginia. My wife, Suzie, noticed oil on the back window of the van. What was happening was the oil was leaking and being blown up against the back of the car. I stopped and added more oil. As we continued driving, the gauge again went down and we added more oil that time and several times after that. Finally we stopped and discovered oil leaking from under the car.

I sought the Lord and He said we should continue on and trust in Him. The whole family prayed fervently. Both Suzie and Rachel, our daughter, received independent visions of angels, one in the car and one outside the car stopping the leak. We used 12 quarts of oil between Cheverly and Clemson! That night we stopped at a gas station in Clemson and when the car was put on a rack the entire bottom of the car was loaded with oil. **But the Lord healed the car and the angels stopped the leak before we got to Clemson.**

We brought it in for servicing the next morning and the mechanic checked for leaks by using a dye and running the engine. He also changed the oil filter but said the oil filter showed no indication of an oil leak. He ran the engine for one and one-half hours and still could find no sign of an oil leak! I told him God had healed our car. As we left, the mechanic confirmed again he had been unable to find a leak and had done nothing to stop it. We drove to Myrtle Beach, used the car during our vacation, drove back to Cheverly, MD and continued to drive the car for another two months before we needed to put in only one quart of oil.

Praise the Lord! He used listening, prayer, two visions and angels to heal our car. You might say the Lord literally gave us the oil of joy!

Circumstances

There are many of us not being led by God through revelation; however, that does not mean that God is not leading us. Always remember, *"A man's steps are directed by the Lord..." (Proverbs 20:24)* If we are walking in the way of the Lord and doing His will to the best of our knowledge and ability, God will create circumstances that will steer us in the ways He wants us to go. Proverbs 16:9 states: *"In his heart a man plans his course, but the Lord determines his steps."* He will bring people and events into our path that will help us to fulfill His will.

Jesus told Peter, a fisherman, that in order to obtain enough money to pay the taxes for both of them, Peter should go fishing. He told him he would catch a fish with a coin in its mouth. Jesus had a word of knowledge, but the Father created the circumstances of having a specific fish, the one with the coin in its mouth waiting to take Peter's bait. We call these kinds of things coincidences when we should really call them *God incidences*.

One day around noon when my daughters were very small, Suzie was thinking she might like to get a toy stove for them. At six o'clock that same day, a neighbor came over and told Suzie they were moving and asked if she would be interested in a free toy stove for the children. Of course God set that up by putting the thoughts in the mind of the unbelieving neighbor to give Suzie the stove. The Lord will often use an unbeliever to help a believer. If you are walking in His ways, you probably have similar stories or have heard others testify to the same things.

Angels

Hebrews 1:14 states the purpose of angels in our lives: *"Are not all angels ministering spirits sent to serve those who will inherit salvation?"* That's comforting, isn't it? Like dreams and visions, angels appear frequently in the Bible.

Examples of angels appearing in the Bible include Gabriel who appeared to Daniel (Daniel 8:15-26), Gabriel who appeared to Mary in Luke 1:26-38 and an angel who appeared to Joseph in a dream. (Matthew 1:20-25)

Be kind because you never know when you may be entertaining an angel. *"Do not forget to entertain strangers, for by so doing some people have entertained angels without knowing it." (Hebrews 13:2)*

One day Suzie stopped to help a woman and her child at the side of the road at the direction of the Lord. After she helped them, she looked back in her rear view mirror and they were not there. They had disappeared. Suzie was unaware she had been entertaining angels.

Cloud by Day and Fire by Night

After the Israelites came out of Egypt, God led them in a most unusual way. *"By day the Lord went ahead of them in a pillar of cloud to guide them on their way and by night in a pillar of fire to give them light, so that they could travel by day or night. Neither the pillar of cloud by day nor the pillar of fire by night left its place in front of the people." (Exodus 13:21-22)*

When the cloud or fire moved, the people were instructed to move; when the cloud or fire stayed, so did the people. This is an Old Testament type of how the Holy Spirit leads His people in the New Testament. Today we don't need to be led by the Cloud and Fire that represents the Holy Spirit because today we have the Holy Spirit within us, and He leads us by the still small voice. When He directs us to stay put, we do not move out. When He says go, we go.

Authorities

God will lead us by those in authority over us. This includes parents, pastors and elders, government leaders and bosses. Romans 13:1-2 is clear:

"Everyone must submit himself to the governing authorities, for there is no authority except that which God has established. The authorities that exist have been established by God. Consequently, he who rebels against the authority is rebelling against what God has instituted, and those who do so will bring judgment on themselves."

Much of the walk God leads us into is a testing of one sort or another. Those individuals God puts in authority over us will without a shadow of a doubt test us. He wants to see how we are going to react to authority. If we can't obey human authorities, how can we obey God's authority? 1 Corinthians 15:46 refers to the physical body, but the same principle applies. *"The spiritual does not come first, but the natural, and after that the spiritual."*

We should be in a position where we are not rebellious to any governing authority. However, there will be times when resistance to authority is in accordance with the will of God. An example that sets forth the principle of obeying God above all else is found in Acts 4:18-20:

"Then they called them in again and commanded them not to speak or teach at all in the name of Jesus. But Peter and John replied, 'Judge for yourselves whether it is right in God's sight to obey you rather than God. For we cannot help speaking about what we have seen and heard.'"

I liken this to the situation where your boss tells you to do one thing and your boss' boss tells you to do something else. You would have to follow the orders of the higher authority. However, caution should be given here to make sure that it is God who is countermanding the orders of someone in authority over you. If a husband ordered his wife to do things that were contrary to the Word of God (e.g. lie, cheat, steal, etc.) a wife would have to be obedient to the Word of God.

The principle remains that we should willingly submit to those in authority over us. The centurion was a man under authority and he recognized Jesus as one who had authority. The centurion said, *"For I myself am a man under authority, with soldiers under me. I tell this one, 'Go,' and he goes; and that one, 'Come,' and he comes. I say to my servant, 'Do this,' and he does it." (Luke 7:8)* Jesus did not contradict the authority structure, but was amazed by the centurion's great faith.

In Romans 1:1 Paul introduces himself first as a servant of Jesus Christ, and then as an apostle. James, in James 1:1 calls himself a servant of God and of the Lord Jesus Christ. The same applies to Peter in 2 Peter 1:1. Finally, Jude, in Jude 1, calls himself a servant of Jesus Christ. These men of God, first and foremost, before any mention of their ministries, acknowledge that they are servants of the Lord Jesus Christ; they all first recognized the authority of their Master, then their ministry. This tells me that they learned humility and submission to God's authority, something we all need.

Urim and Thummim

In the Old Testament, God would speak to the high priest through the Urim and Thummim, which mean *lights* and *perfections.* Exodus 28:30 states:

Also put the Urim and the Thummim in the breastplate, so they may be over Aaron's heart whenever he enters the presence of the LORD. Thus Aaron will always bear the means of making decisions for the Israelites over his heart before the LORD.

The Lord in Numbers 27:21 said to Moses regarding Joshua, *"He is to stand before Eleazar the priest, who will obtain decisions for him by inquiring of the Urim before the Lord..."*

We are not exactly sure what the Urim and Thummim were and how the decisions were made through them, but we do know it was another way God spoke to the people of that day. Now that we have direct access to God there is no longer need for the Urim and Thummim, but it certainly shows another of the numerous ways God led His people.

Prophecy

God spoke through His prophets throughout the Bible, and still speaks through them today. I won't go into detail on prophecy here since chapter six covers prophecy in greater detail, but I wanted to be sure to mention it here as one of the methods God uses to speak to His children.

Speaking Through Animals

Imagine you are nonchalantly riding along on your donkey enjoying the day when suddenly with no warning, he stops in his tracks. Nothing you say or do can get him to move. Angrily, you begin to beat him urging him on when out of the blue he turns his head and speaks to you. That's what happened to Balaam in Numbers 22:23-30. Now that's enough to startle anyone, but Balaam decides to have a conversation with *his* donkey. This was God's way of doing something dramatic to get through to Balaam since previous attempts at direct conversation had failed to get his attention.

I remember one time the Lord told me to speak a word of prophecy in a group. I was afraid and believed that I was not worthy. God said to me, "If I can speak through a jackass, I can speak through you." The Lord's one-line zinger immediately took my fears away. As we listen to the Lord, we will often find He has a great sense of humor and will make us laugh with the things He comes up with.

Fleeces

You've probably heard the story of Gideon and his fleece before God in Judges 6:36-40. Gideon was doubtful that God wanted him to lead the people, so in order to make sure, he asked God to make a fleece of wool wet when he laid it on the threshing floor overnight, leaving the ground dry around it. God did as he requested.

That wasn't enough to satisfy Gideon so he asked the Lord to reverse it; that is, make the fleece dry, but the ground wet. Again the Lord accommodated Gideon. This is how the term *"putting a fleece before the Lord"* originated.

Another example is Abraham's servant in Genesis 24:14 when he asked the Lord:

"May it be that when I say to a girl, 'Please let down your jar that I may have a drink,' and she says, 'Drink, and I'll water your camels too'…let her be the one you have chosen for your servant Isaac. By this I will know that you have shown kindness to my master." Rebekah came and said the exact words spoken by Abraham's servant, who must have been ecstatic when it happened.

Notwithstanding these two successes, I would not include fleeces high on my list of how to hear God speak. I believe many Christians use this method far too often. Know that it is there, but be wary of its use. He spoke through an animal once and through a fleece twice. Does that mean we should expect to hear animals talking half as much as we use fleeces? Of course not; however, it's something to think about. We should not overuse anything in the Bible if it appears infrequently.

Audible Voice

God spoke in an audible voice several times in the Scriptures. John 12:28-30 says,

"Father, glorify your name!" Then a voice came from heaven, "I have glorified it, and will glorify it again." The crowd that was there and heard it said it had thundered; others said an angel had spoken to him. Jesus said, "This voice was for your benefit, not mine."

Jesus was speaking to Saul on the road to Damascus in Acts 9:3-7 and the men traveling with Saul also heard the sound. There were other examples in the Scriptures; however, I believe they are insignificant in number compared to the hearing of the still small voice.

Still Small Voice

The most common way God spoke to man in the Scriptures was through the still small voice. I believe He did not speak frequently in an audible voice, but almost all His conversations were the still small voice within. Why do I believe that? First, the experience of almost all Christians who listen to the voice of the Lord is that He speaks with a quiet voice, almost as a thought in your mind. Most often His voice will sound like your voice.

Rarely do people hear an audible voice. Remember, *"Jesus Christ is the same yesterday and today and forever." (Hebrews 13:8)* He does not change. If He speaks most frequently in a still small voice today, He did it yesterday and He will do it tomorrow.

Another reason for this belief is that *"...The righteous will live by faith."* **(Galatians 3:11)** How much faith would it take if we continually heard a loud booming voice speaking to us from heaven? Not much—we'd be scared stiff. Faith comes when we hear a quiet voice inside giving us direction and wanting us to act on that direction.

Elijah fled from Jezebel and was hiding in Beersheba when he had a conversation with the Lord. 1 Kings 19:12 states: *"After the earthquake*

came a fire, but the Lord was not in the fire. And after the fire came a gentle whisper. *"* That is how the Lord usually speaks to His people. It is like a gentle whisper.

God uses all of the above methods and more to speak to us. Though we cannot tell Him which one to use, the still small voice of the Lord, who led the people much more frequently in the past will still be the most common way to communicate with our God now and in the future.

LISTENING IN THE OLD TESTAMENT

"Pay attention to what I say—listen closely to my words."
(Pro. 4:20)

Chapter Two

GOD INTRODUCES LISTENING

One of the most important things we can do in our Christian walk is to be continually immersed in the written Word of God. How can we love God unless we love His Word? How can we know God unless we know His Word? Every teaching should be consistent with the Bible and you, as a believer, must be sufficiently familiar with the written Word to be able to know whether a message can be confirmed in the Scriptures.

Do an independent study in the Bible on the subject of God's speaking to man and as you do, you will be astonished at the number of times God is speaking in the Bible. In fact, Eerdmans' Handbook to the Bible on page 33 states, "More than 3,800 times words are introduced by such formulae as 'The Lord spoke,' 'Thus says the Lord' and 'the word of the Lord came.'" Imagine that! Over 3,800 times! To gain a new perspective of this, why not consider highlighting the conversations between man and God in the Bible, giving you a whole new appreciation of their interrelationships. You will also see the importance God places in the Bible on His conversations with man. I believe just concentrating on biblical conversations will revolutionize your Christian walk.

Why do you suppose God speaks so frequently in the Bible? I believe He is showing us a pattern of what He considers important and if God considers it important, why shouldn't we?

Many doctrines of churches are based on the existence of only several Scriptures relating to a subject. Listening to the Lord is throughout all the Scriptures, yet so few churches even discuss the subject. It makes sense to me to concentrate on the subjects God concentrates on. Listening is certainly one of them.

As we go to Genesis we will see how God dealt with the saints of old. We'll also be covering some examples of conversations and discussing some of the lessons to be learned from those conversations.

God Introduces Himself as a Speaking God

The Bible begins with an explanation of the creation. In Genesis, chapter one, the Lord indicates He is a God who creates, and He created by *speaking* the world into existence. Verses 3, 6, 9, 11, 14, 20, 24, 26 and 29 begin with the words, *"And God said,"* or *"Then God said."* **Verses 22 and 28 begin with, *"God blessed them and said…"*** Psalms 33:6 *speaks* of His creation, *"By the word of the Lord were the heavens made, their starry host by the breath of his mouth."* In verses 8 and 9 the Psalmist says, *"Let all the earth fear the Lord; let all the people of the world revere him. For He spoke, and it came to be; He commanded, and it stood firm."*

It is no coincidence that God introduces Himself as a God of creation, and that He creates by *speaking* into existence. This is the first impression God wants to give us of Him because first impressions are always important. We often make decisions based on first impressions; a positive first impression on a job interview may make the difference in landing a job.

He wants us to be introduced to Him as a God who creates by *speaking* and He did it over and over again in the first chapter of the Bible. We are created in His image and *we* create by *speaking* His word. No word of God is void of power; as we speak the word He gives us His power is unleashed.

Adam and Eve

God began to reveal Himself in His conversations with man by speaking to the first man, Adam. It's interesting to note that God's relationship with man began with a conversation. Genesis 2:16-17 states:

And the LORD God commanded the man, "You are free to eat from any tree in the garden; but you must not eat from

**the tree of the knowledge of good and evil, for when you eat
of it you will surely die."**

Adam was allowed to have fruit from every tree in the garden except *one*.
Of course, he wanted what he could not have. You will find as you learn to
listen to God that, just as Adam, we want to do what God tells us not to do.
Conversely, we do not want to do what God tells us to do. We have the
Adamic nature and a reluctance to obey God.

We learn through the Bible, and our experiences testify that God does
have our best interests at heart and certainly His commandments are for our
own good. But we aren't always all that interested in our own good; our
inclinations are to rebel and when we rebel we pay the consequences for that
rebellion. Adam did, and I can imagine he was kicking himself later for his
disobedience.

We know Adam told Eve what God had commanded him regarding the
fruit from the tree of the *knowledge of good and evil* because Eve told the
serpent about it. But she was still tempted by the serpent. Genesis 3:1 states:

**Now the serpent was more crafty than any of the wild
animals the LORD God had made. He said to the woman,
"Did God really say, 'You must not eat from any tree in the
garden?'"**

There are several lessons to be learned here. First, God will speak and give
a command or a blessing, and then Satan or one of his demons will put a
question in your mind about what God had actually said. It is no accident that
the first question in the Bible is Satan questioning God, and this is how he
frequently works. The fact that God will speak first then Satan will come to
put doubt or try to steal what God has said or done is confirmed in Mark 4:14-
15 where Jesus says,

**"The farmer sows the word. Some people are like seed along
the path, where the word is sown. As soon as they hear it,
Satan comes and takes away the word that was sown in
them."**

How many of us have had words from the Lord and then later questioned
their validity? Generally speaking, when you receive a word or blessing from
the Lord be prepared for an onslaught of doubt from Satan to try to cause you
to lose your joy and peace. After all, his mission is to steal, kill and destroy.

At the time you were reborn in the Lord, you knew you were a new creature…you were changed…you were saved and your heart was filled with great love and joy. Then thoughts began coming to your mind, bringing doubts. "Was I really saved? Was that really God or just my imagination?" This applies to other areas as well. Perhaps you received the baptism of the Spirit, knew it at the time, but later had thoughts questioning whether you were really baptized in the Spirit. You may have spoken in tongues and later doubted whether you really had tongues. How many of you have doubted healings or deliverances you received because of questions in your mind? The same thing will happen as you learn to listen to the voice of the Lord.

Satan is very subtle and will not come to you and say, "I am Satan." He knows you will be turned off and horrified by that approach. He is a thief who is sneaky and sly. He will do everything he can to try to steal what you receive from God in such a way you won't even realize you are being influenced by the demonic realm. *Remember to doubt the doubts you have about God*…those doubts that have crept into your mind are most certainly from Satan or his demons. One sure way to win the war is to know the ways of the enemy in order to fight him effectively.

The next lesson deals with Eve's repeating what she thought God had said. Genesis 3:2-3 states:

> **The woman said to the serpent, "We may eat fruit from the trees in the garden, but God did say, 'You must not eat fruit from the tree that is in the middle of the garden, and you must not touch it, or you will die.'"**

God did not say anything about touching the fruit. That was added either by Adam when he told Eve what God had said, or later by Eve when she spoke to the serpent. This is something we often do in our listening to the voice of the Lord. We add to the word or we tend to put our own interpretation on the word we hear. As we listen we need to be careful so that we are faithful to the specific direction of the Lord. Many Christians have taken the word that was given to them and added to it so that they, as well as others, were misled to the point of being put into a strait jacket of legalism and bondage.

Satan's response in Genesis 3:4 was,

> **"You will not surely die," the serpent said to the woman. "For God knows that when you eat of it your eyes will be opened, and you will be like God, knowing good and evil."**

God said, *"You will die."* Satan said, *"You will not die."* Here Satan is calling God a liar. Of course, we should expect that from him since he is the father of lies and will try to cause us to question the character of God. He will try to make us believe that God is not truthful and that we cannot trust His promises for our lives. God meant that Adam would spiritually die and he did when he disobeyed.

Another trait of the enemy is to cause us to exalt ourselves. Pride was the cause of Lucifer's downfall and he wants us to also be lifted up to the point where we, too, will fall. Isaiah 14:12-15 provides an account of Lucifer in his prideful efforts to lift himself up to a position equal to God. Verse 14 states: *"I will make myself like the most high."*

Proverbs 16:18 states: *"Pride goes before destruction..."* If you are hearing thoughts that equate you with God, exalt you above your brothers and sisters in the Lord, or cause you to become prideful in your own actions, *be on guard*, for Satan is probably behind it. James 4:10 directs us to *"Humble yourselves before the Lord, and He will lift you up."* The devil wants us to exalt ourselves while the Lord wants the opposite.

Now we see the results of Satan's work in Genesis 3:6, a commentary on how Satan tempts us. It states:

> **"When the woman saw that the fruit of the tree was good for food and pleasing to the eye, and also desirable for gaining wisdom, she took some and ate it. She also gave some to her husband, who was with her, and he ate it."**

Adam and Eve were tempted and fell. Satan also tempted Jesus in a similar way in Matthew, Chapter four, when the Spirit led Jesus into the desert. The lust of the flesh, the lust of the eyes and the pride of life tempted Jesus, as Adam and Eve. He overcame Satan by speaking the written Word. He responded to the first test of Satan by quoting Deuteronomy 8:3. That quote in Matthew 4:4 says,

> **Jesus answered, "It is written: 'Man does not live on bread alone, but on every word that comes from the mouth of God.'"**

Satan tempts us in the same way with the things of the world as shown in 1 John 2:15-16 which states: *"Do not love the world or anything in the world. If anyone loves the world, the love of the father is not in him. For everything in the world…the cravings of sinful man, the lust of his eyes and the boasting of what he has and does…comes not from the father but from the world."*

Now that we know how Satan tempts, it's up to us to learn to overcome his temptation by the Word of the Lord.

After they ate the forbidden fruit, Adam and Eve realized they were naked so they sewed fig leaves together for clothing. I find it interesting that God gave them time to decide what they were going to do. I believe He wanted to see if they would repent and seek Him or hide as they, in fact, did. God came back to the garden in Genesis 3:9 and asked Adam, *"…Where are you?"*

Now God knew were Adam was, just as He knows where we are in our Christian walk, but He wants to see what our reaction is going to be. Adam answered that he was hiding from God because he was afraid. Don't we do the same thing when we sin? God does not want us to hide from Him, but to confess our sins so He can forgive us of our sins and cleanse us from all unrighteousness. (1 John 1:9)

God then asked Adam if he had eaten the fruit. (Genesis 3:11) Adam did not answer the question until he first blamed God and Eve. He said in Genesis 3:12,

> **"…The woman you put here with me…she gave me some fruit from the tree, and I ate it."**

After that Eve did the very same thing and said the devil made her do it. When God confronts you, don't run and hide and don't blame someone else. I have six children and it was amazing how often they blamed each other when they were confronted with something they did wrong. They would not acknowledge their sin, but would shift the blame to their brothers and sisters. Passing the buck is very common in the Adamic nature. We need to be responsible and confess our sins to the Lord; He will quickly forgive us.

Cain and Abel

If we think we have problems with our children, think about Adam and Eve. They had two sons named Cain and Abel. Genesis 4:6-7 state:

In the course of time Cain brought some of the fruits of the soil as an offering to the LORD. But Abel brought fat portions from some of the firstborn of the flock. The LORD looked with favor on Abel and his offering, but on Cain and his offering he did not look with favor. So Cain was very angry, and his face was downcast.

Then the Lord said to Cain, "Why are you angry? Why is your face downcast? If you do what is right, will you not be accepted? But if you do not do what is right, sin is crouching at your door; it desires to have you, but you must master it."

Cain and Abel talked to God probably because their parents taught them how to listen. We should also be teaching our children to do likewise. Let's look at the story. Both Cain and Abel knew from God that the sacrifice to God had to be a *blood* sacrifice. Why do I say that? Hebrews 11:4 states:

By faith Abel offered God a better sacrifice than Cain did. By faith he was commended as a righteous man, when God spoke well of his offerings. And by faith he still speaks, even though he is dead.

Romans 10:17 states: *"Consequently, faith comes from hearing the message, and the message is heard through the word of Christ."* The Greek word used here for *"word"* is Rhema; that is, the spoken word of God. So Abel heard about the need for a blood sacrifice from either his parents who heard from God or from God himself.

Cain also knew since God had said to him, *'If you do right will you not be accepted?"* How did they both know what was the right thing? There were no written records; they only had the teachings of their parents *and* the voice of the Lord. They both listened to God. Abel chose to obey and was commended for being righteous, but Cain chose to disobey by giving God the first fruits of a *cursed* earth because of the disobedience of his father, Adam. Genesis 3:17 states: *"...Cursed is the ground because of you."* I would imagine that if his father had not told him about the earth's being cursed; God certainly would have done so.

Hebrews 9:22 states: *"...without the shedding of blood there is no forgiveness."* Cain's offering was not acceptable because he was disobedient in not bringing a blood offering. Thank God we now have the blood of Jesus. We no longer have to contend with the blood of bulls and goats. He has become our sacrificial offering.

Even though Cain was angry and downcast, God in His mercy gave him another chance. He did not want Cain to continue in his anger. You know the rest of the story. Cain did not heed God's warning and ended up killing his brother.

Again, there are several lessons here regarding listening. First, God tells us what to do and what not to do. He tells us in the written Word and by the Holy Spirit dwelling in us. The Spirit convicts the world of sin (John 16:8) and we are part of that world. He tells us we have the ability to master sin and it's up to us whether we obey or disobey. This is one of the main lessons of the Christian walk. We may choose whom we serve each day, whether the Lord and life or self and death; the lust of the flesh, the lust of the eyes and the pride of life (1 John 2:16) are our downfall. When we serve ourselves we ultimately end up serving Satan. God has given us the freedom to choose. *This day and every day choose life.*

God is no respecter of persons and wants to communicate with all His children. The important thing to remember in listening to the voice of the Lord is obedience. Abel obeyed and was considered righteous. Abraham *believed God and it was credited to him as righteousness* in Genesis 15:6. Cain was a religious person; he believed in God, offered sacrifices to Him and had conversations with Him. Yet he was disobedient to God and jealous of his brother to the point of death. We need to be on guard that we not become jealous and angry at others who find favor with the Lord, but rather, rejoice with them.

Noah

It is interesting to note that over a period of hundreds of years God merely mentioned a number of men in the genealogies in Genesis, chapter six. I believe God will pass over generation after generation until He finds a man who will listen and obey. God used one chapter to cover hundreds of years and the lives of a number of men, and three chapters on one man, Noah, a listener. Genesis 6:22 states: ***"Noah did everything just as God commanded him."*** Noah certainly was not perfect; he drank too much for one thing, at least on one occasion. (Genesis 9:21) Yet, he listened and obeyed.

Imagine being Noah and God tells you to build an ark. Some Bible scholars believe there were no huge bodies of water at that time. Noah, I'm sure, must have wondered about the direction of God, but he was obedient. People taunted and criticized him for the work of building the ark and collecting a zoo; but he obeyed God, in spite of the mocking. Hebrews 11:7 states:

> **By faith Noah, when warned about things not yet seen, in holy fear built an ark to save his family. By his faith he condemned the world and became heir of the righteousness that comes by faith.**

When Noah heard God's plans of judgment and the direction regarding the ark, he was fearful of the coming wrath and obeyed the voice of the Lord. God looks for a person who will obey, even when His direction appears foolish in the eyes of man. It can happen to us as well. God will test us to see whether we will go along with the apparent foolishness of God instead of following the wisdom of man. One time I was ministering to a woman when the Lord told me she had resentment against Stinky. I was very skeptical, but the Lord kept repeating she had resentment against Stinky. Reluctantly, I asked her if she knew someone named Stinky and she said that was a former boyfriend and she did have resentment against him.

It's amazing to realize Noah worked on the ark for about 100 years before the floods came. He followed God and did what he was told; yet the only ones who went with him were those in his immediate family. Obedience to the voice of God may not make you popular or give you a huge ministry as in Noah's case where few believed him.

After Noah, the Bible again has another set of genealogies in Genesis, chapter ten. These cover hundreds of years and again God merely mentions these men in passing...all except one man, Abram who was eventually renamed Abraham by God. It was in Abraham that God found another listener. He is looking for a people, individually and corporately, who will listen to His voice.

Chapter Three

EXAMPLES OF LISTENING IN THE LIFE OF ABRAHAM

I t's amazing how little of a man's life is known in the Bible until God starts speaking to him, or should I say until he starts listening. The first seventy-five years of Abram's life are very briefly described in a few verses at the end of Genesis, chapter eleven. Then exciting things began to happen to him in Genesis 12 as he started listening to the voice of God.

The Call of Abram

The Bible records God's call on the life of Abram in Genesis 12:1-3,

> **The LORD had said to Abram, "Leave your country, your people and your father's household and go to the land I will show you. I will make you into a great nation and I will bless you; I will make your name great, and you will be a blessing. I will bless those who bless you, and whoever curses you I will curse; and all peoples on earth will be blessed through you."**

As you listen to the voice of God, He may direct you to do something specific or as in Abram's case, He may simply tell you to go. Abram had no idea where he was going or what he was to do when he got there. But he passed the first test…obedience to the direction he was given at the time.

Remember, God will always be testing us because we are in the *School of the Holy Spirit.* As in any school we have lessons to learn and if we flunk, we'll have to repeat those lessons over again until we get them right. God doesn't want us to flunk; He wants us to pass so we can go on to more advanced lessons. He wants to know that we are willing to trust Him and not lean on our own understanding.

Also, the Lord made covenant promises to Abraham. He said, *"I will"* six times in the above verses. As we are obedient to God, the Lord will also make covenant promises to us. He has with me, and some of the promises have already been fulfilled. He has told me what He will do without my even asking Him. It's all part of His plan for my life which He has gradually revealed as I take each step of faith.

An example of this in my life was that the Lord, over thirty-five years ago, said that I would be ministering counseling and deliverance to blacks, especially poor black women. At that time, I knew very few blacks. However, the Lord started to bring blacks and, by word of mouth, many more came. I have had healing, counseling, and deliverance sessions with over 3,500 blacks over that period of time.

God made great promises to Abram, some of which, if you analyze them, must have seemed almost unbelievable to him. Can you imagine what Abram thought when God said that *all* the nations of the world would be blessed through him? As it turned out, some of the blessings were fulfilled during Abram's life; however, most of them were fulfilled after he died.

Here's another lesson in listening. God will make promises to you and you will want to see the results immediately. Some of the promises *will* be fulfilled immediately; however, be prepared to wait and trust the living God for the fulfillment of the rest of them. A lot depends on our actions, and a lot depends on timing. God's timing is perfect. He's never early, but He's never late either. He knows the best time for answered prayer. Abram was seventy-five when God said He would make a great nation of him. Most people's lives are over by then, but Abram's family was just beginning, based on a promise from God.

The Lord spoke to Abram again in Genesis 13:14-16,

The LORD said to Abram after Lot had parted from him, "Lift up your eyes from where you are and look north and south, east and west. All the land that you see I will give to

you and your offspring forever. I will make your offspring like the dust of the earth, so that if anyone could count the dust, then your offspring could be counted."

Abram still had no children and by this time was probably in his late seventies. Again, more promises by God with no evidence of the promises' fulfillment. Once more God spoke to Abram about this when he was in his early eighties and this time Abram, in apparent frustration at not receiving the promises, discusses the situation with God in Genesis 15:1-5,

After this, the word of the LORD came to Abram in a vision, "Do not be afraid, Abram. I am your shield, your very great reward." But Abram said, "O Sovereign LORD, what can you give me since I remain childless and the one who will inherit my estate is Eliezer of Damascus?" And Abram said, "You have given me no children; so a servant in my household will be my heir."

Then the word of the LORD came to him, "This man will not be your heir, but a son coming from your own body will be your heir." He took him outside and said, "Look up at the heavens and count the stars...if indeed you can count them." Then He said to him, "So shall your offspring be."

Could there be a little doubt in the mind of Abram when he told God, *"You have given me no children."*? But God overlooked that and again made promises about Abram's offspring. The next verse, Genesis 15:6 is most remarkable in that it states *"**Abram believed the LORD, and He credited it to him as righteousness.**"* Here is a man in later life when most men that age have already died, to whom God made promises three times spread out over a number of years regarding his nonexistent descendants, each time adding more to the promises. No fulfillment of the promises was in sight, yet Abram believed God.

Are we ready to believe the promises of God in the face of circumstances totally contrary to the promises given us by the Lord?

Abram Helps God

Abram was eighty-five or eighty-six when he thought he would help God out. Since his wife Sarai had given him no children, she told him to sleep with Hagar, her maidservant. Abram thought that was a good idea and from that union Ishmael was born; Abram was eighty-six. (Genesis 16:16). But Ishmael was not the child of promise.

Abram was like many of us. God gives us promises that only He can fulfill and we, believing God and His promises, try to help Him out. Some of God's promises are conditional on services or actions we are to perform; some are not. The key is to ask the Lord what we are to do regarding the promises. He may have assignments for us, and then again He may not.

Do not presume you know what you should do to fulfill God's promises or you may create an Ishmael in your life, a thorn in your side or in the sides of others. This could even hinder you from performing what God calls you to do. The Arabs are descendants from Ishmael and they have been a thorn in the lives of the Israelites even to this day. (Don't think I'm anti-Arab since I'm half Palestinian and half Lebanese.)

Child of Promise

God changed Abram's name, which is *exalted father,* to Abraham, which means the *father of many* (Genesis 17:4-5) when He told him he would be the father of many nations. Abraham already had one son, but that son was not the child of promise. The Lord looked into the future and told Abraham what would be; He spoke into existence what was impossible for man to see.

After the Lord changed Abram's name, He spoke to Abraham and told him that Isaac would be the child of promise. This was spoken when Abraham was around one hundred years old and Sarah was about ninety. (Genesis 17:17-19) Since Sarah was past the age of childbearing, God took what was dead and made it alive. He will often fulfill His promises for us just when we think they are impossible to fulfill and all hope is gone. We must die to ourselves and when all our efforts are in vain then God will step in and supernaturally do what He originally promised.

If God has made promises to you, don't give up. Trust the all-powerful God to fulfill all that He promised. It's when things look impossible that He acts; He is an eleventh hour God...sometimes the eleventh hour and fifty-ninth minute.

Intercession for Sodom

In Genesis 18:17-33 Abraham spoke with God and interceded for Sodom asking Him to save that wicked city. He started by asking God to save Sodom if there were fifty righteous men in the city and God agreed. Then Abraham started negotiating with God and said, "How about forty-five?" God agreed. Abraham didn't give up. He went from forty to thirty to twenty, continually talking to God and finally ended up getting God to agree to not destroy Sodom if there were ten righteous men there. At no time did the Lord tell Abraham to stop reducing the number and whenever he lowered the number the Lord agreed to stop the impending judgment on Sodom. Abraham decided to stop at ten. Had he gone on to even one righteous man, his nephew Lot, I'm sure the city would have been saved.

What can we learn from this? First, intercession is often nothing more than engaging in conversations with the Lord. All too often, we pray the prayers we want rather than earnestly seeking the mind of God and then we wonder why our prayers aren't answered. I've heard it said that God doesn't answer our prayers, but He answers His prayers.

If we listen to God and get His heart and mind on the subject, our prayers will be more effective and will get results because they are not our prayers alone; rather they are God's prayers through us. It's not only God's prayers, but also God's purposes through us. Often He chooses to limit His actions on earth to those done through humans. When he tells us to pray for something specific, it is His intention to answer that prayer. He would not tell us to pray for something that He did not intend to fulfill.

Second, don't stop your intercession until the Lord says so, or until it is finished. Pray it through. I experienced this lesson when our former Wednesday night intercession group was praying for a woman whose feet were so swollen we could not see or feel her ankles. The Lord told us to lay hands on her feet and pray for a healing and we obeyed. After a few minutes, the swelling went down and we stopped praying.

The Lord said, "I didn't tell you to stop praying," so we prayed for a few minutes more and the swelling went down further. Again we stopped and again the Lord said He hadn't told us to stop. So we resumed laying our hands on her feet and continued our prayers for healing. In a few more minutes the swelling was completely gone and her feet were normal. That's when the Lord told us to stop. Our prayers, from start to finish took no more than ten minutes, but we learned a valuable lesson. In some groups, this is known as *praying through.* The Lord told us that in the future we should continue to pray for a matter until He tells us to stop.

Sending Hagar and Ishmael Away

Another difficult test came when Sarah decided that Hagar and her son Ishmael should be sent away. (Genesis 21:8-14) God told Abraham to do it, and although he was obedient to the commandment of the Lord, you can imagine how difficult it must have been for him. The lad was his first-born and the first-born had special significance to the people of the Middle East since he was the one who would get the inheritance. For example, if a couple had two sons, the eldest would receive two-thirds and the youngest only one-third.

But Abraham trusted God because he had seen the results of God's promises in the birth of Isaac when he was one hundred and Sarah was ninety. So when God said He would make Ishmael into a great nation, he believed Him.

It's important to remember that God frequently tests us, each time with a new test, often more difficult than the last one. However, as we see His faithfulness, we learn to trust Him more in the things He tells us to do.

Sacrifice of Isaac

In God's direction for Abraham to sacrifice Isaac, God tested Abraham with a really big one. In Genesis 22:2 He told Abraham to sacrifice his son Isaac.

> **"Then God said, 'Take your son, your only son, Isaac, whom you love, and go to the region of Moriah. Sacrifice him there as a burnt offering on one of the mountains I will tell you about.'"**

Abraham had another son, but God calls Isaac *his only son* because he was the child of promise. It was a three-day journey and Abraham had to be thinking about the death of his child of promise. Think about it. First, God has Abraham send away his first-born, and then gives him direction to kill his only remaining son.

Ishmael was gone and God did not bring him back, yet Abraham trusted that God would bring Isaac back if he went through with the sacrifice. Hebrews 11:17-19 talks about Abraham's faith:

> **By faith Abraham, when God tested him, offered Isaac as a sacrifice. He who had received the promises was about to sacrifice his one and only son, even though God had said to him, "It is through Isaac that your offspring will be reckoned." Abraham reasoned that God could raise the dead, and figuratively speaking, he did receive Isaac back from the dead.**

Abraham saw the miracle of God's bringing forth a son when he and Sarah were too old to bring forth life and he knew God could bring forth life in other ways. If Abraham was to be the father of many nations, he would have to have a child and Isaac was that child. God had made him a promise and he was ready to do what He told him to do.

As Abraham bound up Isaac, placed him on top of the wood on the altar and took out his knife to slay him, an angel of the Lord stopped him (Genesis 22:9-10). As a result of his obedience, God gave him this promise, **"I swear by myself, declares the Lord, that because you have done this and have not withheld your son, your only son, I will surely bless you and make your descendants as numerous as the stars in the sky and as the sand on the seashore. Your descendants will take possession of the cities of their enemies and through your offspring all nations on earth will be blessed, because you have obeyed me."** God knew he had found an obedient man. As we also listen to the voice of the Lord, blessings will come as we obey, for us and for our families.

The story of Abraham and his son Isaac became real in my own life with my son Steven, my only son at the time. Steven was six and became extremely ill with a temperature of 103. My wife and I were very concerned. I sought the Lord that morning and all I heard was, "This day I require your son." I came against what I thought was Satan and continued to seek the Lord. Again I heard, "This day I require your son." By now I was convinced the Lord was speaking to me.

Humbly I said to God, "Lord, I believe you are testing me as you tested Abraham with Isaac, but if this isn't a test, and you truly do want my son, I give him to you because he isn't mine to claim. I am only the steward of whomever and whatever you choose to entrust to me." With fear and trembling I waited and waited long agonizing hours that seemed an eternity, hearing nothing from Him. Not knowing what to expect, I could only put my trust in the goodness of a merciful God.

Finally, the Lord said, "This was in fact a test and I am restoring your son to you. I wanted to see if you loved Me more than your son." The fever broke and Steven was immediately healed.

Years ago I learned I was just a steward of what God gave me and I yielded everything I had to the Lord. I told Him my family, my time, my house, my car and my job were His to do with whatever He wanted for His greater glory. Be forewarned, when you do something like this, He's going to take you at your word.

A week later, a brother in the Lord asked me to lend him our station wagon, the only car we had at the time. He wanted to borrow it every Sunday so he could carry his drums to the Mall in Washington, D.C. to witness. I knew right away what the Lord was doing. I had yielded the car to Him and now He was going to use it for His glory. I sought the Lord and He told me to lend the car. I figured I would never be able to use *my car* again on Sunday afternoons, but obeyed the Lord and lent the car. The brother borrowed the car, went to the Mall that Sunday and told me when he came back that he wasn't going to go back and wouldn't need my car after all. I had my car back. Here was another test to see if I would be willing to give up my car, and when I did, He returned it to me.

The Lord wants to know where our hearts are…with Him and His will or with the things He has given us. Once we have shown Him that the car, or Isaac as in the case of Abraham, are not more important than doing His will, He can return it to us. We have proven His will is more important to us than anything else.

Another car incident happened shortly afterward. One evening as I was driving, someone hit the rear of my car at a stoplight. As I was getting out of the car, the driver took off and I was the victim of a hit and run. It was too dark to get his license number so I looked at the newly banged up station wagon and said to the Lord, "Lord, look what he's done to your car." I calmly got back into the car and drove to the prayer meeting where I was teaching. It felt so good to simply give it to the Lord; it was His responsibility and not my responsibility. Later, God provided the funds to get His car fixed.

To end Abraham's story, right after the last successful testing of Abraham, the Bible has a listing of some of the relatives of Nahor, the brother of Abraham (Genesis 22:20-24) Included in that short list is the announcement of the birth of Rebekah, the future bride of Isaac.

Abraham listened to the Lord and was obedient. Therefore, the word of God, *"...through your offspring all nations on earth will be blessed, because you have obeyed me,"* was beginning to be fulfilled. After Abraham's obedience, the bride of Isaac was born. Through their marriage, Jacob later renamed Israel, was born. He became the father of the twelve tribes of Israel. Just as Israel was begotten through the obedience of Abraham, so it is with Jesus and the church.

Because of the obedience of the Son of God, our Lord Jesus Christ, the church, the bride of Christ was born. His obedience brought the church into existence.

As we listen to the Lord, we can ask ourselves, "What will my obedience bring into existence?" You can be sure God has a plan for that.

Chapter Four

LISTENING AND MINISTRY BEGINS AT EIGHTY FOR MOSES

The first eighty years of Moses' life are contained in chapter two of Exodus. He knew when he tried to help the Hebrew slave and wound up killing the Egyptian (Acts 7:24), that even at age forty he had a calling on his life to rescue the Hebrews. However, the fulfillment of that calling did not come about until he started listening to the voice of the Lord at age eighty after having wandered for forty years in the desert. It was then he received specific direction that marked the beginning of his ministry.

You can see the importance of listening to the Lord in the life of Moses and it's just as important in our own lives. *You're never too old to start your ministry or to start listening to the voice of the Lord.*

If you've been wandering around in your Christian walk, knowing you have a calling, but are unable to move effectively in that calling, I suggest you look at Moses' example. Forty years is a long time between knowing you are called and waiting to fulfill that call. Why not cut the time short and start listening? God will direct your path in that calling.

Moses' First Encounter with God

When Moses heard God speaking to him in Exodus, chapter three, his ministry took off. The rest of Exodus and the books of Leviticus, Numbers and Deuteronomy reflect the last forty years of Moses' life, *when he was listening to God.*

The time before a person starts to listen to the Lord is not mentioned by God in the Scriptures, but He makes the point of indicating the time when a person *is* listening to Him as important. There's a pattern God continually uses in telling about the saints of old.

Moses' first encounter with the Lord was in Exodus 3:4 where God tells him who He is.

> **God also said to Moses, "I AM WHO I AM. This is what you are to say to the Israelites: 'I AM has sent me to you.'"**

Our God is the great *I AM*. He is not the *I WAS*, or the *I WILL BE*, but the *I AM*. He is present and active. He is telling Moses that His name means He is always there for him. Moses did not have to fear the future, or anything that Pharaoh could do to him since God would always be present in any circumstance that could arise.

When God told Moses what he wanted him to do, Moses wanted no part of it. He was reluctant, to say the least. Five times Moses tried to back out by making excuses. In Exodus 3:11, Moses asked, *"...Who am I that I should go to Pharaoh and bring the Israelites out of Egypt?"* By that question, we can see that Moses did not know his God very well. When God tells us to do something, it's God Himself who has the power to accomplish that which he directs.

This is an area that causes fear, especially in a relatively new listener. We think we don't have the ability to accomplish God's direction and we don't. But God does, and He will use His supernatural ability through us if we let Him. First, we have to hear and obey to the best of *our* ability, and God will bring about the results He originally said would happen (if He chooses to tell what will happen).

Moses asked God, *"What if they do not believe me or listen to me and say, 'The LORD did not appear to you'?"* **(Exodus 4:1)** That's when God turned Moses' staff into a snake and back into a staff again and made his hand leprous and then healed it. How would you like signs like that to show people that God, in fact, sent you? It didn't impress Moses in the least. He still didn't want any part of it.

In Exodus 4:10, he told God, *"O LORD, I have never been eloquent, neither in the past nor since you have spoken to your servant. I am slow of speech and tongue.*" Now God knew better than that. That was false humility on the part of Moses. Acts 7:22 states: *"Moses was educated in all the wisdom of the Egyptians and was powerful in speech and action."* Moses tried everything he could to get out of God's calling for his life. He even lied.

Moses did not know the power God had to accomplish what He said He would accomplish, but he learned. Moses developed humility to the point where, in Numbers 12:3, it is written *"Now Moses was a very humble man, more humble than anyone else on the face of the earth."* Remember, Moses wrote the first five books of the Bible and he, through the Holy Spirit, called himself the most humble man living. (It should be noted that some Biblical scholars believe that others added this statement at a later date.)

You may think Moses showed arrogance and not humility, but when you lead several million (2.4 million according to some Biblical scholars) people out of bondage and up to the borders of the Promised Land and rely almost exclusively on the voice of the Lord, you do develop humility. You come to realize you can do nothing on your own, but with God all things are possible. You see how helpless you are without God, especially when one considers all the tests God put the Israelites through.

As we are led by the Lord, He will do the same for us. He will show us His miracles in many ways and as we grow older in the Lord and see more of His accomplishments in our lives, humility will be a natural result. We will see, as Moses did, the things God promises come to pass, invariably not the way we believe they will, but indeed they will. We will find ourselves putting exceedingly more trust in God later in our Christian life than at the beginning. Reliance on self will diminish, and greater trust in the Master will gradually take place in our Christian walk.

Moses' Doubts About the Promises of God

God told Moses everything He would do to free His people in Exodus 3:19-20 which states: *"But I know that the king of Egypt will not let you go unless a mighty hand compels him. So I will stretch out my hand and strike the Egyptians with all the wonders that I will perform among them. After that, he will let you go."*

Moses eventually obeyed God and went to Pharaoh. Exodus 5:1-2 says:

Afterward Moses and Aaron went to Pharaoh and said, "This is what the LORD, the God of Israel, says: 'Let my

**people go, so they may hold a festival to me in the desert.'"
Pharaoh said, "Who is the LORD that I should obey him
and let Israel go? I do not know the LORD and I will not let
Israel go."**

Pharaoh hardened his heart and placed additional burdens on the slaves as they made bricks. (Exodus 5:6-18) Subsequently, the Israelite foreman went to Moses and Aaron and angrily condemned them for causing additional burden on the slaves. Moses then went back to God in Exodus 5:22-23 and said:

**"...O LORD, why have you brought trouble upon this
people? Is this why you sent me? Ever since I went to
Pharaoh to speak in your name, he has brought trouble upon
this people, and you have not rescued your people at all."**

One can almost hear the frustration of Moses. Moses doubted God, His promises, and His intentions toward His people. He accused God of not keeping His promises. He was almost at the point of calling God a liar.

God will give us direction and we will obey those directions, but sometimes the results will appear to be disastrous. We will doubt God and question whether or not we heard correctly. Believe me, it will happen. It's happened to me and many others that I know. Remember, God is in the testing business, and He wants to see if we will believe Him in spite of the circumstances which face us.

This happened to Moses, but he didn't stop listening to God simply because he didn't understand. He went on in spite of what he saw before him and we need to do the same. Recently, I heard a sermon where we were admonished, *"Don't doubt in the darkness what God has promised in the light."* You will be tested in the darkness, but remember to believe God's promises rather than the circumstances surrounding you.

Another important lesson is to do the things you are called to do even though there are areas that are baffling to you. Many miracles and judgments took place when Moses simply listened to God and told Pharaoh what God would do if he did not let God's people go. Moses didn't understand the response of Pharaoh, the future plans and direction of God, and all the steps along the way. All he knew was simply to listen to God and do what he was told to do. He walked in the light and understanding that he had. The rest was up to God.

Here's an example of God's promises which characterize what He did with Moses. Some dear friends of ours were ministering in Chicago and finances were tight, to say the least. The husband called me one day and, as I was praying for him, I saw a vision of money coming down from heaven. The Lord said He was going to bless them in abundance financially.

About six months later, after they moved to their house in Pennsylvania, The husband called again. He was not working and finances were worse than when they lived in Chicago. Again, the Lord said the same thing as before.

Seven months later the husband called and said he had a job and had just won about $56,000 in McDonald's Monopoly game. He was an instant winner when he casually opened the game sticker. The couple listen to the Lord and have been faithfully following the Lord's directions for years. God made promises of financial blessings in the midst of dire financial circumstances, not once, but twice. Things got worse after God made the first financial promise, and were bleak when the second promise was made. But Mike and Lisa continued to follow the direction of the Lord in spite of the financial difficulties they were experiencing. God fulfilled His promise, but it was not in the time frame we all expected.

Moses Is Led Each Step of the Way

Moses was given specific directions by God regarding what he was to say to Pharaoh. The continual pattern was that Moses went before God, received His instructions, went to Pharaoh with those instructions, and watched how God performed the miracles which brought the plagues on Egypt. God gave Pharaoh opportunity after opportunity to repent. The first five times Moses went to Pharaoh with instructions from the Lord, Pharaoh hardened his own heart. Then God hardened his heart, then again Pharaoh hardened his heart. God, in His perfect foreknowledge knew that Pharaoh would do this, but He gave Him enough rope to hang himself. Pharaoh could never say that he was not offered an opportunity to turn from his hardened ways. He was shown that the God of Moses was the one and only true God, but he continually rejected him. Today we are given the same opportunity.

We used to attend a prayer meeting/Bible study at the home of our friends, Bill and Diane Lowe. Everyone who attended was born again and spirit filled, trying to walk the Christian walk. Everyone that is, except one man in his thirties who was dating a member of the group, and only came to the study to be with her.

One day, the Lord told me to witness to him and ask him if he wanted to accept Jesus as his Lord. I was going to pray about it, and do it another day; however, the Lord was insistent that I do it that day. I witnessed to him and invited him to accept the Lord and he said, "No, I'm not ready." We left it at that; however, within two weeks, he was sitting in his living room and had a brain aneurysm and died immediately. When he went before the Lord, he could not say he never had an opportunity to receive Him. This incident is a constant sober reminder of the need to be obedient to the leading of the Holy Spirit.

Moses at the Red Sea

Moses and the approximately 2.4 million Israelites were at the Red Sea when God told him the Egyptians were coming. (Exodus 14:4) The people were terrified as they saw the Egyptians marching toward them. (Exodus 14:10) Now these were the same people of God who had experienced the results of the ten plagues in Egypt, and had seen God's hand in removing those plagues. They saw one miracle after another. They even had the cloud by day and the fire by night to lead them. (Genesis 13:21-22) However, they forgot God's power.

We are no different from those Israelites. When we are faced with an immediate crisis, we tend to forget all that God has done for us, our friends and our churches in the past. We approach the new situation with fear and trembling. In Exodus 14:13-14, Moses spoke to the people:

"...Do not be afraid. Stand firm and you will see the deliverance the LORD will bring you today. The Egyptians you see today you will never see again. The LORD will fight for you; you need only to be still."

Is this the same Moses who was so afraid in Exodus chapters three and four? What changed his attitude? He saw the fulfillment of the many promises God gave him and he saw the miraculous judgments which took place when he only spoke the word given to him by God. He had learned through the experience of listening to the voice of the Lord that God is faithful to His promises. He was fearful before he really knew God, but now, having learned the faithfulness of God, was able to calm the fears of those under his charge. God is not looking for ability, but rather, availability.

As we continue listening to the voice of the Lord and believing His promises, we will see the results and our faith will increase. As we trust more, we will be more obedient in different situations and we will see still more results. As our faith increases, our trust in the living God will grow, and He will be able to trust us with more and more. What began as fear will finish as faith.

God, in Exodus 14:16 said to Moses, *"Raise your staff and stretch out your hand over the sea to divide the water so that the Israelites can go through the sea on dry ground."* Moses again listened and obeyed God and the supernatural miracle of the parting of the Red Sea took place.

God Again Tests the Israelites

Three days after the parting of the Red Sea and the total destruction of the Egyptian army, the Israelites started their grumbling. They were out of water and they were thirsty. The waters at Marah were bitter, so God told Moses to throw a piece of wood into the water to make it sweet and drinkable. He then said a remarkable thing in Exodus 15:25-26.

> **Then Moses cried out to the LORD, and the LORD showed him a piece of wood. He threw it into the water, and the water became sweet. There the LORD made a decree and a law for them, and there he tested them. He said, "If you listen carefully to the voice of the LORD your God and do what is right in his eyes, if you pay attention to his commands and keep all his decrees, I will not bring on you any of the diseases I brought on the Egyptians, for I am the LORD who heals you."**

He gave the Israelites the promise of being disease free if they obeyed Him. These verses speak for themselves. Will we harken to them and *listen carefully* and do what He wants us to do, realizing that all of God's directions and our obedience is part of a life long test? God does not change. What He said then applies to us now. Let listening and obedience become our life in Christ.

From Marah, they went to Elim, then to the desert of Sin where the Lord provided a different test in Exodus 16:4-5.

> **Then the LORD said to Moses, "I will rain down bread from heaven for you. The people are to go out each day and gather enough for that day. In this way I will test them and see whether they will follow my instructions. On the sixth day they are to prepare what they bring in, and this is to be twice as much as they gather on the other days."**

This time the Lord tested the Israelites with a different kind of test. He wanted to see if they were willing to rely on His promises for daily provisions including gathering twice as much on the sixth day to cover the Sabbath. Of course, some disobeyed taking more than their daily share, planning to have some leftover for later. But the left over manna became full of maggots and began to smell.

Jesus is our daily bread and we need a fresh portion of Him each day; He is new every morning. Too often many of us rely on yesterday's blessings as we live in the past. We find ourselves wanting to be independent of the Lord and so do not seek fresh direction or *"manna from heaven."* He is the bread of life and we need His spiritual bread every day. When Jesus was tempted by Satan in the desert, he was hungry. Jesus quoted part of Deut. 8:3 which states, *"man does not live on bread alone, but on every word that comes from the mouth of God."* This is true of us individually and corporately. When we live in our past blessings, our walk begins to smell. We need God's new blessing each day.

Another testing came when the Israelites were out of water again at Rephidim, and they quarreled with Moses blaming him (Exodus 17:1-2). God told Moses to take the same staff he had used to strike the Nile and bring plagues upon the Egyptians, and to part the Red Sea, and strike the rock, which brought forth life-giving water to God's people.

Later, at Kadesh, again there was no water, and the people gathered in opposition to Moses and Aaron (Numbers 20:2-5). They quarreled with Moses and made him angry. The Lord said to Moses in Numbers 20:8:

> **"Take the staff, and you and your brother Aaron gather the assembly together. Speak to that rock before their eyes and**

you will pour water out of the rock... Jesus

it will pour out its water. You will bring water out of the rock for the community so they and their livestock can drink."

Moses disobeyed God's new commandment and in his anger toward the people he took his staff and struck the rock two times. The Lord told Moses to *speak* to the rock; not strike it with the staff. (Numbers 20:9-10) God had used the staff to perform miracles before and Moses was trusting in the staff more than in the word of God. He probably thought, I used the staff at the parting of the Red Sea, and at Rephidim when the Lord brought forth water when I struck the rock, **why not now?** He trusted in the old tried and true ways; while God wanted him to trust Him in a totally different way and to merely *speak* to the rock. *Always be ready to obey something new.*

What is remarkable is that God honored Moses' striking of the rock in spite of his disobedience. Because of his disobedience, Moses was forbidden from entering into the Promised Land. I used to think the judgment of God was exceedingly harsh; however, now I understand that Moses was God's leader and he had to set an example for the people. He saw many miracles of God when He was totally obedient to the voice of the Lord and should have learned the lesson of full obedience by this time.

We all tend to get into habit patterns and believe what worked so well in the past will work the same way in the future. This is not always so. We must learn to rely on the living God and not on past successes through God. He will always do new things in our lives to get us away from trusting in methods, objects, or historical success. He wants us to trust in Him and His word only and will often change what He has us do. The Bible is filled with examples of this. All the wars in the Bible are different, all the healings and deliverances are different, and the examples are all different. God is a God of variety and we are creatures of habit. He will break that habit only if we let Him.

God Continually Led the Israelites in Desperate Situations

Here is an interesting thing. Remember, God led the people with a cloud by day and fire by night. It was God who led the people to the Red Sea with the sea in front and Pharaoh's army behind. God led them to the bitter waters of Marah and it was God who led them when they did not have water on several occasions. God led them each step of the way. What is remarkable is that He led them to places that seemed impossible.

However, God always led them to miraculous results and escape. He caused the Egyptian army to drown. He provided a tree to throw in the water to make the water sweet. He provided manna from heaven. He made water come out of the rock. All of these were supernatural events.

These are examples of how the Lord will work in our lives today. We, at times, will be led into seemingly impossible situations. We will cry out in desperation and the Lord will deliver us supernaturally. Often, we are in continuous testing situations, just as the Israelites.

A Friend of God

"The Lord would speak to Moses face to face, as a man speaks with his friend."
Exodus 33:11.

Moses developed a friendship with God because he was in constant communication with Him. No one can be considered a friend unless and until there is a close relationship. Moses is our example. Many of us would like to be like Moses, God's friend. But we cannot do it unless and until we are willing to spend time in His presence, to learn about Him, and to have Him learn about us. I know you want that relationship with God; otherwise, you would not be reading this book. Let's start by getting into many conversations with the living God and drawing closer to Him so that we, too, can be called a friend of God.

Disobedience in Entering the Promised Land

The people grumbled after the twelve spies came back from exploring the Promised Land and gave their bad report. (Numbers 13:31-33) Only Caleb and Joshua were men of faith and believed that God would prevail over the enemy. After Moses reported God's displeasure at their lack of faith to the people and told them not to go into the Promised Land, they were determined to go anyway. Numbers 14:41-43 states:

> **But Moses said, "Why are you disobeying the LORD'S command? This will not succeed! Do not go up, because the LORD is not with you. You will be defeated by your enemies, for the Amalekites and Canaanites will face you there. Because you have turned away from the LORD, He will not be with you and you will fall by the sword."**

God will honor our obedience; however, it has to be in His timing. The Israelites were told that God was not in the attack and that they were disobedient, yet they went anyway. We have to learn that obedience to the Lord is not at our convenience and whenever we get up enough nerve to do what He told us to do. It may be too late by then.

Life and Death, Blessings and Curses

At the end of his ministry and life, Moses called the Israelites together and gave them a sermon. Deuteronomy 30:19-20 says,

> **"This day I call heaven and earth as witnesses against you that I have set before you life and death, blessings and curses. Now choose life, so that you and your children may live and that you may love the LORD your God, listen to his voice, and hold fast to him. For the LORD is your life…"**

Moses is telling the people to choose which way they will go. Just as the Israelites had a choice, so we, too, have a choice. We can choose life or death, blessings or curses. The key is whether or not we choose to listen to the voice of the Lord. When we listen and obey, we have life and blessings abundantly. Moses learned the lessons through the many experiences he had with and without the leading of God. What he learned, he now wants to impart to others. Are we ready to learn from his experiences? Jeremiah 17:5-8 says,

> **"This is what the Lord says: "Cursed is the one who trusts in man, who depends on flesh for his strength and whose heart turns away from the LORD. He will be like a bush in the wastelands; he will not see prosperity when it comes. He will dwell in the parched places of the desert, in a salt land where no one lives. But blessed is the man who trusts in the Lord, whose confidence is in him. He will be like a tree planted by the water that sends out its roots by the stream. It does not fear when heat comes; its leaves are always green. It has no worries in a year of drought and never fails to bear fruit."**

I do not want to be cursed by trusting in man, no matter how spiritual that man may appear to be. I want the blessings of God, but it follows that I must trust Him.

Deuteronomy 28:1-14 sets forth the blessings that will come upon us and overtake us *and our children* if we will listen to the voice of the Lord. Further, Deuteronomy 28:15-68 sets forth the curses if we ignore the Lord. I want the blessings; therefore, listening to the Lord is an absolute necessity in my life. I urge you to search out on your own all the conversations Moses had with God and as you do you will discover many nuggets on listening that will enrich your life as well.

Chapter Five

JOSHUA, GIDEON, SAMUEL, DAVID, AND SOLOMON

These Old Testament Saints started their ministries by listening to God and following His direction. They knew that without Him they could do nothing even though at times they tried, but failed miserably. The Bible is filled with examples. Here are more to show that God wants us to always be led by His Spirit.

Joshua

Joshua knew only God could bring the nation of Israel into the Promised Land. He was one of the two spies who, forty years earlier, had had faith that God would bring His people into the Promised Land at that time. But because of their disobedience they were forced to wander in the desert for forty years, Joshua with them.

Even though he was obedient, he still wandered in the desert with those who were disobedient. He was ready to go into the Promised Land forty years earlier, but was unable to do so because of the disobedience of the many. We, too, may be obedient but we may be hindered because of the disobedience of those around us. Joshua eventually went into the Promised Land with the Israelites, chosen by God to be their leader.

During the time he and the people were in the desert, he saw many miracles of God. He had been under the tutelage of a great listener, Moses. He saw what happened when Moses obeyed the Lord and what happened when he didn't. He was there when God told Moses he could not enter into the Promised Land because of his disobedience in striking the rock rather than speaking to it and he knew the power of both obeying the voice of the Lord and the consequences of disobeying the Lord. His background in Egypt and forty years in the wilderness with Moses was the preparation he needed in order to become the leader of the Israelites.

The first recorded events in the leadership of Joshua was his listening to the Lord and getting guidance for the people. (Joshua 1:1-9) The Bible shows that Joshua started his ministry by talking to the Lord and is the first thing God deems important in showing us the start of Joshua's ministry. His relationship to the Lord and obedience to His directions are brought out in the book of Joshua.

God told him to have the priests step into the waters of the Jordan (Joshua 3:7-8); a different test from what Moses was directed to follow. The Lord didn't tell Joshua to lift up his staff, hit the water, or speak to the water as He told Moses. God responded to those *steps of obedience* by causing the river to cease to flow upstream. The Lord knew that the people had to be shown that the power of God was with Joshua just as it had been with Moses. Remember that you cannot live on the accomplishments of your predecessor. The Lord will always have a new set of steps for a new leader.

Later was the test of Jericho. The Lord told Joshua: *"See, I have delivered Jericho into your hands...." (Joshua 6:2)* He said that it was done *even before* the Israelites had begun their war with Jericho. It is past tense. Before they did anything, God had already given the city into their hands.

When God tells us to do something, the results are already established in heaven. He's looking for our obedience and when He gets it, His plan will be accomplished through a human being.

God told Joshua to march around the city once each day for six days and seven times on the seventh day. (Joshua 6:2-5) Joshua told the people not to talk until the seventh day. The reason for this was that the people probably would have been complaining and murmuring just as their fathers had done. They were their fathers' children, and God and Joshua both knew they had to keep quiet or the same scenario could develop for them as happened to their fathers. You can't complain if you can't talk.

Can you imagine what the Israelites would have said if they talked? The conversation could have gone something like this. *"Why are we doing this?" "We never did this when Moses led us."*

"How are we going to fight a battle this way?" "Grumble, grumble." God knew them. They were their father's children. Since they could not talk, they could not complain. Further, they were obedient because they saw how God used Joshua to stop the river from flowing. When they obeyed the Lord in walking around the city for seven days, the walls came tumbling down. First comes obedience and then comes the results.

Later, in Joshua, chapter nine, Joshua failed to seek the Lord regarding the treatment of a group of people called the Gibeonites. The Gibeonites were very clever and deceived Joshua into believing they came from a long distance. The Israelites did not know that the Gibeonites lived in part of the land that was to be given to them by God. So they went ahead and made a pact with the Gibeonites without asking God first. They gave them permission to live in the land and even though they were deceived they had to honor their commitment. Had they sought the Lord before, they would not have made the agreement with the Gibeonites.

There is always a very simple pattern. When you seek the Lord and obey, God's results occur. When we do whatever we believe we should, even though it *appears* to be a good thing, and God is not in it, He will not guarantee the results. In fact, disaster may be the result.

Gideon

Gideon was not a person of great importance, but simply a farmer from one of the least of the tribes. You might say he was a nobody. He had lived under the bondage and control of despotic foreign leaders, the Midianites, where he learned to be afraid, and his approach to God was one of fear. In Judges, chapter six, the angel of the Lord appeared to Gideon. (Many Bible scholars believe that any time the *angel of the Lord* appeared in the Old Testament, it was really the appearance of Jesus.)

Although several supernatural events occurred such as fire flaring from the rock to consume the meat and the bread when Gideon prepared a sacrifice, and dew on the fleece with the ground dry and vice versa, Gideon was still fearful. He continued to be afraid when God reduced his army from 30,000 troops to 300. With this small number of troops, Gideon could not take credit for the victory, for the victory would be the Lord's. God said if he was still afraid, he should go down to the camp of the enemy, the Midianites.(Judges 7:10)

When he went down, God had him listen to the conversation of several enemy soldiers. As he listened, he found they were more afraid of him than he was of them. Gideon knew God had set up that conversation specifically for him, and that God was in control. As a result, Gideon's confidence in the Lord grew. Because his trust in the Lord was strengthened, Gideon went ahead at the direction of the Lord and had complete victory.

As we are led by the Lord, we will constantly find that the Lord's timing is perfect. One summer our family went to Dewey Beach in Delaware for a week's vacation. This bright sunny day the Lord told my wife and me to walk to Rehoboth Beach and witness on the way. We were led by the Lord to each person we witnessed to; however, we saw no apparent results.

When we got to Rehoboth, the Lord said we should sit down on a certain bench. Within one minute, three joggers passed the bench. As they were running, one jogger was speaking to the others and said clearly, *"Have faith in God."* That was all we heard as they ran by. The Lord told us He set up that very brief encounter. He had us sitting on the bench at the exact time when one jogger told the other joggers to *"Have faith in God."*

He wanted us to know that He was in control. Even though we didn't see any results from the witnessing we did, God wanted us to know that the witnessing was not in vain. It accomplished His purpose, and we should always have faith that the Lord is in control. Praise the Lord! The Scripture that came to mind is Isaiah 55:10-11 which says,

> **As the rain and the snow come down from heaven, and do not return to it without watering the earth and making it bud and flourish, so that it yields seed for the sower and bread for the eater, so is my word that goes out from my mouth: It will not return to me empty, but will accomplish what I desire and achieve the purpose for which I send it.**

We are no different than Gideon. We are often afraid when God directs us to do something. God knows this; but, He wants us to trust in what He says to do rather than to conjure up fears that will never come to pass. As we trust His spoken word, He puts together events in our lives we know are from God. As a result, our faith is strengthened and our fears lessen.

Most of us are somebodies that God takes and makes into some bodies, maybe not some bodies in the world, but some bodies in His kingdom, which is more important. But it will only come with obedience.

Samuel

Moses was eighty years old when he began to hear from God. But Samuel was only a boy and though the Bible is not clear as to his age, it does refer to him as a boy (1 Samuel 3:1). If you can read this book, you're neither too young nor too old to begin to hear from your heavenly Father. Even as a young lad, Samuel was taught by Eli that God was speaking to him. Samuel, at first, thought Eli was calling him, but Eli told him it was the Lord and told Samuel to simply say: *"Speak, for your servant is listening." (1 Samuel 3:10)*

Even though I will be teaching a different method to help in listening to God in chapters 10 and 11, this is one excellent way to begin hearing from Him. The key to listening is doing whatever works for you as long as you are listening to the Lord.

God gave Samuel a hard word to give to Eli regarding his disobedient sons (1 Samuel 3:11-14). Eli knew Samuel had a word for him from the Lord and had to urge Samuel to tell him what it was. Reluctantly, Samuel told Eli what the Lord had told him about his sons and it proved to be a confirmation of a word another man of God had given Eli (1 Samuel 2:27-36). The people had also complained to Eli about the wicked deeds of his sons (1 Samuel 2:22-23), so this was not new to Eli. It was simply a confirmation of what Eli had already received from the Lord.

God gives people a number of chances to repent. Eli knew he had to discipline his sons, yet he failed to respond to what the people were saying, and, more importantly, to what was said to him twice prophetically from the prophets of God. One of the characteristics of God, and a fruit of the spirit, is patience, and God is continually demonstrating patience with His people. God also gives us many chances to repent so we will have no excuse when the judgment of God comes upon us for disobedience.

If the Lord gives us a word for others, we should not be afraid to give it. Generally, it is confirmatory to what someone has already given them through another word, what God had spoken to them directly, or what is happening in their lives. There will be times when it will be a new word to the individual; however, it is generally confirmatory.

Samuel continued to be used by the Lord. He continued to follow the voice of the Lord and to lead the Israelites accordingly. One of the most dramatic instances where the Lord used Samuel concerns King Saul and his disobedience in 1 Samuel 15:20-23:

> **"But I did obey the LORD," Saul said. "I went on the mission the Lord assigned me. I completely destroyed the Amalekites and brought back Agag their king. The soldiers took sheep and cattle from the plunder, the best of what was devoted to God, in order to sacrifice them to the LORD your God at Gilgal."**

> **But Samuel replied, "Does the LORD delight in burnt offerings and sacrifices as much as in obeying the voice of the Lord? To obey is better than sacrifice, and to heed is better than the fat of rams. For rebellion is like the sin of divination, and arrogance like the evil of idolatry. Because you have rejected the word of the LORD, he has rejected you as king."**

Saul was told to kill all of the Amalekites, but he didn't. He said he did, but he brought back the king. There were also other Amalekites whom he failed to destroy and David had to finish the job that Saul failed to do (2 Samuel 1). In addition, and of great importance, Saul was later killed by an Amalekite (2 Samuel 1:5-10); that which he failed to destroy, in the end destroyed him. He was commanded to kill the sheep and cattle, but chose the religious way, and decided to sacrifice them, against the specific direction of the Lord. He said he was obedient, but he was only partially obedient. Partial obedience is really disobedience. Because Saul rejected the word of the Lord, he was rejected as king.

It's important to remember that leaders in the body are required to be examples to the people. If the people see obedience, it will help them to be obedient; whereas, if they see disobedience to the word of the Lord and see the leaders getting away with disobedience, it will lead them to do the same. God must deal harshly with the disobedience of leaders to show the church what to expect. Public disclosure of the sins of many Christian leaders has caused the body to have a healthy fear of the Lord. What God did then, he can also do now.

Samuel led by example by listening to the Lord and doing what he was told; however, he could not bring his own sons to the same point of obedience (1 Samuel 8:1-3). They chose to go their own way and consequently lost their right to be the spiritual leader their father had been. Samuel also saw what happened to Eli's sons. That should have been a warning to him regarding his own sons; yet, Samuel's sons were similar to Eli's in their disobedience to the Lord. His sons accepted bribes and perverted justice as well. (1 Samuel 8:3)

We can have the greatest ministry and many people may look up to us in awe, but imagine our heartbreak when our own children do not follow after the Lord. One of the greatest desires of all Christians with children is that their children love the Lord with all their heart, mind, soul, and strength. No matter what our part is in the body of Christ, we must not neglect our children. One of our greatest ministries is to them. All too often we become so immersed in our public ministries that we forget our most important ministry is to our families. Let us learn the lessons of the Bible to help our children know and follow the way of righteousness.

David

David was a great listener. All you have to do is look at all the prophetic psalms written by him. He had to be hearing from God to record all the events fulfilled in the life of Jesus. One of the best examples is Psalm 22 which gives very specific detail of the agony of Jesus on the cross. The first verse of the psalm was quoted by Jesus at His crucifixion: ***"My God, my God, why have you forsaken me?"***

Jesus knew that the Jews knew the Psalms in great detail, and He was pointing to that Psalm as the fulfillment of the agony He was then going through. David had to have received divine direction from God in order to write it. The 23rd Psalm is one of the greatest, most memorized of all the Psalms and is a perfect example of how Jesus, our Great Shepherd, leads and guides us.

In Psalm 3:4 David cried: *"To the LORD I cry aloud, and he answers me from his holy hill."* **Further, in Psalm 27:7 David cried:** *"Hear my voice when I call O LORD; be merciful to me and answer me."* **Again in Psalm 5:3 David said:** *"In the morning, O LORD, you hear my voice; in the morning I lay my requests before you and wait in expectation."* David arose early, made petition before God and waited for His response.

David sought the Wonderful Counselor in Psalm 16:7. He says: *"I will praise the LORD, who counsels me; even at night my heart instructs me."* David sought the Lord in the morning and at night and was constantly listening before the Lord. He is an example for us all.

Psalm 25 gives us insight regarding David's relationship with God. Verses 4 and 5 state: *"Show me your ways, O LORD, teach me your paths; guide me in your truth and teach me, for you are God my Savior."* And in verses 8 and 9 David stated: *"Good and upright is the LORD; therefore he instructs sinners in his ways. He guides the humble in what is right and teaches them his way."* David expected to be guided, taught, and instructed by the Lord—and he was.

Psalm 143:8 and 10 continue with the same message. *"Let the morning bring me the word of your unfailing love, for I have put my trust in you. Show me the way I should go, for to you I lift up my soul. Teach me to do your will, for you are my God; may your good Spirit lead me on level ground."*

The same theme is set forth in Psalm 32:8 when God spoke to David and speaks to us when He said: *"I will instruct you and teach you in the way you should go; I will counsel you and watch over you."*

And again in Psalm 34:4 David related his continual seeking the Lord. He says: *"I sought the LORD, and he answered me; he delivered me from all my fears."* Psalm 86:7 says: *"In the days of my trouble I will call to you, for you will answer me."*

Also in Psalm 34:11, the Lord is speaking about His wisdom when He says, *"Come my children, listen to me; I will teach you the fear of the LORD."*

Psalm 139 is one of my favorite psalms. In verses 17 and 18, David declared the numerous thoughts he received from the Lord. *"How precious to me are your thoughts, O God! How vast is the sum of them! Were I to count them, they would outnumber the grains of sand. When I awake I am still with you.* " David was constantly in the presence of the Lord. He couldn't even count the gems of wisdom which the Lord had given him.

My prayer is that we have the same relationship with the Lord that David experienced. He awoke each morning with thoughts from the Lord and went to sleep at night in conversation with Him.

Lord, let this be our experience as well. Bring us to that place of intimate times with you. O Lord, give us the same heart that David had for you!

David often inquired of the Lord through the high priest and prophets, asking specific direction regarding the many battles he fought. He also received a prophecy from Nathan the prophet in 2 Samuel 7:5-16 which provided a number of undeserved promises. Because David was a man after God's own heart, the Lord blessed him, the nation, and his children. God promised him that He would make his name great, that He would provide a place for the nation Israel, that He would plant them so they could have a home, that He would protect them from being disturbed by wicked people, that God would give David rest from his enemies, and that He would raise up offspring to succeed him and establish his kingdom. Further, he, and his son Solomon, would be the ones to build a house for God. In addition, God promised that when David's offspring did wrong He would punish them with the rod of men. He also promised that the house of David would endure forever. What promises! Let's look at their fulfillment.

God certainly made David's name great. All of the promises concerning Israel were fulfilled for a season; however, because of the disobedience of subsequent leaders and the people, God sent enemies to discipline the Israelites.

David had rest from his enemies until the time he had Uriah the Hittite killed in battle so that he could have Bathsheba for himself. God sent Nathan with another prophecy in 2 Samuel 12:7-14. Part of the word of the Lord in 2 Samuel 12:9-10 says:

> **Why did you despise the word of the LORD by doing what is evil in his eyes? You struck down Uriah the Hittite with the sword and took his wife to be your own. You killed him with the sword of the Ammonites. Now, therefore, the sword will never depart from your house, because you despised me and took the wife of Uriah the Hittite to be your** own.

God may give us a word about the future that will come true if we continue on in obedience; however, disobedience may well cause the promises to be null and void. Promises we receive from the Lord are often conditional on our continued obedience.

There is a Biblical principle that is unchanging. What we sow, we will reap; whatever we do to others will be done to us. Here are several Biblical examples: *"Blessed are the merciful, for they shall be shown mercy."* *(Matthew 5:7). "For if you forgive men when they sin against you, your heavenly father will also forgive you. But if you do not forgive men their sins, your Father will not forgive your sins." (Matthew 6:14-15). "Do not judge, or you too will be judged. For in the same way you judge others, you will be judged, and with the measure you use, it will be measured to you." (Matthew 7:1-2). "Remember this: whosoever sows sparingly, will also reap sparingly, and whosoever sows generously will also reap generously." (2 Corinthians 9:6).*

David sowed the death of Uriah and reaped war for both his household and country for the rest of his days. God does not renege on His promises; we make the promises null and void by our rebellion, disobedience and sin. However, God is faithful even though man may not be. Finally, the House of David certainly will endure forever, since Jesus is from the house of David.

Solomon

Solomon observed his father listening and he did likewise. However, he was not as consistent as David had been. There are two examples of listening to the Lord in the life of Solomon. The first was in 1 Kings 3:9-14 which states:

> **"So give your servant a discerning heart to govern your people and to distinguish between right and wrong. For who is able to govern this great people of yours?"**

> **The Lord was pleased that Solomon had asked for this. So God said to him, "Since you have asked for this and not for long life or wealth for yourself, nor have asked for the death of your enemies but for discernment in administering justice, I will do what you have asked. I will give you a wise and discerning heart, so that there will never have been anyone like you, nor will there ever be."**

Solomon was humble at the beginning, knowing he could not govern the people with his knowledge and wisdom alone. He asked for discernment (some versions indicate wisdom) and he received more than he asked for.

I have found that the principle of asking for others rather than for self pleases the Lord and He will often bless in abundance those individuals who are unselfish and look out for the good of others in their prayers. I have seen numerous occasions when individuals praying for the needs of others have received blessings in abundance. Job was a good example. He was healed when he prayed for his friends.

Solomon received what God had promised. He became the wisest man who ever walked the face of the earth. People came from all over the known world to hear the Wisdom of Solomon. He received such wealth that even silver was looked down upon, since gold was so plentiful. He had one recorded conversation with the Lord and his whole life and kingdom were blessed. He obeyed the Lord for a season and reaped the rewards.

After God raised Solomon to be king, Solomon fulfilled the promise of God which was given to David for him to build God's temple. When the temple was completed, the glory of the Lord filled the temple so completely the priests could not stand, but fell on their faces.

When we, in cooperation with God, complete tasks or projects God has given us to do, we will see God's result and even experience His presence at times. The key is constant obedience—something that Solomon did not continue during his days.

Another example of listening occurred later in his reign. In 1 Kings 9:4-7, God told Solomon:

> **"As for you, if you walk before me in integrity of heart and uprightness, as David your father did, and do all I command and observe my decrees and laws, I will establish your royal throne over Israel forever, as I promised David your father when I said, 'You shall never fail to have a man on the throne of Israel.'"**

"But if you or your sons turn away from me and do not observe the commands and decrees I have given you and go off to serve other gods and worship them, then I will cut off Israel from the land I have given them and will reject this temple I have consecrated for my Name. Israel will then become a byword and an object of ridicule among all peoples."

What did Solomon do? He saw the promises of God fulfilled in his kingdom, yet he did not continue to follow the one true God. Unfortunately, later in his life he acquired 700 wives and 300 concubines, many of whom were not Israelites. These wives brought their gods with them and turned Solomon's heart away from the living God. He followed the false gods Ashtoreth, Molech, and Chemosh (1 King 11:1-8). God told him specifically the consequences of serving other gods; but he did not heed His warning. God became angry at Solomon and the judgment He warned about came upon Israel.

God will often warn an individual, church, or nation about the consequences of their disobedience, giving them an opportunity for repentance—yet, historically, the pattern has been that they continually go astray. Here we have the wisest man in the history of the world. He knew the results of past disobedience of the Israelites, he knew the results of the sin of his father and mother and the resulting death of his brother; he knew the blessings he received because of the obedience of his father David, and yet he ignored God's warning.

God will warn in a very specific area, knowing full well that the warning will be disregarded; however, when judgment comes, the individual, church, or nation cannot say they never knew. Heed well the warnings of the Lord, for we know they could come to pass.

Years ago, I was ministering to a Christian who was a practicing homosexual. The Lord delivered him, but with the deliverance came a warning. If he continued in homosexuality, he would get herpes. He did not believe the warning. Several years later, he called and said that he had herpes. He had been unwilling to give up homosexuality. After ministering to him again, the Lord gave me a word and warned him that if he continued in homosexuality, he would get AIDS. Again, he did not heed the warning. About three years later, he called and said he was HIV positive.

I somberly relate this example so you can understand God does not change. He punishes sin. We are not exempt from the judgments of God because we are Christians and are His children. If we are warned by the Lord, we need to heed the warning. If we do not, we bear the consequences of our disobedience. Judgment first comes to the household of God.

Finally, we must all learn that if and when we become successful, whether in the spiritual realm or the secular one, we must acknowledge the source of our success. It is always God who raises us up, we cannot do it ourselves. We must always be ever thankful to our Lord who is responsible for whatever success we have in this world. Never turn away from the living God, as did the wisest man who walked the earth.

Chapter Six

THE PROPHETS ARE LED BY GOD

There is no group in the Bible which highlights listening to the Lord more than the prophets. The prophetic books of the Bible and parts of the Bible during the reign of the kings of Israel exemplify the constant communication God had with His prophets.

There is a tendency to set the prophets aside as having a special place in the interaction between God and man; however, we should not do so. Any individual can have the same intimate relationship that most of the prophets had with God.

They were in a place of prayer and prayed expectantly as they listened to the Lord. They listened and obeyed. They went where He sent them and said what He wanted them to say. They are a picture of His ultimate servants, the kind of relationship God wants each of us to develop with Him. He wants us to come before Him just as the prophets of old, to listen and obey.

True vs. False Prophets

Ezekiel is an example of a true prophet. Ezekiel 2:1-3 states:

> *He said to me, "Son of man, stand up on your feet and I will speak to you." As he spoke, the Spirit came into me and raised me to my feet, and I heard him speaking to me. He said: "Son of man, I am sending you to the Israelites, to a rebellious nation that has rebelled against me; they and their fathers have been in revolt against me to this very day."*

You can see that true prophets stand in the presence of the Lord, hear the voice of the Lord, and are sent by the Lord. We do not have time in this book to detail the numerous times words are given from God to a *man of God* or to a *woman of God* as there are also women prophetesses. They hear the word and are the mailmen of the Lord, delivering the message to whomever the Lord chooses.

Let's see what the Bible calls a false prophet. Jeremiah 14:14 states:

> ***Then the LORD said to me, "The prophets are prophesying lies in my name. I have not sent them or appointed them or spoken to them. They are prophesying to you false visions, divinations, idolatries and the delusions of their own minds."***

A true prophet is appointed by God, hears God speaking to him, and is sent by Him to do His will. False prophets are not appointed by Him, do not hear Him speak and are not sent by Him. Believers who prophesy, whether appointed by God as a prophet or are simply prophesying because God has chosen to use them, have to hear from God; they must hear in order to know they are appointed as prophets, and to know when they are sent. In order to give a message from God, they have to hear that message. Hearing is absolutely necessary according to the Bible.

You may wonder why I am emphasizing this area so much. The reason is there are numbers of people in the body who are supposedly delivering *"a word from the Lord"* who have not heard from God. They may hear one or a few words and start speaking as if they had the whole message. They may have a vision and speak based on *their* interpretation of that vision. If we are to be true to the Bible, we must hear the word and deliver it at the time, place, and to the person or groups the Lord directs. When I prophecy, I am simply told by the Lord who the message is for and when I should deliver it. Then I listen and the Lord gives me a sentence which I speak. Then I listen to the next sentence and speak it. I continue to do this until I hear no more. The prophecy is then over.

If an individual is not given the full message by the Lord, but only a vision or part of a word, that person should explain what was from the Lord according to his/her understanding. It is important not to attribute to the Lord that which could very well be of one's own self.

The words we hear can be from the Lord, from our own mind, or from the demonic realm. Of course, the worst scenario would be that they would be from the evil one. We all are capable of deception, and unfortunately, there are those who are being deceived by Satan, and in turn, deceiving others. This will be addressed in more detail in a later chapter.

Isaiah

Isaiah's story in 2 Kings 20:1-6 states:

> *In those days Hezekiah became ill and was at the point of death. The prophet Isaiah son of Amoz went to him and said, "This is what the LORD says. Put your house in order, because you are going to die; you will not recover."*
>
> *Hezekiah turned his face to the wall and prayed to the Lord, "Remember, O LORD, how I have walked before you faithfully and with wholehearted devotion and have done what is good in your eyes." And Hezekiah wept bitterly.*
>
> *Before Isaiah had left the middle of the court, the word of the LORD came to him; "Go back and tell Hezekiah, the leader of my people, 'This is what the LORD, the God of your father David, says: I have heard your prayer and seen your tears; I will heal you. On the third day from now you will go up to the temple of the Lord. I will add fifteen years to your life..."*

God honored the repentance of Hezekiah, changed His mind and let him live. And though He gave him the desire of his heart, it certainly was not the best for the nation. Later, Hezekiah showed the envoys from Babylon all the riches of the treasury and they reported back to their Babylonian leaders. Eventually all of the riches were carried back to Babylon in fulfillment of another word from Isaiah.

Furthermore, during Hezekiah's fifteen additional years of life, he fathered Manasseh who eventually became the worst king Judah had ever had. If Hezekiah had accepted the original will of the Lord when He was going to take him home, Manasseh never would have been born and history might have been different.

We need have no fear of dying since death has no sting for us. We merely graduate to glory. It may be in our own best interest and those around us to accept the will of the Lord. We are better off with His will and His timing for our graduation than our own desires in a matter. He knows the present and the future and what is best in all situations. We may be asking for the desires of our heart and unfortunately for all concerned, get what we ask for.

There have been about five situations when people have come to me and asked me to pray for someone to be healed and raised from impending death. I will always seek the Lord as to how to pray. In each of those cases, the Lord wanted to take them home. At the direction of the Lord, I related God's intentions and, if they were willing, led them in a prayer to release their loved ones to the Lord. All of their loved ones were Christians and all died within two days after they were released to the Lord.

I've seen situations where the Lord supernaturally raised people from their death beds, and I am willing to pray for miraculous healings when the Lord leads me to do so. However, the key is to seek the will of the Lord in every situation.

Isaiah was a listener and encouraged others to listen. In a message from the Lord, Isaiah 55:1-2 states:

> *"Why spend money on what is not bread, and your labor on what does not satisfy? Listen, listen to me and eat what is good, and your soul will delight in the richest of fare. Give ear and come to me; hear me, that your soul may live..."*

God is saying for us to listen and he repeats it by saying, *"Listen, listen."* God has to keep saying it since we are so slow to hear. We have two ears and one mouth so shouldn't we be listening at least twice as much as we speak?

Further, Isaiah 30:21 states: *"Whether you turn to the right or to the left, your ears will hear a voice behind you, saying, 'This is the way; walk in it.'"* Isaiah was constantly hearing from the Lord and so should we.

Jeremiah

God often will lead by examples that we are familiar with so we can have a better understanding of what He is teaching us. The beginning of Jeremiah, chapter thirteen, is a good example of this. God told Jeremiah to take the linen belt he was wearing around his waist and to hide it in the crevice of a rock. After many days, God told him to get the belt. After being subjected to the elements for some time, the belt had become ruined and completely useless. Then the Lord spoke the meaning of the belt to Jeremiah. He said in Jeremiah 13:9-11:

> *"This is what the LORD says: 'In the same way I will ruin the pride of Judah and the great pride of Jerusalem. These wicked people, who refuse to listen to my words, who follow the stubbornness of their hearts and go after other gods to serve and worship them, will be like this belt—completely useless! For as a belt is bound around a man's waist, so I bound the whole house of Israel and the whole house of Judah to me," declares the LORD, "to be my people for my renown and praise and honor. But they have not listened."*

God very plainly says those who do not listen to Him are completely useless. Some other Bible translations say, *"Good for nothing."* That's probably where the term *"Good for nothing"* came from and it hit me like a ton of bricks when I first saw this Scripture. God calls us *"good for nothing"* and *"completely useless"* if we do not listen to Him. All our efforts in the kingdom will be in vain if we don't listen to God and obey Him and when we permit our hearts to be stubborn, we are virtually wasting our time. I'm not saying God will not honor our efforts, but He looks for and longs for those of His children who will hear and obey.

Another well-know example of God's showing us godly principles by the things of this world is in Jeremiah 18, the story about the potter and the clay. We will only look at part of the word the Lord spoke to Jeremiah. Jeremiah 18:1-6 states:

> *This is the word that came to Jeremiah from the LORD: "Go down to the potter's house, there I will give you my message." So I went down to the potter's house, and I saw him working at the wheel. But the pot he was shaping from the clay was marred in his hands; so the potter formed it into another pot, shaping it as seemed best to him.*
>
> *Then the word of the LORD came to me: "O house of Israel, can I not do with you as this potter does?" declares the LORD. "Like clay in the hand of the potter, so are you in my hand, O house of Israel."*

Jeremiah did not immediately grasp the full understanding of what the Lord was going to show him. He was told to go first and observe, and then the Lord brought forth the message. Frequently, this will be the case in our own lives. We will not know until we are willing to go in obedience to His direction. Too often, we want the whole scenario laid out for us, but that is not the way of the Lord. He wants us to walk in faith, trusting Him each step of the way.

He uses common, ordinary experiences to teach us lessons. The impact of this simple Bible lesson is enormous. We know what happens to clay in the hands of a potter. It's formed into the image the potter wants it to be after he has kneaded it and shaped it. The clay does not rebel, but simply yields to his hands. God has taken what we know and used it as an example for teaching us. He molds his people, but we have to be as clay in His hand. It's up to us to yield to the Maker as He does what He wants. Clay is dead and without life and, in like manner, we also must die to our ideas and plans, yielding every step of the way to the unfolding of the Lord's master plan for our life.

Recently, the Lord told me that I had to die to my prophetic ministry. He would not give me any prophetic messages during the services. I kept asking the Lord if I had a word for the people and He would say no. I asked Him why He would not give me a prophetic message and He said that, *"Dead men don't talk."* He would not expound on the subject. I knew that it was His ministry through me and not my own. Therefore, if He chooses not to use me for a season in the prophetic ministry, that's His choice. My responsibility is to hear and obey. However, if He chooses to use me in that manner again, He'll let me know.

Throughout the Scriptures, God has taken familiar things and taught us lessons about them. Whether it is the potter and the clay, a light hid under a lamp stand, a woman with a lost coin, the relationship between the shepherd and the sheep, or whatever, the Lord will use topics we are familiar with to make His point. He did it in the Bible and He does it in our lives today.

Ahijah

Ahijah is certainly not one of the Major Prophets. In fact, you could say he was one of the most Minor Prophets among the Minor Prophets. However, God worked in the same way regardless of the extent of his exposure in the

Bible. Ahijah had a word for Jeroboam who rebelled against the kingdom of Solomon. I Kings 11:29-33 says:

> *About that time Jeroboam was going out of Jerusalem, and Ahijah the prophet of Shiloh met him on the way, wearing a new cloak. The two of them were alone out in the country, and Ahijah took hold of the new cloak he was wearing and tore it into twelve pieces. Then he said to Jeroboam, "Take ten pieces for yourself, for this is what the Lord, the God of Israel, says: 'See, I am going to tear the kingdom out of Solomon's hand and give you ten tribes. But for the sake of my servant David and the city of Jerusalem, which I have chosen out of all the tribes of Israel, he will have one tribe. I will do this because they have forsaken me and worshiped Ashtoreth, the goddess of the Sidonians, Chemosh the god of the Moabites, and Molech the god of the Ammonites, and have not walked in my ways, nor done what is right in my eyes, nor kept my statutes and laws as David, Solomon's father, did."*

This prophecy eventually came true and Jeroboam, although he certainly was not a righteous man, became the first king of the ten tribes of Israel. The Lord sent Ahijah to the exact place where he would meet Jeroboam and he spoke the words that came to pass. This was also fulfillment of the word the Lord spoke to Solomon in 1 Kings, chapter nine.

God will do the same thing today. He'll send you exactly where He wants you to go and give you the words He wants you to speak. One example of this in my life happened one evening when the Lord sent me to a city twenty-five miles away. As I was driving down the road, He told me to go into a certain restaurant. I was not hungry, but he told me to go and order something. I obeyed although I did not understand at the time. As I was ordering, a pastor I had known when he was an assistant pastor at another church came to the ordering line and asked for his wife's purse, which had been left there. Since we had not seen each other for several years we sat down and talked, and I had a prophecy for him and his church. God set up that encounter.

God had told me where to go and I went in His timing and *"happened"* to be at the ordering line just when the pastor came by. The pastor would have been there less than one minute just to pick up his wife's purse had I not been there at that exact time.

Our responsibilities as Christians, whether we are prophets or not, are to:

a) be in the presence of the Lord,
b) listen to the words the Lord speaks to us,
c) go where the Lord sends us, and
d) speak only the words the Lord would have us speak.

When we are obedient, God, who is all-knowing, will create the circumstances for us so that the purpose of our mission will be fulfilled. We will almost never know the full details of the direction and the reasons for directions unless and until we have obeyed his voice.

The Man of God and the Old Prophet

1 Kings, chapter 13, has another story about Jeroboam and several prophets. A man of God from Judah was directed by the Lord to go to Bethel. We never find out his name, only that he is called *the man of God.* He was given a prophecy against the altar and Jeroboam which stated:

> *O altar, altar! This is what the LORD says: "A son named Josiah will be born to the house of David. On you he will sacrifice the priests of the high places who now make offerings here, and human bones will be burned on you."*

Jeroboam was angry at what the man of God was saying, stretched out his arm, and commanded that he be seized. Immediately, his arm shriveled. Jeroboam asked the man of God to intercede and his arm was healed after he prayed for Jeroboam. He was grateful and wanted the man of God to come home with him to eat and receive a gift (1 Kings 13:1-7).

The man of God in 1 Kings 13:8 said:

> *Even if you do give me half your possessions, I would not go with you, nor would I eat bread or drink water here. For I was commanded by the word of the LORD: "You must not eat bread or drink water or return by the way you came."*

An old prophet from Bethel heard what happened, went after the man of God, and invited him to come home with him and eat with him. The man of God told the old prophet the same words he told Jeroboam. But the old prophet lied to the man of God and in verse 18 said:

"I too am a prophet, as you are. And an angel said to me by the word of the LORD: 'Bring him back with you to your house so that he may eat bread and drink water.'"

Unfortunately, the man of God believed him, went back to eat and drink and received a prophecy from the old prophet in verses 21 and 22 which stated:

"This is what the LORD says: 'You have defied the word of the LORD and have not kept the command the LORD your God gave you. You came back and ate bread and drank water in the place he told you not to eat or drink. Therefore, your body will not be buried in the tomb of your fathers.'" The man of God died on the way home because of his disobedience.

The old prophet who gave the man of God a false prophecy was indeed a prophet because the second prophecy he received did come from the Lord and came true. Both Jeroboam and the old prophet wanted to associate themselves with the man of God when his word against the altar came true.

Where was the old prophet when Jeroboam was sinning against the Lord? Why didn't he receive a word from the Lord? He lived right there. Since he so easily lied, I believe he was comfortable with both Jeroboam's sin as well as his own. Could it be that his sin caused God to stop using him? However, he still wanted to bask in the glory of a demonstrated true prophecy by being associated with the man of God.

The man of God wanted to be accepted by one of his peers, another prophet. He also trusted the supposed word of the Lord from that person rather than trusting the word he received directly. This can be a problem with many people. They'll go miles to see a prophet and seek a word from God from him rather than hearing for themselves. We must learn to place more trust in our own hearing and not in another person's hearing. I have learned not to go to hear anyone unless the Lord directs me to. I won't even go up for prayer unless He directs me to. This may seem radical to some, but I have learned to trust the Lord rather than trust in man.

Finally, after all the prophecies Jeroboam received, he still didn't change his ways. Verse 33 says:

"Even after this, Jeroboam did not change his evil ways, but once more appointed priests for the high places from all sorts of people. Anyone who wanted to become a priest he consecrated for the high places."

Jeroboam's son became sick and he sent his wife to Ahijah, the prophet who originally gave him the prophecy that he would be king. A long, harsh word came forth for Jeroboam and his family from the Lord in 1 Kings 14:7-17 because of his unrepentant sin.

We can see the miracles of the Lord and in spite of that, continue to sin. It's so important that we see our sin and repent. God is patient; but his patience will come to an end. May the example of Jeroboam be a solemn reminder of our need to repent.

Jonah

Jonah was told by God to go to Nineveh to prophecy to them because of their sin. However, Jonah refused to obey. As a result, as he was fleeing the Lord by taking a ship to Tarshish, a violent storm caused the ship to almost be destroyed. Cargo was lost and great fear came upon the sailors. To make a long story short, after becoming fish dinner, he became fish vomit and the Lord gave him a second chance to obey his command. Obediently he went to Nineveh, and prophesied that the city would be overturned in forty days (Jonah 1-3).

When we choose to disobey the Lord, we may put other people at risk. The sailors were not responsible for Jonah's disobedience, but they and the owner of the cargo paid a great price for his disobedience.

God is a God of second chances. He sent Jonah again even though he chose originally to disobey and He will do the same for us. There may be times when you know God wants you to do something, but for whatever reason, you decide not to do it. Often you'll feel miserable knowing you chose to disobey the Lord. The consequences of disobedience will generally not be as severe as Jonah's disobedience, but like Jonah, invariably you will get a second and third chance to do what He asked you to do.

Finally Jonah was obedient to the Lord's word, went to Nineveh and preached as in Jonah 3:4 where he said: **"Forty more days and Nineveh will be overturned."** Jonah did not tell the people to repent, but because they feared the Lord, they made the decision to do so. As it turned out, this prophecy did not come true and the city was not overturned in forty days. Why not? Was Jonah a false prophet? No, it was the mercy of God that caused the word not to be fulfilled. The people were repentant and threw themselves on God's mercy. Repentance will always bring God's mercy and will stay the hand of judgment. Nineveh was eventually destroyed, but not until many, many years later.

God does not want to destroy anyone. His desire is for all men to come to the knowledge of Him and when there is true repentance, He will honor it. But we cannot repent for our children or grandchildren. You can see this in the story of the Ninevites: the people of Jonah's day repented while their descendants did not, causing the judgment of God to eventually come upon Nineveh.

Micaiah

The work of the prophet is set forth most succinctly in the words of Micaiah the prophet. He said, speaking of Ahab the King of Israel in 1 Kings 22:14:

> *"As surely as the LORD lives, I can tell him only what the LORD tells me."*

Whatever a prophet gives to a person should be *only* that which is received from the Lord.

Transition to the New Covenant

The point I am trying to make, not only in the lives of the prophets, but also in the lives of all God's children, is the importance of listening to God. Examples of listening fill the pages of the Bible. I have touched on some examples of listening by a few prophets, but there are so many more examples of listening given in the Bible for you to discover.

Examples of listening abound in the Old Testament, but what of the New Testament? They abound there also. In fact, listening should be more prevalent in the New Covenant since we now have the Holy Spirit in us.

In the New Covenant the Spirit of God is in us and wants to speak to us. We have every right to be expectant as we continue to study listening in the lives of the New Testament saints, our Lord Jesus Christ, and the Holy Spirit.

LISTENING
IN THE NEW TESTAMENT

"I want you to know, brothers, that the gospel I preached is not something that man made up. I did not receive it from any man, nor was I taught it; rather, I received it by revelation from Jesus Christ." (Gal. 1:11-12)

Chapter Seven

THE SAINTS
IN THE NEW TESTAMENT

You have seen what a vital part listening played in the Old Testament. What about the New Testament? Actually, there should be more listening by the saints of God as a result of the New Covenant. When Jesus died on the cross, the veil of the Temple was rent or torn from top to bottom (Matthew 27:51). This action signified we now have access into the Holy of Holies, into the very presence of God. Hebrews 10:19-22 states:

> *Therefore, brothers, since we have confidence to enter into the Most Holy Place, by the blood of Jesus, by a new and living way opened for us through the curtain, that is, his body, and since we have a great priest over the house of God, let us draw near to God with a sincere heart in full assurance of faith, having our hearts sprinkled to cleanse us from a guilty conscience and having our bodies washed with pure water.*

Here are several more Scriptures on our access to the Father. Ephesians 2:18 states:

 "For through him we both have access to the Father by one Spirit." Also verse 3:12 states: *"In him and through faith in him we may approach God with freedom and confidence."*

Though God dwelt in a physical temple in the Old Covenant, He now dwells in us, his spiritual temples, since our bodies are now the temple of the

Holy Spirit. He communicated with the priests in the Holy of Holies, but now He communicates with His kingdom of priests (us) directly and not through an earthly high priest. *Isn't that exciting?! We can have a closer walk with God than the saints in the Old Testament!*

John the Baptist

For the most part John is not thought of as a listener; however, John 1:32-34 states:

> ***Then John gave this testimony: "I saw the Spirit come down from heaven as a dove and remain on him. I would not have known him, except that the One who sent me to baptize with water told me, 'The man on whom you see the Spirit come down and remain is he who will baptize with the Holy Spirit,' I have seen and I testify that this is the Son of God."***

First John acknowledges that he was *sent* by God to baptize. He did not do it on his own. John had to know how to listen to God to know that he was sent and for other directions in his ministry. John would not have known the called One was Jesus unless the Spirit revealed it to him. Often, we will not understand something, but God, through a word of His knowledge will reveal what we need in a certain situation. John was walking as God wants us to walk—by listening, believing and trusting in His word.

Philip

Philip was directed by an angel to go south to the desert road that goes down from Jerusalem to Gaza (Acts 8:26). Now Philip had been used by God in preaching to help bring revival to Samaria. The Spirit had been moving and people were being saved, baptized, and filled with the Spirit, and witnessing signs and wonders. Philip could have asked God why He was taking him from the revival to lead him onto a lonely road in the desert, but he didn't. The Spirit told Philip to join a chariot (Acts 8:29) and he did not hesitate.

As he ran up to the chariot, *coincidentally* an Ethiopian eunuch, a minister of the queen, was reading Isaiah 53:7-8, the famous passage which foretells about Jesus, the sheep being led to slaughter. Philip asked him if he understood what he was reading and the eunuch, with the perfect lead-in to witnessing said, ***"How can I....unless someone explains it to me?"* (Acts 8:31)** What a setup by God. After Philip finished witnessing, he was translated away by the Spirit.

When God leads you, He has a good reason for you doing what He wants you to do. The natural man would say it's not right to leave a revival while it's still going on, but the Spirit had other ideas. He brought Philip to the right place at the right time to witness to the eunuch exactly while he was reading the right passage in Isaiah. He prepared the eunuch's heart to be receptive to the message and then confirmed it with a supernatural event, the whisking away of Philip. You don't forget something like that.

But first comes the testing of the listener. God will give you a command and He wants to see if you will carry it out or if you will pit your intelligence against His. Philip could have said to the Lord, *"You don't want me to witness to a black man, do you?"* He also could have believed the message belonged only to the Jews which was standard theology among Jews and Jewish believers back then, but he didn't. He, too, did not let tradition get in the way of spreading the gospel. God wants to see whether we have faith in the Spirit's direction (like Philip) or in our own analysis of the situation.

Ananias

Now we come to an obscure saint called Ananias. He only appears in Acts. Chapter 9:10-15 states:

> *In Damascus there was a disciple named Ananias. The LORD called to him in a vision, "Ananias!" "Yes, Lord," he answered. The Lord told him, "Go to the house of Judas on Straight Street and ask for a man from Tarsus named Saul, for he is praying. In a vision he has seen a man named Ananias come and place his hands on him to restore his sight."*

> *"LORD," Ananias answered, "I have heard many reports about this man and all the harm he has done to your saints in Jerusalem. And he has come here with authority from the chief priests to arrest all who call on your name."*

> *But the LORD said to Ananias, "Go! This man is my chosen instrument to carry my name before the Gentiles and their kings and before the people of Israel."*

Notwithstanding his protestations, God still told Ananias to go. Interestingly, He did not tell him that Saul had been converted on the road to

Damascus. Why not? It's another example of testing by the Lord. The Lord will never give us the complete picture. He'll just give us what He thinks we need to know for the immediate assignment at hand.

I'd like to bring out several other points on Ananias. First, as I stated earlier, this is his only appearance in the pages of the Bible, and yet he was used by God to minister to one of the most prolific writers of the New Testament. Why is that? God will use anyone who is obedient to His leading and not just those in leadership positions. *That includes all of us as well!* We don't know where our next obedience will take us or the implications it will have for the next person we are affecting.

Second, here's another example of pitting our intelligence against God's wisdom. Ananias protested the direction of the Lord and had what he believed was a rational counter to what God wanted him to do. Wouldn't you do the same? God, of course, knew better, but He wanted to see if Ananias would be obedient in spite of appearances, or if He would have to use another who would be more open to the leading of the Holy Spirit.

Third, don't let your fears of what you know or don't know stop you from doing the will of the Lord. Ananias was afraid of Saul because of what he had done to other Christians. He was probably afraid of losing his own life as well. In spite of his fears, he chose to be obedient and reaped the rewards.

Fourth, God used this obscure saint to restore the sight of Saul, give him a message from the Lord, and pray for him to receive the baptism in the Holy Spirit. Again, we don't have to be a spiritual giant to be used of God; we only have to be available.

Peter

Peter walked with Jesus. Through watching Jesus as He was led by the Spirit, he learned that to be a disciple of Jesus is to listen to God. He learned by the example of following a leader who listened to God. This is the same pattern Joshua learned as he followed Moses, who was following the leadings of God.

When Peter was on the roof of a house in Joppa praying, he had a vision and the Spirit spoke to him regarding the meaning of the sheet coming down from heaven. Then the spirit directed him to go with the men who were downstairs. Acts 10:19-20 states:

While Peter was still thinking about the vision, the Spirit said to him, "Simon, three men are looking for you. So get up and go downstairs. Do not hesitate to go with them, for I have sent them."

When Peter went downstairs, He had the confidence necessary to immediately tell the three men that he was the man they were looking for. Why? He was familiar with the voice of the Lord. Because he had been led by the Spirit before, he didn't have to say, *"Is that really you, Lord?"* The spirit told him there were three men downstairs and that they were looking for Peter, and indeed, that was their mission. The Spirit did not tell him the purpose of the trip but left that up to the three men. When Peter found out he was to go to the house of a Gentile, he could have said that Jews don't go into the houses of Gentiles because they were unclean. However, what God had called clean was now clean. He trusted more in the direction of the Spirit than in the traditions of man. He was being led on a missionary trip by the Holy Spirit.

You will find that the Holy Spirit will often go against religious traditions which have no basis in the Scriptures. Jesus came to set the captives free, and part of that freedom is the traditions men have set up in their religions. Be open to the work of the Holy Spirit wherever that work will take you.

Now here is an interesting thing. We have looked at parts of Acts, chapters eight, nine and ten, and we found that in all three instances of evangelism, men of God were led by the Holy Spirit into witnessing situations. They listened to the Spirit and obeyed, even though they may have had reservations at the time. All three of them could have argued with the Lord that these people are not the ones to hear the message. Only Ananias did, but, in the end, he too was obedient. God wanted to show us that His message is for all people. Finally, before you go out to witness, get directions from the Holy Spirit. *He will lead you to the right place, the right people, in the right time.*

Paul

Paul became a listener. It started on the road to Damascus when he heard the audible voice of the Lord (Acts 9:4-6). It was reinforced when Ananias told him the Spirit sent him to Paul after Paul received the same information from the Lord in Acts 22:10. As a result of Ananias' obedience to the Lord, Paul received the Spirit and also was healed of blindness (Acts 9:17). I'm sure

Paul discovered the value of listening to the Lord when his eyes were literally opened and he immediately saw that power followed listening. This is a lesson we all need to learn. The church has generally been powerless through the years because, for the most part, leaders have not been tuned in to God.

Paul demonstrated listening to the Lord a number of other times in the book of Acts. In Acts 18:9, the Lord spoke to Paul in a vision and told him not to be afraid. Many times the Lord or an angel will tell a saint of God not to be afraid in the Scriptures. The reason for this is most of us are fearful people and have fears of the future and the unknown that we need to overcome. If you are in the Lord for any length of time, He will invariably tell you the same thing. He's constantly trying to teach us to have faith in him and not to fear the circumstances surrounding us. As we grow in the Lord, we will learn to trust him more and our fears will dissipate; but it doesn't happen overnight.

In Acts 16:6, Paul and Barnabas were forbidden by the Spirit to speak the word in Asia. You will often find the Spirit will direct you not to go to a certain place. Some people will say they received a check in their spirit about doing something or going somewhere. When that happens, get into a conversation with the Lord and find out what he wants or doesn't want. The Spirit warned Paul to get out of Jerusalem because they would not receive his testimony about Jesus. (Acts 22:18)

There are two points to make here. First, the Spirit will not only warn us to not go into a place, but also will tell us to get out of a place when it is expedient to do so. Second, The Spirit will tell us when it's fruitless to continue witnessing. God knows when the message is reaching the heart and when it is falling on deaf ears. *Let's listen to God and save our energy.*

Notice that in many instances, there is an economy of words by the Lord. Sometimes He will speak at length and other times He will simply give you a one-liner. Remember that the one-liners are extremely important too since they have the wisdom, knowledge and power of God behind them.

Paul also talks about listening in Galatians 1:11-12. It states:

> *I want you to know, brothers, that the gospel I preached is not something that man made up. I did not receive it from any man, nor was I taught it; rather, I received it by revelation from Jesus Christ.*

Paul had to be listening to the Lord in order to receive the messages he preached. The Christian doctrine that we so strongly believe was given to Paul directly by the Lord Jesus Christ. Paul, in talking about mature saints, said in Romans 8:14:

> **"Because those who are led by the Spirit of God are sons of God."**

The meaning of the word *sons* here is mature sons. Not babies in the Lord. Paul would not have said that unless he was experiencing being led by the Lord. The most effective way to be led by the Spirit of God is by listening to the voice of the Lord.

Other Listeners

In Acts 15:28-29, the church leaders heard from the Holy Spirit regarding the specific restrictions God wanted to place on the body of Christ. They said:

> *It seemed good to the Holy Spirit and to us not to burden you with anything beyond the following requirements: You are to abstain from food sacrificed to idols, from blood, from the meat of strangled animals and from sexual immorality. You will do well to avoid these things.*

The Holy Spirit will speak to us through other Christians as well. In every city Paul went, the Holy Spirit warned him that prison and hardships faced him. (Acts 20:23) That means a number of unnamed Christians were also giving Paul the same confirmatory words from God. Another obscure Christian named Agabus prophesied to Paul and provided further confirmation of what was to befall him in Jerusalem. (Acts 21:10-11) Those who were giving prophecies to Paul had the same message in every city. They were all hearing from the Lord.

Many Christians hold a special place in their hearts for Mary, the mother of Jesus, and rightly so. Let's look at the last recorded words she spoke in the Bible. At the marriage which took place at Cana, *"His mother said to the servants, 'Do whatever he tells you.'"* (John 2:5) I think it is significant that the last recorded words of Mary in the Bible were to instruct the servants to listen to Jesus. We are the servants of God, and we also are instructed to do whatever He tells us. For those who love Mary, let's follow her last instructions. *I will do whatever you tell me* 9/28/13

97

I've discussed a number of Christians, some of whom played a rather insignificant role in the leadership of the new church and yet God spoke to them. This is important since God speaks to not only the leaders, but also to the followers, the masses of Christians who hear from the One who is the head of the body and who will direct the body as He chooses.

The Great Faith Chapter

If someone were to ask you what the great faith chapter in the Bible was, you would most likely say Hebrews, chapter eleven. Although this chapter is not an example of New Testament saints listening to God, it is an example of the New Testament writer pointing to Old Testament examples of faithful followers of God for the benefit of the New Testament saints.

You will find that most of the examples in this chapter are testimonies of nothing more than Old Testament saints listening to the voice of the Lord, believing and obeying. Although we will be looking at many examples, I ask you to go back to the Old Testament yourself and closely examine the examples set forth in Hebrews, chapter eleven. It will build your faith regarding listening. Let's briefly look at the *Hall of Fame* of the Biblical characters who make up that chapter.

Hebrews 11:4 speaks of Cain and Abel and the conversations the Lord had regarding the offering. Enoch is mentioned in verses five and six, although there is no statement of a conversation between Enoch and God, Genesis 5:24 speaks of Enoch walking with God. You could infer that if he walked with God, he also talked with Him, since there was no recorded Bible at that time.

Hebrews 11:7 refers to Noah. We know that Noah listened to God since Genesis 6:22 says, ***"Noah did everything just as God commanded him."*** Obviously, Noah was a listener.

The next saint, Abraham, in Hebrews 11:8-19, also listened to God. Thirteen chapters of Genesis are devoted to the life of Abraham, another listening man.

Isaac, in Hebrews 11:20 had to be listening to God to know the future blessings for his sons Jacob and Esau. Isaac heard from God and gave the blessings as he heard them. Isn't it amazing that of all the things which could have been put in the faith chapter about Isaac, an example of listening was chosen by God?

Again the same is true of Jacob in verse 21. God chose an example where Jacob prophesied of the future of the sons of Joseph. He had to be hearing from God in order to do so.

Verse 22, regarding Joseph, is the first verse not directly related to his listening to the Lord. But it is related to the promises made to Abraham who listened to God.

Not all of the verses regarding Moses, verses 23-29, are related to listening; however, some of them are. The activities in verses 27 through 29 are directly related to listening by Moses.

Verse 30, relating to Joshua and the fall of Jericho, is again an example of listening.

I could go on to the other saints, but I believe you get the picture. Faith and listening to the voice of the Lord are very closely related. If you want to be a man or woman of faith, you need to develop a listening ear.

Finis

These are just some of the examples in the New Testament about listening. There are others, but we will not go into all of them. Suffice it to say the early church listened to the Spirit. Now the question is *"Will the latter church do the same?!*

Chapter Eight

THE FATHER, JESUS, AND THE HOLY SPIRIT

We can get a better understanding of the nature of God by seeing what the Father, His Son Jesus, and the Holy Spirit say and do regarding listening in the New Testament. We will see that each person of the Trinity does not lord it over the others, but points to the others, and is submissive to the rest of the Godhead. We have to learn by example that we also have to be more cognizant of others and not lift ourselves up. The Godhead does not, and we need to follow their example. Let's look at the Father, Jesus the son, and then the Holy Spirit in relation to listening and submissiveness.

The Father

As soon as Jesus was baptized with water by John, the Father spoke about Jesus, His son. He said, in Matthew 3:17: *"...This is my son, whom I love; with whom I am well pleased."* The Father did not point to Himself, but to His precious son.

In the beginning of the Old Testament in Genesis, God spoke the world into existence. In the beginning of the New Testament, when His son Jesus was beginning His ministry, the Father spoke to us in an audible voice about His beloved Son. He pointed us to Jesus.

At the Transfiguration, the Father was speaking to Peter, James, and John about Jesus in an audible voice. He said, in Matthew 17:5: *"This is my Son, whom I love; with him I am well pleased. Listen to him!"* Again our heavenly Father was pointing to His beloved Son.

His message to the three disciples was short and to the point. When they heard a voice from heaven saying that Jesus was the Son, they knew He was the Son of God. Next to the sonship of Jesus, what does the Father consider to be important in this encounter? He told them to *listen* to Jesus. That should tell us of the importance the Father places on listening. He tells all His children to listen to Him.

Jesus

In everything we do, Jesus should be our example. He is God incarnate, and He came to earth to show us how to enter into a godly walk. Scripture says He is the first of many brethren; therefore, there should be others following after Him. Since He was without sin and we are sinners, we can never attain to the perfection of Jesus; however, we can follow Him and accomplish many of the things He accomplished. In fact, He said we would accomplish greater works than He did.

Jesus chose not to walk in His deity, but to walk in His humanity while on this earth. That is important for us to comprehend because if He walked as God and I would have to follow the example of a deity, I, and everyone else, would be in trouble. We cannot do the same things God could do and Jesus knew that; therefore, He chose to walk as a man. He was still God, but walked in submission to the Father and the Holy Spirit to show us the way.

Let's see how He walked. We'll not be covering all the aspects of His time on earth but concentrate on some Biblical examples illustrating His listening to the other Persons of the Godhead and some instructions for us. We'll also look at Jesus' role as Chief Shepherd and the relationship He has with us, His sheep.

When He was at the temple at the age of twelve, His parents were frantically searching for Him. They finally found Him in the Temple. He told Joseph and Mary in Luke 2:49: *"Why were you searching for me?" he asked. "Didn't you know that I had to be in my Father's house?"* He knew at that time that God was His Father; however, He didn't begin His public ministry until about eighteen years later. In the meantime He was studying and memorizing much of the Old Testament, building His relationship and talking with His Father.

I want you to look at the pattern of Jesus' listening in the book of John. Many times He told His followers about His direction from the Father. John 4:34 states: *"My food," said Jesus "is to do the will of him who sent me and to finish his work."* There are several verses that really hit me as I studied them. John 5:19 says:

> *Jesus gave them this answer: "I tell you the truth, the Son can do nothing by himself; he can only do what he sees his Father doing, because whatever the Father does the Son also does."*

Jesus is telling us that He is submitted to the will of the Father and does not do *anything* on His own. His Father has to lead Him each step of the way.

John 5:30, another even more amazing verse, says,

> *"By myself I can do nothing; I judge only as I hear, and my judgment is just, for I seek not to please myself but him who sent me."*

Think about these verses. *Jesus Christ, the Son of God, God incarnate, could not do anything on His own authority. He had to hear from the other Persons of the Godhead!* He walked the earth listening for direction in His ministry. If Jesus Christ is our example, and He should be, we should be doing the same thing. How many times have we marched ahead doing God's work without getting direction from God? We should be getting direction from the Spirit before we move out. *If Jesus listened, we should also listen. If Jesus could do nothing without direction from the Spirit, neither can we.*

Here's another verse about Jesus' mission in John 6:38: *"For I have come down from heaven not to do my will but to do the will of him who sent me."* John 7:16 is another verse about Jesus' dependence upon His Father. It says: *"...My teaching is not my own. It comes from him who sent me."*

And in another place, Jesus affirms His lack of authority without the Father. John 8:28-29 states:

> *So Jesus said, "When you have lifted up the Son of Man, then you will know who I am and that I do nothing on my own but speak just what the Father has taught me. The one who sent me is with me; he has not left me alone, for I always do what pleases him."*

Jesus, when He walked the earth, spoke what His Father told Him to speak and went where His Father told Him to go. He was totally submitted to the will of His Father.

But He does not stop there. In John 12:49-50 He said: *"For I did not speak of my own accord, but the Father who sent me commanded me what to say and how to say it. I know that his command leads to eternal life. So whatever I say is just what the Father has told me to say."* Jesus wants to drum in the message that He does not act on His own, but is a servant of the other persons of the Trinity. We not only can know what to say, but the Spirit will show us how to say it, just as Jesus taught us in the preceding verse. We can actually get the tone that God wants to convey in His messages. We, too, can be servants of God, submitted to His feelings and His leading. Believe me, it *can* be done.

In the garden of Gethsemane, Jesus said in Mark 14:36: *"... Yet not what I will, but what you will."* He yielded His will at the cross, but it also was an everyday experience with Him. In the same way, we are to yield our wills to the Lord telling Him we are putting aside our own will and desires to seek His will only. It was Jesus' walk and it has to be our walk as well.

Jesus says in John 14:15: *"If you love me, you will obey what I command."* Think of that! Our love for Jesus is demonstrated by our obedience to Him, just as Jesus' love for the Father was demonstrated by His obedience.

Have you ever thought what you could give God? We make a big deal about giving Him our tithe, but it's all His anyway; He allows us to give back a portion of what is already His. *The only thing I can give God that He doesn't already have and cannot get from any other source is my obedience.* Sure, He can get someone else to obey Him in the same area in which I was being led to be obedient, but it's that person's obedience not mine. The only way I know how to prove my love for God is through my obedience.

Another remarkable verse is John 8:47 which says,

> **He who belongs to God hears what God says. The reason you do not hear is that you do not belong to God.**

Think of that verse for a moment. When I looked at that verse, I knew that listening to God was important. Jesus did not mince words, but told it like it was. More than anything, I wanted to belong to God and made the decision that I had to be a hearer of God. I want all of you to have that desire also.

There are several more examples in one of the greatest prayers in the Bible, Jesus' prayer to His Father in John, chapter seventeen. In verse four, Jesus said: *"I have brought you glory on earth by completing the work you gave me to do."* Jesus was totally obedient to the Father, and, as a result, the Father received glory. If we want Jesus to be glorified in us, we must be obedient to Him.

John 17:7 says: *"Now they know that everything you have given me comes from you."* **John 17:14 states in part:** *"I have given them your word...."* Again, Jesus keeps saying over and over that whatever He gives forth, He first receives from the Father. He is our pattern, our example, the first of many brothers.

Jesus then says in John 17:18: *"As you have sent me into the world, I have sent them into the world."* His life with the Father is the pattern for our life with Him. He could do nothing on His own, neither can we. The words He spoke were from His Father and the words and messages we speak should be from Him. He was so connected to the Father that the Father's words were part of Him. *We should be so connected to Jesus that His words become part of us. Are we willing to be so tied to the Lord that when the world sees us, they see Jesus? The Lord is ready and willing. Now it's up to us.*

Another important example in listening is in Matthew 12:46-50:

> *While Jesus was still talking to the crowd, his mother and brothers stood outside, wanting to speak to him. Someone told him, "Your mother and brothers are standing outside wanting to speak to you."*
>
> *He replied to him, "Who is my mother and who are my brothers?" Pointing to his disciples he said, "For whoever does the will of my Father in heaven is my brother and sister and mother."*

He was not putting down his mother and brothers; rather, He was making the point that those who are in the family of God are doing the will of God. His family relationship with his Father was one of obedience and He teaches us that our family relationship to the Godhead should also be one of obedience.

How can we fully do the will of God unless we know what it is? Certainly, the Bible gives us much of His will; however, it does not give us all the everyday details for our lives. We need to be led by the Spirit, but we cannot be led by the Spirit continuously unless we are listening to Him. There will be more about *Knowing the Will of God* in chapter eighteen.

Examples in the Life of Jesus

How did He know what to do or what to say regarding people and situations? He was listening to the Spirit and following directions. Matthew 17:27 states:

> ***But so that we may not offend them, go to the lake and throw out your line. Take the first fish you catch; open its mouth and you will find a four-drachma coin. Take it and give it to them for my tax and yours.***

Can you imagine telling Peter, a fisherman, to go fishing and in the mouth of the first fish he catches would be a coin which would be enough to pay the taxes? Jesus even gave the specific amount of the coin. How did He know that the first (not the tenth or some other number) fish Peter caught would have a coin in its mouth? That obviously was supernatural knowledge the Holy Spirit gave Him. That exact fish had to be at the exact place at the exact time when Peter was there.

Why didn't Jesus pray for Lazarus immediately when he found out he was sick? Why in John 11:17 did He stay away from Lazarus for four days? Jesus went where the Father told Him to go and He wasn't told to go immediately. Timing is always important to God. The greater glory to God came when Jesus raised Lazarus from the dead. Had Jesus gone immediately and prayed for a healing, it would just be another healing along the way, but the Father had a better idea.

How did Jesus know when to lay hands upon the sick, speak a word of healing from a distance, cast out a demon, forgive sins and subsequently heal, put mud in the eyes of a blind man, or rebuke a fever, etc.? He did it by the direction of the Father who was speaking to Him as to what to do and say and where to go. He wants to do the same with us and He will if we are submitted to the direction of the Spirit.

How did Jesus in Mark 14:30 know that Peter would deny Him three times before the cock crowed? This was a future event. How could He know it? You might say, "Well, He was God." But, He was walking in human form for our benefit. He chose to walk in His humanity and not in His divinity, so it had to be the other Persons of the Godhead who told Him of future events.

How did Jesus in John 1:47 know that Nathanael was a man in whom there was nothing false? The Holy Spirit told Him. How did Jesus know that the Pharisees were trying to trick Him? Again, the Spirit told Him.

How did Jesus know in Luke 19:30-31 that a colt which no one had ever ridden would be tied up just as the disciples entered the village for His triumphal entry into Jerusalem? You guessed it.

These are only a few examples of many where Jesus simply followed the instructions of the other Persons of the Godhead. He was in total submission to the Father and the Holy Spirit.

The Shepherd of the Sheep

Jesus used many examples of situations the people were familiar with in order to teach biblical principles. Sheep were everywhere, and people knew what transpired between the shepherd and the sheep. God used the example of the shepherd leading the sheep in the Old Testament in Ezekiel chapter 34. Specifically in Ezekiel 34:23, where He said: *"I will place over them one shepherd, my servant David, and he will tend them; he will tend them and be their shepherd."*

This prophecy was fulfilled in Jesus. In John 10:14-16, Jesus said:

> *"I am the good shepherd; I know my sheep and my sheep know me—just as the Father knows me and I know the Father—and I lay down my life for the sheep. I have other sheep that are not of this sheep pen. I must bring them also. They too will listen to my voice, and there shall be one flock and one shepherd."*

And again in John 10:27, Jesus said: *"My sheep listen to my voice; I know them, and they follow me."*

The people knew that mature sheep will follow the voice of the shepherd. Here, Jesus, in calling Himself the Good Shepherd, is telling the people that

He is the fulfillment of Ezekiel 24:13, and that, like natural sheep which listen to their shepherd, so too, do the spiritual sheep listen to their Shepherd, Jesus. Again, let's think about what Jesus considers important. He is revealing that He is God's Shepherd over the sheep and in the next breath, He speaks of His sheep listening to Him. If Jesus sees it important to listen, so should we.

The lambs do not know the voice of the shepherd because they're too young and need to follow the older sheep. However, when the lambs mature, they see the older sheep following the voice of the shepherd, and they begin to do the same. They learn the voice of their natural shepherd, as we have to learn the voice of our Shepherd, Jesus.

He said there would be one flock and one shepherd, and He is that Shepherd. It is His intention that all in the Kingdom of God listens to this one shepherd, Jesus.

Are we lambs following older sheep, hoping they are following the voice of the shepherd, or mature sheep who have learned and now follow the voice of the one true Shepherd, our Lord and Savior, Jesus Christ?

The Holy Spirit

The Holy Spirit is the third person of the Trinity. His work is similar in nature to that of Jesus, but He is called the *Counselor.* John 14:16-17 says: ***"And I will ask the Father, and he will give you another Counselor to be with you forever—the Spirit of truth…"*** A counselor is one who gives advice. The person being counseled will always be in conversation with the counselor. Other translations use the word *Advocate.* A lawyer is a counselor and an advocate on our behalf. If we have legal problems, we discuss the situation with our lawyer, and he gives us expert advice. He also acts as our defender or advocate. This is what the Holy Spirit does.

John 14:26 is another verse where Jesus was talking about the Holy Spirit. It says: ***"But the Counselor, the Holy Spirit, whom the Father will send in my name, will teach you all things and will remind you of everything I have said to you."*** Here you have Jesus, the Wonderful Counselor, pointing to another person in the Godhead and the Holy Spirit, also Counselor, pointing back to Jesus. Again, you see the Godhead deferring to one another and in submission to one another.

There is a similarity between the Spirit and Jesus. The Spirit is called teacher as was Jesus, who was called *Rabboni*, or teacher. A teacher teaches a class by talking and using a textbook. The Holy Spirit talks to us and uses the greatest book, the Bible as a textbook for our lives. A teacher needs both and so does the student. We need to be immersed in the Bible, our textbook, and also God, our teacher.

When we were in school, we learned the lesson and then were tested on how well we learned. The same thing applies in the school of the Holy Spirit. We are taught spiritual lessons and then given tests on the lessons we've learned. But remember, He's not out to flunk us, but to have us learn our lessons so we can move up the spiritual ladder.

When we are taking a test in school, the teacher is silent and often will not answer questions during the testing period. This is not always the case with the Lord during our times of testing. He may not necessarily give us the answers we think will help us while we're being tested, or get us out of the test, instead we may hear words like, *"Trust me"* or *"Have faith in me,"* more often than we would like and that may be all the guidance we'll get from the Spirit at that time. One of the reasons is we've already learned the way out of the situation, and the Lord wants us to merely apply the Biblical solution or simply to continue to follow the direction He's given us.

Here's a remarkable verse about the work of the Holy Spirit. John 16:13 says:

> **But when he, the Spirit of truth, comes, He will guide you into all truth. He will not speak on His own; He will speak only what He hears, and He will tell you what is yet to come.**

Here we have the third person of the Trinity totally submitted to the other persons of the Godhead. The Spirit, just like Jesus, will not speak on His own authority. He will hear and then speak. Two persons of the Godhead doing exactly the same thing, submitted to each other. *Shouldn't we also follow the example of total submission to the Godhead? Shouldn't we listen to the Spirit and then follow the leading we receive?* When we go off on our own, we, in effect, are saying we do not need God for this particular situation, we can do it ourselves. If Jesus and the Holy Spirit could do nothing on their own authority, how could we think we can?

The Holy Spirit wants the churches to hear what He is telling them, and He makes that very clear in the Book of Revelation. There are messages to seven churches, which really signify the church universal. At the end of each message, the Spirit says the exact same thing. In Revelation 2:7, 2:11, 2:17, 2:29, 3:6, 3:13, and 3:22, the words are, *"He who has an ear, let him hear what the Spirit says to the churches."* This message is repeated over and over again. Why would that be? Could it be that maybe the Spirit has to keep drumming the message in because we don't get it? God wants us to incline our ear toward Him so we can have His mind for the church, *all* the time, for *all* the churches, in *all* the ages.

Can we honestly say we're submitted to God if we do not listen to the Him and follow His guidance? If not, we can change. Perhaps we're not listening now, but we can decide to begin to listen. If this is what you want, let me lead you in a prayer about listening.

> *Father, I want to lead my life submitted unto You. I know that I need to be led by the Holy Spirit. I need to hear from You on a daily basis. Lord, open my ears that I may hear. My earnest desire is to hear from You and follow Your leading. I want to show my love for You by my obedience to You. May You hear my prayer in the name of Your precious Son, Jesus.*

LEARNING TO LISTEN TO THE LORD

"Dear friend, do not believe every spirit, but test the spirits to see whether they are from God, because many false prophets have come into this world." (1 John 4:1)

Chapter Nine

WAYS TO TEST THE SPIRIT

So often I hear saints of God questioning or doubting the words they are receiving from Him. They're not sure whether they come from themselves, from a messenger of Satan, or from the Holy Spirit and they sincerely want to follow the Lord, but do not want to be deceived or to deceive others. That attitude is both understandable and commendable. There are so many people who say they are hearing from God and we sometimes question if, in fact, they are. We wonder, if others can be deceived, why we can't be deceived as well.

There are times when we will be deceived. How do we avoid this? There are a number of tests we can and should apply in deciding whether the words we receive are, in fact, from God.

The Written Word

First and foremost, the word we hear must be consistent with the written revealed Word of God, the Bible. The Lord will not, and cannot, contradict the Bible. If we hear something which is contrary to the Scriptures, we have to question what we are hearing. Jesus Christ is the truth and the Bible is a revelation of Jesus who is the truth. If the written Word of God is the truth, any contradiction to that Word is a lie. Satan is the father of lies and will always try to distort the truth.

Let me stress the need to be sufficiently familiar with the Bible in order to tell whether a spoken word is consistent with the written word. To take it one step further, if we are not continually reading, studying and meditating on the Bible, I guarantee we will be misled. I've seen it happen. Sometimes Christians can develop arrogance believing they do not need the written Word, since they are being led by the Holy Spirit. There was a man I taught to listen to the Lord who stopped reading the Bible and was led into error, but thankfully, he saw the *error* of his ways and returned to the written Word. *Do not fall into that same trap. We need the Spirit and the Word!*

Peace

Another way to test the Spirit is to make sure peace is associated with the message. Jesus said, *"Peace I leave with you; my peace I give you. I do not give to you as the world gives. Do not let your hearts be troubled and do not be afraid." (John 14:27)* Romans 8:6 for those who are led by the Spirit says, *"The mind of sinful man is death, but the mind controlled by the Spirit is life and peace; the sinful mind is hostile to God."* Remember also that one of the fruit of the Spirit in Galatians 5:22-23 is peace. Psalm 85:8 says: *"I will listen to what God the Lord will say; he promises peace to his people, his saints—but let them not return to folly."*

Therefore, when you receive a word from the Lord, there should be peace which accompanies the word. If there is no peace, be on guard.

Now this may not always be true in the beginning stages of listening when you will not have peace receiving a message from the Holy Spirit. The reason for this is not the Holy Spirit, nor is it that the word is not from the Lord, but our lack of knowledge and confidence in who God is, our own fear of failure, or fear of man. I've experienced this and I know others have as well. We had apprehension and doubt and did not initially have peace, but that changed in time with experience and as our confidence increased. When you learn more about the faithfulness of God, His kindness and goodness, and His trustworthiness, doubts of God letting you down will diminish.

A good example is Moses. He dug in his heels and did not want to do what God wanted him to because he did not really know who God was. He was a reluctant servant; but, as he learned more about his God, his doubts, and I'm sure, lack of peace, disappeared. The same is true of Gideon. He was fearful and did not have peace; however, the Lord gave him confidence when He led Gideon to the camp of the enemy and he heard their fear of him. (See chapter five).

The same thing will happen to us. Often we will start in fear, but end in faith, knowing the Lord will sustain us. When we walk in obedience to the Lord, we will see our peace grow as our love for Him and understanding of His ways grow.

Gentle Leading

The next test is also a test of the nature of the Spirit. Jesus is the Lamb of God. A lamb is gentle, and so is the Holy Spirit. Gentleness is another fruit of the Spirit and will be another of the ways we will know we are being led by God. He will woo you gently and will never force you to do anything. His desire is for His children to want to be led by Him. He will gently lead you as you are going about your business if you are attuned to Him.

One time I was reluctant to do what the Lord wanted me to do. He said, *"You NEVER HAVE to do what I want you to do."* The emphasis was added by the Lord as He spoke to me. He does not force us, but gently leads us.

God will not drive you; however, Satan will and does. If you feel intimidated, feeling as if you were driven, it is not the Lord. He is gentle and humble of heart and we will find rest for our souls (Matthew 11:29). If the voice you are hearing is continually insistent and compels you to act, watch out! If you feel driven by the voice you are hearing, it is not the Lord. It may be the evil one.

Patience

We have another fruit of the Spirit. Are you getting the picture? The direction we receive from the Lord is consistent with all of the fruit of the Spirit. God does not change. His character does not change. And what we receive has to be consistent with the very nature of God.

God is in no hurry. To him, a day is like a thousand years (2 Peter 3:8). That doesn't mean He doesn't have a timetable for words to be acted upon or delivered. He does. What it does mean is that He wants us to be led by His spirit as much as we are willing to yield our lives to Him. If we are unwilling to be led; the patient Lord will wait and continue wooing us. As I have said before, we are in the school of the Holy Spirit. Our schoolwork is individualized by the Lord, our teacher. We advance to newer and tougher subjects based on our learning of the subject matter and passing the tests given by our teacher. We progress at our own pace, while our teacher is always patiently encouraging and guiding us in our Christian walk.

The Lord is not short with us, but continually shows patience in spite of our frequent failings. Satan, on the other hand, is impatient and demands instant obedience. Always ask yourself whether the leading you are getting is patient toward you.

Love

God is love and any word we receive from the Lord will reflect that most important characteristic of God. Does the word we receive show a love for us and others? Or is it hateful, judgmental, or vindictive? Love covers a multitude of sins (1 Peter 4:8), and God will always do the gentlest, most loving thing to turn us or other individuals around. We should do the same. We all have sin in our lives. Public exposure of one person's sin through *a word from the Lord* should be rare. Remember the woman caught in the very act of adultery? Jesus said in John 8:7: ***"...If any one of you is without sin, let him be the first to throw a stone at her."***

When we receive a word, is it hateful or tender? Will it harm and cause confusion to others, or will it be comforting? Know that God is the God of all comfort (2 Corinthians 1:3), and His word will also be a comfort to us and others. That does not mean that all the words we receive are wishy-washy, gooey words, but we will see and know whether the words are from the Lord by the love shown forth.

There will also be words of tough love when there is a need to apply discipline to the situation. But even the words of discipline will be given in a way where there is an answer or a way out of a problem. God will always give us hope for the future. If a hard word is given which does not give hope, watch out. It may be the judgmental attitude of the evil one or the individual giving the word.

Also, love will not cause harm to ourselves or others. If we hear words that say we should harm ourselves or take our own lives, or harm others or kill others, that is not God. These are Satanic words and should not be obeyed. If you hear harmful words as those above, stop listening. Get help. You need deliverance before you engage in listening again. You may need professional help. God is light and in Him is no darkness.

Humility

The Holy Spirit will always lead us in ways which will bring glory to the Lord and not to ourselves. Satan, on the other hand, will try to get us to exalt ourselves. He tried it with Eve when he told her she would be like God. He tried it with Jesus when he tempted Him in the desert, and he'll try it with us. The pride of life is one of the common ways we will be tempted by the evil one. *We must look to the leading we are receiving. Does it point to Jesus and exalt Him, or to ourselves and our position?*

Jesus Christ humbled himself, taking the form of a servant (Philippians 2:7), and became the example of how we should act as servants. His desire was to do the will of the Father, and not His own will. His life in the Spirit was filled with obedience and was obedient unto death. He knew that God was His father and that He could call down ten thousand angels at Calvary if He wanted, but He chose death for our sakes. Jesus humbled himself and He was exalted. God wants us to humble ourselves and He will exalt us.

One time I had a humbling experience from the Lord. He sent me to a prayer meeting on a Friday night to deliver a prophecy on humility. Afterward, some of the brothers and sisters came up to me and thanked me for the word of prophecy. I am ashamed to say I was proud of that prophecy on humility! It was the practice following the meeting for some of the brothers and sisters to put away the approximately 300 chairs, a thankless job, but one that needed to be done. Because of my pride, the Lord told me to move the chairs. I reminded Him of the beautiful prophecy He had me give on humility. He said He wanted me to put the lesson on humility into practice by putting away the chairs. God is in the humbling business.

Another time the Lord sent me to three different meetings on three consecutive nights, a Cursillo meeting, a Full Gospel Business Men's meeting, and a prayer meeting. Each time, the Lord told me to sit in the back, and each time I was called forward to speak or pray. I asked the Lord why this was happening. He said He wanted me to humble myself, and He would do the exalting. He did the same thing three nights in a row to show that He was in control. We never have to put ourselves forward. Just walk in humility and the rest is up to the Lord in His timing. All we need to do is to obey the Lord and He will further reveal the next part of His plan for us in His perfect timing.

Witness of the body

Matthew 18:16 says in part: *"…so that every matter may be established by the testimony of two or three witnesses."* Our Christian walk is not that of the lone ranger. We are part of the body of Christ, and what we receive and pass on to others should be confirmed by others in the church. Others in the Lord also have the Holy Spirit, and He will bear witness to them regarding the words we speak. Another verse on the subject is 1 Corinthians 14:29 which states: ***"Two or three prophets should speak, and the others should weigh carefully what is said."*** If there is no witness, and we hear or think others are not as spiritual as we are, *we must be careful!* Satan will try to separate us from the rest of the believers. He wants us to think we're better or more spiritual than they are. It's all part of his work to divide the body.

That doesn't mean there will always be confirmation with *all* believers within the body of Christ. There may be some who will not hear what the Spirit is speaking to the church or there may also be those, both within and outside our particular body of believers, whose eyes are blinded and whose ears cannot hear because they choose not to hear. However, as a general rule, if there is no confirmation by a number of other believers, we should not move out on important words we are hearing without first spending much more time in prayer.

What happens when a word is given and parts of the body bear witness to it and parts do not? The word should to be submitted to the local church where it is up to the pastoral staff to decide what action, if any, is taken. Often a decision may be made to wait to see whether the word is fulfilled. Time will tell. Also remember that nobody is infallible. The mistake could be made by the giver of the word, the body, or the leadership. The key is to deal with the situation in a loving Christian way.

Inner Witness

When we receive a word, whether directly or from another, there is an inner witness, a knowing that the word is from the Lord. If we have an uneasy feeling, we should check the word out further by testing more thoroughly. When others give us a word, the Holy Spirit within us should give us a feeling of acceptance or rejection of the word. This is only one of many tests. We should not always go by feelings, for feelings can be deceiving. But this is a valid test and cannot be ignored.

Asking the Spirit to Confess That Jesus Christ Has Come In the Flesh

In Chapter ten, I will discuss testing the spirit using the verses in 1 John 3:24 through 4:3. This is an important test and I recommend its use whenever we begin to seek the Lord. I will not go into detail here. However, based on my experiences with a number of people, it is important to consider using this test to avoid the possibility of deception by the evil one speaking to us. All tests should be applied when we are hearing from the Lord.

Acceptance by Authorities over Us

When we receive a word, there will be times when spiritual authority to whom we are submitted needs to be informed of the word before we speak it. We should not hesitate to submit a word we receive to them for their prayerful consideration. They are there to watch over our souls and the flock of God, and should be in a position to help confirm the word or apply understanding or interpretation to that word.

Although this is a valid test, caution must be used. We must be careful not to allow a situation like the one that arose in the 1970s and 1980s, the discipleship movement, in which leaders put themselves in the place of God by teaching that God only spoke through them. God speaks to all of His children and not just the leaders. Remember, the Lord is my shepherd, no shepherd is my Lord.

The same attitude of submitting spiritual matters is true of our parents. They are there to help us and are interested in the best for us. We should not hesitate to seek their counsel about spiritual matters, even if we believe we are more spiritual than they are. God will often speak through parents on our behalf, even though they may not know they are being led by God. Where marriage is concerned, we should be especially careful to ask their permission and receive their blessing. Often love is blind and our parents will see things that we conveniently ignore about our prospective mates.

Confirmation

One of the ways to know that we know that a word we may be receiving is from the Lord is by the confirmation we receive regarding that word. Frequently the word is confirmed as we're reading the Bible. The spirit may give us a certain word or Scripture as we are seeking direction, and shortly thereafter, we'll come upon that Scripture in our reading.

In addition, prophecy is usually confirmatory. Unknown to the one giving the word, the word given may have already been spoken to the individual or to the church. Remember that in every city he visited, Paul heard the same word regarding his eventual persecution and trials? Those people giving the word did not know similar words were given in other cities. However, Paul, the recipient of the words, knew. The Holy Spirit thought it was important for Paul to hear many times what was to befall him.

Another way to know you are continuously being led by the Spirit is the confirmation which often comes after the Spirit leads in a certain way. An example would be for the Spirit to tell us certain things and within a short time, you listen to a Christian radio station and hear a message on the same subject. The Lord may lead us to read an article in a Christian magazine on the same subject or He may confirm the word He gave by an experience which takes place to show us that the word is from the Lord. These are just several of the numerous ways the Spirit will speak to us with confirmation coming from another unexpected source shortly thereafter. The reason I bring this up is that this occurs frequently if a person is led by the Spirit. The fact it happens so frequently will show us it is the spirit who is continuing to lead us. The Lord knows we need reassurance that the words we are hearing are, in fact, from the Lord. Therefore, frequent confirmation occurs.

If a word we hear is not confirmatory, do not dismiss it out of hand, but ask the Lord for a confirming word to be given. Let Him choose the method of confirmation. He will constantly surprise us.

Track Record of Those Who Give Words

We will come across numbers of people in the body who prophesy. After listening to their prophecies over and over, we will discern the accuracy of their words. If they have been consistently off the wall, we'll know it and we can disregard what they say. On the other hand, there are those who have developed a reputation of accuracy which will cause us to have greater faith when they deliver a word of prophecy. These generally are individuals who have shown faithfulness in a local body, and the Lord can trust them more and more because of this faithfulness.

Character

Finally, let's look at the life styles of the ones delivering words in a church. What is their life at home like? Are their children well behaved and, of great importance, are they believers? Are they respected in the community and in the church? Do they hold responsible positions in the business world or their jobs? And especially, is the fruit of the Spirit being manifested in their lives? Are they reliable and dependable?

God will speak through anyone; but the individuals who grow in the Spirit and yield to the Spirit will grow in maturity. There are a lot of Christian flakes who turn people off by their lifestyle. We need to see a continual growth in individuals to have greater assurance that the words they are speaking are from the Lord.

However, remember that no one is perfect. God is still dealing with all of us. Even if you have not arrived in a certain area, do not lose heart. And certainly do not stop being led by the Holy Spirit. If you continually submit yourself to the Lord, He will use you. And while He is using you, He will also be working on you to wash and cleanse you.

I know a man who refused leadership in the church because his children were disobedient. He was a very mature Christian, and I knew the Lord wanted Him in a leadership position. However, he refused. That man's children were trained up in the way they should go. Eventually, when they grew older and matured, they all became solid Christians. God knew what would happen and wanted that man to be an elder because of the wisdom he had learned throughout his years of walking with the Lord.

I sought the Lord regarding this man since I knew he would have been a good elder. The Lord reminded me of the many disobedient children He had and asked me if that meant He shouldn't be the Head of the Church. He who began a good work in His children, will continue it until He comes back.

Conclusion

Remember that the tests of the Spirit are not absolutes. They are important guides and we should be aware of all of them. However, there will be times when answers will not be absolutely clear. We will speak further of problems in listening in chapters thirteen through fifteen.

Chapter Ten

LEARNING TO LISTEN

We have come to the point in this book in which I will be teaching you to actually listen to the voice of the Lord. I will be discussing each step and the Biblical basis for it. There will be some of you who believe these steps are not necessary; but I believe they have proven to be most effective in learning to listen as well as being a protection against further deception. *However, this, or any other method, is not a fool proof way to hear from God.* Satan or his demons will try to deceive us whenever we use any method of listening to the Lord. We must be on guard at all times.

Some hear by saying the same words that Samuel said when he was trying to hear God. He said, *"Speak for your servant is listening." (1 Samuel 3:10)* Others hear when they speak in tongues and wait for the interpretation. Still others hear when they are in the quiet of their prayer closets or in a quiet church service where the Lord speaks to them. Some go off to a place of solitude for a short season. Others hear after times of praise since God inhabits the praises of His people. There is no set way to hear from God. Try my method; but, if you are more comfortable with another method, use what works best for you.

Christians hear from God in numerous ways. However, the way I will be teaching is one way which has helped thousands of earnest Christians begin that close intimate relationship with the Lord for which they have yearned. One of the reasons is that the use of questions in seeking the Lord and waiting for the Lord's immediate response will often result in a continuous conversation with Him.

How God Speaks

We need to have a better understanding of the nature of the still small voice. Below are a few pointers regarding how to know that the voice you're hearing is the Lord's.

1) The voice of the Lord is generally a still small voice to the hearer. It will not be a booming voice, but almost like a thought or a gentle whisper in your mind. Rarely do people hear a loud, audible voice. The voice will usually be manifested as a thought, and especially initially, you may confuse the Lord's voice with your own thoughts.

2) The use of questions to communicate with the Lord is a good way to hear from God. God is a perfect gentleman and He generally wants us to initiate the conversation. He will not force Himself on us. He wants us to seek Him. That is why the method of asking the Lord questions works well in learning to listen to the Lord. A good biblical example of this is the story of Abraham interceding for Sodom. He kept asking the Lord questions as to whether He would destroy the city if there were 50, then 45, then 40, etc. righteous men in Sodom. God kept responding to Abraham's questions. You will find that God will almost always respond to the questions we ask of Him.

3) When the Lord has something to say, he will generally speak immediately after you ask a question. Expect the answer to come immediately. In fact, you may hear an answer before you ask the question. Often it will be the Lord's voice first, and afterwards Satan will come to confuse and try to steal by creating doubts about the Lord's voice.

4) The answers generally will be short at first, so do not expect a long dissertation. Later, when you get to know one another, He will, at times, speak at great length. Ask the questions aloud so you will more easily distinguish your thoughts from the voice of the Lord.

5) The Lord's voice will not drive you, but will be gentle, loving, patient, and will reflect the fruit of the Spirit, as set forth

in Galatians 5:22-23. However, there will be times (although rare) when the Lord will speak in an angry tone because of continued disobedience.

6) You will find that conversations with the Lord will come so easily you'll believe (or a demon will try to make you believe) it's too easy and is not the Lord speaking to you. Don't you believe it. I believe that normal Christianity should easily include conversations between God and man.

Before you start to learn to listen to God, make sure that you have asked Jesus into your heart and made him your Lord and Savior. If you have not done so, go to the Preface and read the prayer near the end of the Preface. Become one of His children, not just His creation.

Learning to Listen

I have found that many Christians who had never listened before or who had difficulty in listening have easily learned to listen by following these simple steps. *Please just read the first three steps and do not actually DO the steps until you get into the directions in the fourth step.* The steps are as follows:

STEP 1—WE ASK GOD TO STILL OUR VOICE AND THE VOICE OF SATAN AND HIS DEMONS.

There are three voices we must recognize—our voice, the voice of Satan and his demons, and that of the Holy Spirit.

Let's discuss each one individually. First, we have our own voice—our desires, will, ideas, and imaginations. We have our own desires and God will give us the desires of our heart. However, the Bible also says, *"The heart is deceitful above all things and beyond cure. Who can understand it?" (Jeremiah 17:9)* I don't want the desires of my heart if my heart is deceitful above *all* things. I may very well be in deception if I ask for my desires. I want to be in a position to always say, *"Not my will, but thine be done."* Not too many people attain to that all the time. I certainly don't. However, that is the place to be when we are seeking the Lord.

Let me give you an example of why it is important to try to eliminate our own desires in listening to the voice of the Lord. Suppose one of my children came to me and asked, *"Can I go to the candy store?"* I might reluctantly give my permission. But if my child should ask what I want him to do today, I might say, *"Clean your room."* Do you see the difference?

On the one hand, I was giving permission for my child to fulfill the desires of his/her heart. On the other hand, the child is fulfilling my desire. Now isn't that what we want in our relationship with God? We have to be in a position where we can honestly say, *"I don't care what you want me to do, I'll do it and I'll go wherever you want me to go."* Are we ready to yield to God and be His servant?

The Bible says, ***"We demolish arguments and every pretension that sets itself up against the knowledge of God, and we take captive every thought to make it obedient to Christ." (2 Corinthians 10:5.*** This is another reason for having our voices stilled. We are to strive to take captive every thought that races through our minds and as you know, our minds can wander all over the place. We need to discipline our thoughts and bring them into captivity, so we yield our minds to God and ask Him to still our voice.

We are to also ask Him to still the voice of Satan. Satan spoke in many places in the Bible and we certainly do not want him interfering in our conversation with the Lord. The example that best stands out of all of Satan's conversations is the temptation of Jesus in the wilderness in Luke chapter four. Other examples include when He spoke to God before and during the testing of Job (Job chapters one and two), Satan's conversation with Eve (Genesis 3:1-5), the conversation of Jesus with the demons in the Gadarene demoniac (Mark 5:6-13), and Jesus' telling Peter that Satan had asked to sift him. (Luke 22:31)

The reason we can ask God to still our voice and the voice of Satan and his demons is that God has ultimate authority over us and over Satan and his cohorts.

STEP 2—WE STILL THE VOICE OF SATAN AND HIS DEMONS

I use both *belts and suspenders* for assurance that I'm hearing the Lord. By that I mean I want to take as many precautionary steps as I can in order to assure myself that when I am listening to the Lord, it will be the Lord's voice I hear. Therefore, even though I asked God to still the voice of Satan, I still look for as many safeguards as I can in listening. For this reason, I include another step to protect against problems in listening.

Jesus has been given all authority in heaven and on earth. He also gave us authority. He said that *"...As the Father has sent me, I am sending you." (John 20-21)* He said in Matthew 10:1: *"He called his twelve disciples to him and gave them authority to drive out evil spirits and to heal every disease and sickness."* Luke 10:20 states: *"However, do not rejoice that the spirits submit to you, but rejoice that your names are written in heaven."* We have the necessary authority to still the voice of the enemy. We need to exercise that authority.

STEP 3—CONFESS OUR SINS

This next step is a very important step. Psalm 66:18 says: *"If I had cherished sin in my heart, the Lord would not have listened."* If He does not hear us, He will not answer us. *I've found in my own listening and in teaching others to listen that the one biggest stumbling block in hearing from the Lord is unconfessed sin.* I advise people that if you do not hear, assume first that there is sin blocking you from hearing. Let's delve into this further.

The high priest in the Old Testament had to make atonement for the sins of the people. He could not enter into the Holy of Holies unless or until the sins of the people were dealt with by sacrificing a lamb or goat. The Holy of Holies is the place where the high priest heard from God. He could not enter in or listen to God unless sin had been covered by the blood. When Jesus died on the cross, the veil to the Holy of Holies was rent or torn from top to bottom. This signified that we now have access to the Father and can now enter into the very presence of God.

Jesus became our sacrificial lamb. John the Baptist said in John 1:29: *"...Look, the Lamb of God who takes away the sin of the world!"* Through Him we have forgiveness of sins. However, we have to appropriate that forgiveness by asking to be forgiven. God has found a way! *"If we confess our sins, he is faithful and just and will forgive us our sins and purify us from all unrighteousness." (1 John 1:9)*

I have found we often need the help of the Holy Spirit to show us our sins. John 16:8, speaking of the work of the Holy Spirit, says, *"When he comes, he will convict the world of guilt in regard to sin..."* We are part of the world and He will convict us of our sins.

First, I ask people to privately confess any know sin. I have them do this privately since love covers a multitude of sins. I don't need to know their sins.

Then,, I have them ask the Lord to *"Show me any unconfessed sin."* The Holy Spirit will then speak quietly and gently about any unconfessed sin. Usually, you will hear a thought in your mind naming a particular sin. For example, you might hear the thought *lust* and immediately you recognize that you are guilty of that sin. You then ask the Lord to forgive you of the sin of lust. You then ask the Lord, *"What else, Lord?"* He will then proceed to show you the sins you need to confess before Him. Continue on until you hear no more sins or He says something like, *"That's all my child."*

Another verse on dealing with unconfessed sin is in 1 John 3:21-22. It states:

> **"Dear friends, if our hearts do not condemn us, we have confidence before God and receive from Him anything we ask, because we obey his commands and do what pleases him."**

It's important to see that this comes before the next step of testing the spirit at the end of 1 John 3 and the beginning of 1 John 4.

STEP 4—TESTING THE SPIRIT

We're going to go through the next step a little differently from the previous steps. Please follow closely. Let's begin at the second sentence of 1 John 3:24 and go through 1 John 4:3. It states:

> *And this is how we know he lives in us: We know it by the Spirit he gave us. Dear friends, do not believe every spirit, but test the spirits to see whether they are from God, because many false prophets have gone out into the world. This is how you can recognize the Spirit of God. Every spirit that acknowledges that Jesus Christ has come in the flesh is from God, but every spirit that does not acknowledge Jesus is not from God. This is the spirit of the antichrist, which you have heard is coming and even now is in the world.*

Some other versions of the Bible use the word *confess* instead of *acknowledge*. The words are synonymous; however, I use the word confess when testing the spirit since I am looking for an actual confession by the Holy Spirit.

At this point I would like you to proceed with the first three steps. First, say aloud, *"Father, in Jesus' name, still (or quiet) my voice and still (or quiet) the voice of Satan and his demons."* Second, say aloud, *"I command Satan and his demons to be still (or quiet) in Jesus' name."* Third, say, *"Lord, show me any unconfessed sins."* Then confess your sins as He reveals them to you. When you do not hear any more sins, continue on.

Fourth, ask the spirit, *"Will you confess that Jesus Christ has come in the flesh?"* NOW LISTEN. You should immediately hear, *"Yes,"* or *"Yes, I confess."* Now most people, when they hear that thought, will think it's their own thought. But remember, you have stilled your own voice and the voices of Satan and his demons. If you think it's yourself speaking, be assured that most people think this also. Now, I want you to go on to chapter eleven. You can come back to the rest of this chapter after you finish chapter eleven.

For those who heard nothing, remember to first assume unconfessed sin. Go back and ask the Lord to show you the sins preventing you from hearing from God. The Holy Spirit may now reveal some unconfessed sins. (I found that, at times, people will now begin to hear the Lord speaking.) After confessing your sins, test the spirit. If the Holy Spirit now confesses that Jesus Christ has come in the flesh, you may go on to the next chapter.

If you still hear nothing, command the spirits that are blocking you from hearing from God to leave you in Jesus' name. Try testing the spirit. If you hear, go on to the next chapter.

Some people who still hear nothing continue on with the questions in the next chapter and start hearing the Lord. However, in all instances of listening, remember the other ways to test the Spirit in chapter nine. Be aware that Satan or his cohorts will try to attack you in the thought process. He is a thief and will try to make you believe you are being led by the Lord, when, in fact, you are being led by the powers of darkness. Therefore, be aware of all the tests of the Spirit whenever you try to listen to the Lord.

If you still hear nothing, don't be alarmed. I have worked with a number of people who could not hear initially, but eventually became excellent hearers. Sometimes it is necessary for prayers for you to get your spiritual hearing. Ask the Lord to give you ears that you might hear Him. Remember, **"...Seek and you will find..." (Matthew 7:7), and "...he rewards those who earnestly seek him." (Hebrews 11:6)**

Finally, I will discuss the last situation. If you asked the Lord to still your voice and the voice of Satan and his demons and you received an answer such as *"No,"* or *"No, I will not,"* you need to stop listening at this point. You are listening to the evil one and deliverance is needed. **PLEASE READ WHAT I AM ABOUT TO SAY WITH AN OPEN MIND.**

Many different Christian groups believe that Christians cannot have demons. They are very sincere in their convictions; however, they are incorrect. I have been involved in thousands of deliverances (the casting out of demons) with born-again and spirit-filled Christians. Some of them also did not believe that Christians could have demons. As they were delivered, and the demons left them, their belief changed. Jesus came to set the captives free, and they were being set free. These brothers and sisters changed their study of God as they were experiencing their deliverance.

Let's discuss some biblical examples of demons and Christians. Ephesians 4:26-27 states:

> *In your anger do not sin: do not let the sun go down while you are still angry, and do not give the devil a foothold.*

Paul is talking to Christians in the book of Ephesians. Verse 20 states: *"You did not come to know Christ in that way."* Paul is telling Christians that anger left unchecked gives the devil a foothold.

Another scriptural example of this is Cain, who was warned by God that **"...sin was crouching at your door; it desires to have you, but you must master it." (Genesis 4:7).** An *"it"* cannot have desire; however, a living creature, in this case, Satan, can. Chapter two goes into more detail on this. Satan's desire is always for human beings. Satan wants to enter us and use us for his evil desires. Sin is the legal right that Satan has in his battle against us.

King Saul is another example. He was anointed king, he prophesied, yet, when anger got the best of him **"...an evil spirit from God came forcefully upon Saul." (1 Samuel 18:10)** Anger which is not dealt with became the door for the demons to enter.

Another example of the consequences of unforgiveness is shown in the parable in Matthew 18:23-25. In this parable, the Lord forgave his servant ten thousand talents (the equivalent of millions of dollars) because he pleaded with him to do so, yet he wouldn't forgive a fellow servant the equivalent of one day's wages (a few dollars). When the Lord found out about it, he was angry since he had forgiven that servant, but the servant would not forgive another. Therefore, he turned him over to the jailers to be tortured. Those are demons. If we do not forgive, we give the devil a foothold and demons have a legal right to torment us. Anger and unforgiveness have caused untold numbers of Christians to be tormented by the evil one.

James 4:7 says for us to *"submit yourselves, then, to God. Resist the devil and he will flee from you."* James is speaking to Christians since non-Christians not only do not believe in God, but they certainly do not submit to Him as well. Those Christians who continually resist God will be a target of Satan and his attacks. The reason we have to resist the devil is that if we don't he will attack us. The best defense against those attacks by the devil is our submission to the Lord.

Another example is in 1 Peter 5:8 which states: *"Be self-controlled and alert. Your enemy the devil prowls around like a roaring lion looking for someone to devour."* The devil's legions, the demons, look for an opening and continuous sin is that opening, whether we are Christians or non-Christians. Continuous lack of self-control is an open door for the enemy to come in.

Another scripture is 1 Timothy 4:1 which states: *"The Spirit clearly says that in later times some will abandon the faith and follow deceiving spirits and things taught by demons."* In order to *abandon* the faith, they had to be *in* the faith in the first place. These Christians were being led by demons.

1 John 3:8 states: *"He who does what is sinful is of the devil because the devil has been sinning from the beginning. The reason the Son of God appeared was to destroy the devil's work."* Those who continue in sin are of the devil and will continue to do the things of the devil. John is speaking to Christians in this epistle.

Paul was being tormented by a demon in 2 Corinthians 12:7 which says: *"To keep me from being conceited because of these surpassing great revelations, there was given me a thorn in my flesh, a messenger of Satan, to torment me."* Since it was in his flesh, the demon was inside Paul.

When Jesus was talking about His death and resurrection in Matthew 16:21, Peter took Jesus aside and said, *"Never Lord! This shall never happen to you!" (verse 22)* Jesus in the next verse said, *"Get behind me, Satan! You are a stumbling block to me..."* Obviously, Jesus knew Peter wasn't Satan, but He recognized that a spirit working through Peter was trying to stop Him from the finished work of the cross. These are just a few of the biblical examples of demonic interference with Christians.

Too many Christians in the body of Christ believe they are being led by God when it is, in fact, evil spirits doing the leading. One of the prime reasons for this is the false doctrine that Christians cannot have a demon. Christians often will not deal with the reality of demon involvement in their lives. I'm not going to go into any further details about deliverances. I'll make it the subject of another book. Suffice it to say that if you heard voices or thoughts denying Jesus, you need deliverance. Put away your theology and find someone in your town who can help you get set free. Do not continue listening until the demons are cast out. You should continue to read and learn about listening, but do not put it into practice until a later time.

And please do not be alarmed. Deliverance is very common in many churches and, I believe, since approximately one-fourth to one-third of Jesus' ministry consisted of casting out demons, the church should be much more involved in this ministry. Look at the bright side. Deliverance is only one step on the way to having a close, intimate relationship with the Holy Spirit.

The Beginning of Your Journey

Now that you have begun to listen, chapter eleven has more questions for you to ask the Lord in helping you on your new journey. The best of your Christian walk is yet to come. You now have communication and a new relationship with the Creator of the Universe.

Chapter Eleven

QUESTIONS TO ASK THE LORD

Now that you've learned the preliminary steps, we will begin to ask the Lord a number of questions. This will help you to become familiar with His voice and start you on the way to a new relationship with the Lord. Let me recap some of the things I said at the beginning of chapter ten to help you in listening.

The Lord's voice is not a loud booming voice, but rather a still small voice coming as a thought to your mind. You may have doubts that it's the Lord speaking, but as you continue, your faith will grow and you'll realize it is, in fact, the Lord talking to you. He will generally speak almost immediately after you ask the question. Also, He is a Lord of few words, so do not expect a long dissertation, especially at the beginning of your listening. Usually He will speak in a few short sentences, but this will change later as you develop a deeper relationship with Him.

I have included explanations with some of the questions in order to give a better understanding of why I asked the question in the way I did. I also have expanded on some of the questions based on the response from the Lord. This will aid in obtaining a clearer understanding of His specific direction.

Please follow the steps I will be discussing, since they will help build your confidence that it is, indeed, the Lord answering you. Get a ruler, a book or something to block the text after each question.

As you read each question, cover the text below the question. Read the question aloud and immediately listen to the still small voice of the Spirit.

After you get an answer, read the text for that question. Use this same procedure for the other questions in this chapter.

REMEMBER TO COVER THE TEXT BELOW THE QUESTION

1. Lord, how can I get to know you better?

If you are reading this before you get an answer, stop and ask the question again. Once you get an answer, read on. Most people will get an answer related to the Bible. They will hear *"Read My Word," "Read the Bible,"* or something similar to that. I would say about seventy-five percent of the people I have taught to listen will hear an answer related to the written Word. However, others may get answers such as *"Draw close to me," "Listen to me,"* or *"Do not doubt that it is Me."* I cannot put God in a box and tell you He won't answer anything else. He is sovereign and I cannot predict all His ways. I know by my own experience, most of the answers should fall into the above categories. Sometimes, more experienced listeners will receive answers which will be different.

As we move on to the next question, remember to cover the text below the question.

2. Lord, is there anything you want to tell me?

If you hear "Yes" then ask, "What is it?" About half of the people will get an answer such as *"I love you."* It always amazes me how the creator of the universe wants to tell His created beings that He loves us! We know about God's love intellectually, but we need to know it in our hearts. Many Christians have doubts about God's love for them. God knows this and He wants to reassure us of His great love for us. More amazingly is that we are asking the Lord if there is *anything* he wants to tell us and He tells us of His love for us.

You may get other answers such as *"Do not fear,"* or *"Trust me."* If He's telling you that, it's because He knows you have a problem in this area and He's working to overcome it. He wants you to trust in Him more. If He says, *"Trust me,"* ask the Lord the specific areas where you do not trust Him. Now on to the next question. Again, please cover the answer.

3. What would you have me do today, Lord?

Go to the Lord with neutral questions, that is, questions without a predisposition to what you want to do. For example, if you say, *"Lord, is it all right for me to go to the prayer meeting tonight?"* He might say *"yes"* because He wants to give you the desire of your heart. However, your desire should be His desire, so instead, ask a question like, *"What would you have me do tonight."* He may say to go to the prayer meeting, but He may also tell you to stay home and love your kids or clean your house. Sometimes our unsaved loved ones become jealous of the religious activities that take you out of the house. Get specific directions from the Lord regarding what to do. He loves your unsaved members of the family, and staying home to take care of their needs rather than going to church activities five days a week might be the will of the Lord. On the other hand, you may want to stay home and the Lord wants you to go to a church service. The key, as always, is to do whatever He tells you to do.

He might also tell you to do the things you were intending to do anyway. He could already have put the thoughts in your head without your knowing it. So you might think you are merely hearing your own thought, but it may be the Lord, confirming what you already were going to do.

If you do not hear anything, don't worry. He hasn't given you any assignment. Go on to the next question.

4. What would you have me do to expand your kingdom?

Often, the Lord will say something like, *"Tell others of my love,"* or *"Witness to other people."* Often, this is the first question in a series of questions on the subject. I like to get specific at this point and ask Him, *"Is there anyone specifically you want me to talk to or witness to?"* Ask that question now. He might give the name of a particular person. I would then ask something like, *"What should I tell them?"* then *"Should I give them a particular book, tract, or should I just tell them about my experiences with you?"* The Lord's answer will frequently cause me to ask another question. Also, get the timing for the witnessing. Ask the Lord when you should do it.

A word of caution at this point. Sometimes there is a tendency to become fearful of the Lord and be led by fear rather than love and a desire to be obedient to Him. In fact, many people go through the early stages of listening and being obedient out of fear, expecting they will receive a harsh judgment if they do not obey. God loves you and He wants to motivate you by His love.

If you are in the beginning stages of listening, don't worry. God is most patient. I'm saying your motivation should be one of a desire to be a servant of the Most High, a desire to serve our wonderful Lord. Don't be afraid to witness to the person the Lord puts on your heart. Learn not to have a greater fear of man than fear of the Lord.

5. What activities in the church do you want me to add or to eliminate?

meet the need when I can

If you are a sincere Christian (and you probably are or you wouldn't be trying to learn more about listening to the Lord), you want to eagerly serve both the Lord and other Christians. There is often a tendency to become so involved in the *"work of the Lord"* that we forget about the *"Lord of the work."* We become involved in projects that are worthy and then ask the Lord to bless the project. We have it backwards. What is important is to have the Lord direct us in *what He wants us to do rather than what we want to do.* There is always so much to do, but what is His will for us now?

He may say, *"I want you to teach."* Ask Him who He wants you to teach and when He wants you to teach them. He may tell you to get involved in an area that you were already thinking about. There is a tendency to believe the thoughts were your own because you had the thoughts before. He probably put the ideas in your mind before, and you didn't know it was the Lord. He often will lead us without our knowledge, so don't be concerned that you were already thinking the thoughts you receive. Also, we need to continue to ask the Lord various questions regarding the situation. Too often we stop and move out on direction which is not complete. We need to continue to ask questions until we are sure we have the mind of the Lord on a subject.

6. What question do you want me to ask you?

am I aligned
yes at the moment

You may hear a question. If you do, then ask it even if you have doubts about the question. For example, the Lord might give you the question, *"Do you love me?"* as a question He wants you to ask Him. You might wonder why the Lord would have you ask that question. Ask it anyway. Again the Lord frequently wants to tell us about His love. By the way, this is one of the most frequent questions the Lord has people ask Him.

If you didn't get an answer, (and many people do not), simply go on to the next question. You didn't get an answer because the Lord did not want to give you a question. You don't need to make a big deal out of not receiving an answer.

7. I have difficulty with _____. What should I do? (Insert the name of the person you are having difficulty with at the time.)

Be firm He love him

He may say to *"Love them,"* or *"Forgive them."* He might also have you pray for those who persecute you. (Matthew 5:44) He may have you bake a cake, walk the extra mile, call them, write them, or just try to be a friend, etc. Whatever the Lord says to do, do it even though you may have doubts about its effectiveness.

8. My pastor is not leading the church the way I think it should be led. What should I do about it?

Expect to hear something like, *"Pray for him,"* Submit to him and say nothing," or *"Serve him and the people with love and with your whole heart."* Remember, all authority is from God and whoever resists that authority is resisting God. (Romans 13:2) There are too many disgruntled, complaining Christians and not enough who will serve with a heart of love even though they do not agree with all the things a pastor does or does not do in a church.

The Lord may have you tell the pastor the specific areas of concern, but once you have done that, leave it up to the pastor and the Lord. You have delivered your message. Leave it at that. There will be times when the message is unheeded and your concerns continue. Again, ask the Lord what He wants you to do. As before, follow the Lord's direction. There are some pastors who feel uncomfortable in receiving a word in this manner. Sometimes it's because they have not experienced listening. Be patient and not judgmental.

Understand that submitting to authority is first and foremost submitting to the will of the Lord, and generally that will mean that He will have us submitting to those in church and secular authority.

John continue to Emmys   Be the example

9. What should I do to help _____ know you? (Insert the name of a loved one or someone you are concerned about).

We all want our loved ones and friends to become children of God. That is one of the strongest desires of Christians. So naturally we want to do whatever we can to help them become Christians. There is also a tendency for us to botch it up and sometimes even drive them away from the Lord because of our zeal. That's why it's important to get directions from the Lord on how to proceed. He may give answers such as, *"Pray for their salvation,"* *"Let Me handle it,"* *"Love them,"* *"Be an example to them,"* *"Yield them to me,"* or *"Stop nagging them,"* or *"Give them to me."* The important thing is to do what He is telling you to do and to leave it in His hands. Of course, continually seek Him for He may give you other assignments regarding that person; however, don't keep trying to do it on your own.

Many times, before we act, the Lord will have us pray for that person. How many of us came to the Lord because we had a mother or friend faithfully praying for us? If someone is unsaved, we know we have an obligation to pray for that person. If we do not, who will? God wants all men to be saved and come to the knowledge of the truth. (1 Timothy 2:4) His desire is our desire. We should begin attempts to reach our loved ones with prayer even if we don't get a specific word from the Lord on the subject since we know we are praying His will.

10. What particular book, Bible chapter, magazine, TV program, radio program, tape, or other material do you want me to read, hear, or see?

When we are studying or in prayer, we often get involved in a religious routine which does not permit the entrance of the Holy Spirit. Sometimes we say we want to be led by the written Word and we exclude any other leading He may want to give. God will often lead us by quickening a certain Scripture; however, He may choose to lead us by way of a teaching tape, a message on TV or radio, a book, a magazine or booklet, or another way. *Don't limit God by saying you want to be led in only one way!* If the direction is not specific enough, keep asking the Lord for more direction. I can't tell you how many times the Lord has told me to turn on the radio and the message I heard was exactly what was needed at the time.

11. Who would you have me pray for, Lord?

God will probably give you a name immediately. Don't be surprised if it's someone you are already praying for. After you get the name(s), ask the Lord, *"How should I pray for that person?"* He might say something like, *"Pray for salvation,"* *"Pray for a healing,"* *"Pray that they come to know me,"* or *"Pray in the Spirit."* Pray as He leads you. That does not mean He will not answer prayers unless He tells you how to pray for a person, but I would rather pray based on the knowledge of the Lord rather than on my own knowledge.

12. Please disclose anything about my life that displeases you.
God will probably show you an area that you already know is a problem area. The Lord may simply give you the name of the sin He wants you to overcome. He may also simply give you a biblical response such as, *"Flee youthful lust," "Trust me,"* or *"Fear not for I am with you."* He will not give you something that is contrary to the Scriptures.

He may, instead, show you an area you did not think was important, but God Himself did. After He shows you the area, ask Him, *"What should I do to overcome it?"* What you need to do now is follow through with His direction.

13. I'm having difficulties at work. What direction do you have for me regarding my work situation?
Often, what we are looking for is a way of escaping because we think the grass is always greener on the other side. We believe if we had another job, boss, wife, house, church, etc. things would be better. Do not be surprised if the Lord keeps you on your job to learn submissiveness and to learn to be content, whatever the circumstances. (Philippians 4:11) He may tell you to look for another job. If He does, then do so. If He wants to keep you where you are for a season, accept that as the will of the Lord for you right now.

14. Should I stay in my present job or look for another? If another, what kind of job should I look for and how should I go about doing it?

The key to our life is to be in the will of the Lord and keep in obedience to His leading. If he tells us to stay where we are, then we should happily do so even though we may dislike the job. If the Lord tells us to stay, then do so with joy. If He tells us to look around for another job, then get further direction as to the specifics. If no specific direction is given as to where to look, or the specific kind of job, then look based on your sanctified common sense.

Look in employment fields where you are experienced. When you receive a job offer, seek the Lord before accepting it. Wait until the Lord gives you specific steps. Often, the Lord will create the right job opening only after He tells us to look for a job and we step out in faith. As long as you are trying to be obedient to the best of your ability and knowledge, God will honor your attempts.

If you are a listener and do not hear anything regarding a change of job, it often means the Lord isn't ready to give you direction to move. I suggest you stay put and learn whatever lessons the Lord has for you on your present job.

15. What area of ministry are you calling me into? *Restoring*

Again, the Lord may speak to you about something you already know you should be involved in, or an area in which you may already be working. Study as much about the ministry as you can. He will lead us by His Spirit, but He also wants us to learn from others who have been successful in that particular ministry. *I already know as I will open it up to you*

16. Lord, what direction do you have for me regarding my ministry?

We may already know we have a calling in a certain ministry, but we need to continue seeking the Lord and obtaining His direction each step of the way, just as Moses did. We should not be anxious if we do not receive more specific guidance. Do not despise small beginnings. As long as we are listening to the Lord and obeying to the best of our understanding and ability, we are in His will. Also, we should realize His direction for us will change during our lives. Our ministry may change. We should be open to the Lord and not be afraid to follow the new direction.

17. What message do you want me to teach for my sermon, Bible study, Sunday School class, or youth group?

God knows what is needed, and if we consult Him, He will surely determine the subject of the message. Once He has given you the subject, get more specific with Him regarding the details of the message. Let God be the literal head of the church. Let us be followers of the living God. I always seek the Lord regarding my teachings. He knows exactly what is needed.

Sometimes the Lord will wait until the eleventh hour before giving you the message. Trust Him for He knows what He is doing. He wants to be in control and not us and our plans.

18. What direction do you have for my future education? What school do you want me to attend, and what should my major be?

The Lord may give you specific direction now, or He may wait. Sometimes the waiting is because we do not have all the material we need to know about the various schools He wants us to be interested in. In the case of all of my children, the Lord gave them specific schools. Their majors were also chosen by the Lord.

If God does not give you a specific school, ask Him if He is leaving the decision to you. Also ask the Lord if He has plans other than school for you at this time.

19. What curfew should I set for my children?

You may wonder why I include this in the list. It is because the Lord has set the curfew for each of my children, and it has worked out wonderfully. Generally, they have obeyed the time set forth by the Lord, but there have been times when they have not. The Lord provided the punishment as I sought Him for direction. As obedience continued to take place, the Lord extended the time.

I have found the Lord often is more lenient with my kids than I would have been. However, my children have grown up to make me very proud, and the Lord had more to do with it than I did. He knew when to be stern and when to be lenient. I strongly recommend that you literally let the Lord be the head of your house. After rearing six children, I have found that the *"Heavenly Father"* knows best.

20. What can I do to help me love my wife as Christ loved the church? (For a man) What should I do to submit to my husband? (For a woman)

Often, we are blind to our shortcomings, blind to what it takes to please our spouses. However, God is not. He knows what needs to be done. Expect his answer to be simple and one of service such as, start to do the list of chores your wife has been asking you to do, or, make him his favorite dinner. Once I asked the Lord what I should do for my wife, and he said for her to buy two pairs of shoes. After I told her what the Lord said, my wife said she needed two pairs of shoes but didn't think we could afford them. Can you imagine how she felt when she was shopping for shoes knowing she was in the perfect will of the Lord?

21. Are there any Scriptures you want me to study today?

He may give you one or a number of verses to read and study. Often, they will have a theme to them. After you read the verses, seek the Lord again and discuss the verses and the reason He gave them to you. Ask Him what He wants you to do regarding the verses, book of the Bible, or the theme he gives you. He may also give you a page number and lead you to the verse(s) you need at that time. Be open to whatever He chooses to do.

Infrequently, you will hear verses which do not exist. Go back to the Lord for clarification. It often is because of our mistakes in hearing. This will be addressed in more detail in Chapter 14.

22. Is there anything else you want to tell me now? Another question could be *"Speak, for your servant is listening."* *Continually look to me & not others.*

Be open to anything the Lord has for you. I like to end my conversations with this question just in case I missed anything.

I was through with writing the book and the Lord told me to add the following question to this list.

23. Do you want to have me buy this book and give the book to someone else? If the Lord says, "Yes," then ask him to give you the name(s) of the people to whom he wants you to give the book.

Thrust of the Questions

God blessed Solomon when he asked for wisdom and discernment for the people instead of asking for himself. When we ask the Lord questions, the thrust of the questions should be for the benefit of others and for the good of the kingdom of God. God wants us to be servants of all, and we need to be concerned with the body. I generally try not to ask many questions for my benefit, for I know that God will take care of me as I concern myself with the needs of others. As our desire for service to God and others increases, God will more than meet our needs.

Chapter Twelve

PRACTICE LISTENING
TO THE LORD DAILY

Once we start to listen, one of the most important things we need to do is to continue listening on a daily basis. It is necessary to familiarize ourselves with the voice of the Chief Shepherd. John 10:27 states: *"My sheep listen to my voice; I know them, and they follow me."* To make sure we are listening to His voice, we have to get to know His voice, and the way to do that is to be with Him continuously, as sheep are daily with their shepherd. Time spent cultivating a relationship with the Lord on a daily basis will ensure that we know His voice.

We do not forget to brush our teeth daily, we eat our food daily (we would never forget to eat!), and we should be in the written Word of God daily in order to get our spiritual food. We also need to practice listening *daily* so we can be led anew each day, so that the walk we have each day with the Shepherd is fresh and exciting.

Bread from Heaven

Jesus said in Matthew 4:4, in which He quoted Deuteronomy 8:3, *"...man does not live on bread alone but on every word that comes from the mouth of the Lord."* Bread was one of the staple daily foods of the Middle East. Bread will sustain a person's hunger every day, but Jesus said that was not enough. We also need spiritual food, and we need it every day. He is the Bread of Life. We live only in Jesus, and life comes from His Word, whether spoken or written. We cannot have life apart from Him, and we need Him daily. We talk about the need to be in the Bible on a daily basis and that same need applies to listening to Him on a daily basis.

Another example of this is in Exodus, chapter 16. The Lord tested the Israelites when they were hungry, and He chose to provide them with bread from heaven. Exodus 16:4 states:

> *Then the LORD said to Moses, "I will rain down bread from heaven for you. The people are to go out each day and gather enough for that day. In that way I will test them and see whether they will follow my instructions."*

God tested them to see if they would trust Him on a daily basis. They were to go out and collect enough manna to sustain them for that day only. Some of them collected more than they needed, and the manna turned to maggots and smelled by the next morning. They needed a fresh supply each day. In the same way, we need a fresh supply of the Lord each day. We can't live on yesterday's supply.

And what is the bread from heaven in the New Testament? John 6:35 and 38 have the answer:

> *Then Jesus declared, "I am the bread of life. He who comes to me will never go hungry, and he who believes in me will never be thirsty...For I have come down from heaven not to do my will but to do the will of him who sent me."*

Jesus is the one who sustains us. He is our spiritual bread and we are to partake of that bread daily.

When Jesus' disciples asked Him how they should pray, He answered in part in the Lord's Prayer by saying: *"Give us today our daily bread." (Matthew 6:11)* That bread is food for our body and the bread that comes down from heaven. Jesus, when asked how we should pray, said we should pray and ask the Father daily for Jesus, our bread of life.

We live by God's spoken and written Word to us. It is life and sustenance to our bodies, soul, and spirit. We need to continually feed on the spiritual bread from heaven, our Lord and Savior, Jesus Christ.

The Vine and the Branches

Another way to see the need for daily feeding in the written Word and conversation with the Lord is by studying the analogy given in John, chapter 15, the analogy of the vine and the branches which Jesus uses to get His point across. Just as in the analogy of bread, raising grapes and tending to vineyards was understandable to most of the people during the life and times of Jesus. He tied their understanding of the grapes, vines and branches to the spiritual in John 15:1-10 which states:

> *I am the true vine, and my Father is the gardener. He cuts off every branch in me that bears no fruit, while every branch that does bear fruit he prunes so that it will be even more fruitful. You are already clean because of the word I have spoken to you. Remain in me, and I will remain in you. No branch can bear fruit by itself; it must remain in the vine. Neither can you bear fruit unless you remain in me.*

> *I am the vine; you are the branches. If a man remains in me and I in him, he will bear much fruit; apart from me you can do nothing. If anyone does not remain in me, he is like a branch that is thrown away and withers; such branches are picked up, thrown into the fire and burned. If you remain in me and my words remain in you, ask whatever you wish, and it will be given you. This is my Father's glory, that you bear much fruit, showing yourselves to be my disciples.*

> *As the Father has loved me, so have I loved you. Now remain in my love. If you obey my commands, you will remain in my love, just as I have obeyed my Father's commands and remain in his love.*

In the natural, a drying-up and death process occurs whenever there is a separation of an entity from its life-source. In the vine/branches analogy, this occurs when the branch is separated from the vine. When it is cut off, it dies immediately unless it is somehow restored to its source of life. What is true in the natural is also true in the spiritual. Without continual connection with the source of life, we spiritually die. We are not led by the Spirit when we've cut ourselves off from the Spirit. We are led only by ourselves and our past leadings of the Lord. The Lord is fresh every morning, new every morning, and we need to connect to that newness. If our Christian walk is stale, it's not because of the Lord, it's because of us.

The branches are continuously fed by the vine. The source of life does not stop, and it is the same way with the Lord. Our continuous feeding by the Lord, both through the written Word of God and the spoken word, will assure that our walk will be God-led and will have the power of the Lord behind our steps. Apart from Jesus who is our life, we can do nothing (John 15:5). But with Him all things are possible. (Mark 10:27)

Let's look at an Old Testament verse where the Lord speaks about the identity of the vineyard. Isaiah 5:7 states: ***"The vineyard of the LORD Almighty is the house of Israel, and the men of Judah are the garden of his delight."*** However, the Lord cut off Israel since they did not bear fruit. Now Christians are that vineyard. We Christians now have been grafted in as shown in Romans 11:17-18 which states:

> *If some of the branches have been broken off, and you, though a wild olive shoot, have been grafted in among the others and now share in the nourishing sap from the olive root, do not boast over those branches. If you do, consider this: You do not support the root, but the root supports you.*

We now share in the nourishing sap from the olive root, which is Jesus, the ***"Root of Jesse" (Romans 15:12)***. We will receive daily nourishment from Jesus if we come to Him daily. He is the root that supports us if we will allow Him to do so. He won't break us off unless we choose by our turning away to be broken off. A broken branch just lies on the ground, completely dead by itself. It doesn't take long for a branch no longer connected to its life source to dry up. We are dead in ourselves and our works, but alive in Him; and its our daily choice who we will follow this day.

Be connected to Jesus every day and let the life of the Almighty God continually flow through you. It's a daily choice, so choose life this day and every day hereafter, to be continually led and fed by our precious Lord.

Today, If You Hear His Voice

Let's turn now to Hebrews 3:7-8 where Psalms 95:7-8 is quoted. It states:

> ***So, as the Holy Spirit says, "Today, if you hear his voice, do not harden your hearts as you did in the rebellion, during the time of testing in the desert."***

The Holy Spirit didn't say it only once in Hebrews, but He said it in Heb. 3:7, Heb. 3:15, and again in Heb. 4:7. Could it be that perhaps God was trying to make a point by repeating it two times? He wants us to hear His voice daily, and when we do, to not turn away in disbelief.

Again, the plea is in both the Old and New Testaments. It appeared once in Psalms and three times in Hebrews, so if we don't get it the first time, God repeats the message. And yet, how many of us really listen to God on a daily basis? This is something we need to do.

We need to develop a new habit pattern of listening, just as we have the habit of brushing our teeth, showering, driving to work or anything else that has developed and continues in our lives. How much more must we develop a continual habit pattern of communing with the Lord in His written Word and directly through listening?

Some will say that we should not be legalistic in our approach to the Lord. While that is true, we cannot ignore the fact that if we do not establish new spiritual habit patterns or routines, we often neglect or forget Him.

David was a man after God's own heart and he said in Psalms 5:3: *"In the morning, O LORD, you hear my voice; in the morning I lay my requests before you and wait in expectation."* He placed God as his first priority. David sought the Lord in the morning as well as other parts of the day.

Isaiah 50:4-5 states:

> *The Sovereign LORD has given me an instructed tongue, to know the word that sustains the weary. He wakens me morning by morning, wakens my ear to listen like one being taught. The Sovereign LORD has opened my ears, and I have not been rebellious; I have not drawn back.*

Isaiah listened to the Lord morning by morning and established a set pattern for being instructed by Him. Isaiah had an instructed tongue. That means he received direction from the Lord as to what to say and spoke just as the Lord told him to. As he listened each morning to the specific direction of the Lord for that day, he said he had not been rebellious and did what the Lord told him to do. He did it and so can we. We should practice listening on a daily basis, have an instructed tongue, do what the Lord says and not be rebellious.

Daniel prayed three times a day (Daniel 6:10); Peter and John went to the synagogue at the hour of prayer; Acts 3:1 shows us that Peter prayed at 3:00 pm in the afternoon. There was a set time for prayer. Muslims often pray more than Christians do and they have set times for prayer. Jesus spent whole nights with His Father in prayer. On the eve of His death on the cross, He asked those with Him in the garden if they could not tarry but one hour.

Prayer has many forms, but we won't go into all of them here; however, one of the most common is simply conversation with the Lord. When we go into our time of prayer, take time to converse with the Lord. Learn what is on His heart, and don't just say canned prayers. Let's get the mind of God during those precious moments.

Some people are morning persons and are wide awake early each day while others don't get started until much later. Some thrive during the night, but whether it's in the early morning hours, the middle of the day, the cool of the evening, or whatever time, the *when* is unimportant. What is important is that we pray on a regular basis.

How can we expect Jesus to be our friend if we don't communicate with Him? We don't ignore our friends when they're waiting for us to initiate conversation, yet we do this to the Lord. Stop each day and find quality time for the person we want to be our dearest friend, our Lord and Savior, Jesus Christ. Get to know the Holy Spirit as well. He's there all the time for us. Let's find time in our busy schedule for conversations with our God.

The Light We Need for Today

God knows the heart of man. He also knows man would ignore Him if we didn't need Him. There's a certain amount of selfishness in the heart of man and sometimes our motives for seeking God are not exactly righteous. In spite of this, God will still meet us wherever we are in our Christian walk.

He'll generally give us the light we need for today and not the whole picture at one time. If He were to give us the whole scenario at once, we wouldn't need Him anymore. We'd have our marching orders and know the full plan He has for us, so there would no longer be a need to fellowship with Him since we would already know what the future holds. He'll give us direction based on either our present need or to fulfill His plan for us at the time.

He will give us the light we need for the moment we need it. Psalms 119:105 says: ***"Your word is a lamp to my feet and a light for my path."*** In days of old, there were no streetlights. When people went outside at night, it was pitch dark except for the light from the moon and stars. So when they walked with a lamp, they had to hold it in front of them in order to see a few steps at a time, and this gave only enough light to see what was just ahead. The light could not pierce the darkness beyond because the glow it gave forth was too weak.

God is the light of the world and He will light our paths. He'll sometimes give us general directions of where He would like us to be in future years, but He doesn't give the specifics at the present time. Rather, He waits until we need it in the future. What the Lord generally does is give the specific steps He wants us to take for today, not for tomorrow, next week, or next year. He may do so occasionally, but the more usual pattern is for Him to give us His direction for that day. We may want to know everything about the future; but the Lord will not tell us to the extent of our desire.

A friend of mine, who formerly had been a missionary for four years, was working at the U.S. Office of Education with me. His twenty-one-year-old son had just died in an automobile accident, and both he and his wife were grief stricken. It's always most difficult to know what to say to someone who has lost a loved one. There are few words that can be spoken at a time like that to help relieve the grief. I asked the Lord to help me help my friend in some way.

That night the Lord told me to listen to a cassette tape a member of our prayer group had given me. She had been told by the Lord to do so the previous Saturday. The tape was by Loren Cunningham of Youth with a Mission and was on *"Relinquishment."* Loren related several instances of how we are only stewards of what the Lord has given us in this life. He specifically witnessed about an automobile accident in Mexico which nearly claimed the life of his wife, and how he relinquished her to the Lord. The Lord gave him his wife back, as the Lord will often do when we relinquish something or someone to Him. Then again, He may not give us back whatever or whoever we relinquish to Him. It's His choice—not ours.

The Lord immediately told me to give that tape to the grieving friend. Later, this friend said that of all the things people said or did during this grieving time, nothing comforted him and his wife more than that tape.

I received the light needed to help my friend on the evening I cried out to the Lord for what to say to him. The Lord prepared the situation ahead of time by having another saint give me the tape before it was needed, and then He had me listen to the tape the day before I gave it to my friend. Had I not been listening to the Lord, I would have missed His needed guidance that day and would not have been able to provide the comfort so desperately needed.

God is the God of all comfort, and He gives us what we need when we need it. All He wants us to do is be open to His leading.

Active Communication Is Necessary to Build a Relationship

Many marriages, including Christian marriages, are in serious trouble. Divorce is rampant, and we see many shaky marriages even where divorce is not being considered. The reasons are many and varied; however, sex, money, problems with children, and lack of communication head the list. Let's deal with the last issue.

Taking your partner for granted, selfishness, lack of time together because of busy schedules, our own agendas, and an unwillingness to discuss and resolve unsettled issues are often reasons behind the lack of communication between husband and wife. There is also a lack of understanding the needs of the other spouse.

I have been in hundreds of counseling sessions where the wife says her husband doesn't communicate with her and he's perplexed because he believes he does. I've found the needs and expectations of both spouses are different, but the lack of discussing and understanding those needs creates tensions and unhappiness. We cannot build a solid marriage unless this critical area of communication is satisfactorily dealt with. We can be in a marriage and be strangers to one another.

In the same way we can have a personal relationship with God, be born-again, a child of God, and still be separated from Him. We know *about* Him, but we don't know Him. We cannot be a friend of God unless we decide to cultivate a relationship with Him. He won't force Himself on us, and if we choose to develop a relationship, He'll be there, waiting and very willing to have the kind of relationship we need.

There are those who believe God needs our friendship. I disagree. If God needed anything, He would be less than complete, and in Him there is no lack.

He chooses to let us share in His infinite wisdom, knowledge, and life and we can choose life if we want it. To choose life is to choose the Lord.

Here are some more natural examples to understand the need to follow Him daily. What would happen if we didn't talk to our husband or wife at all during only one day? Our relationship would be strained to say the least. The same is true of any relationship where the individual is present and we choose not to talk. Is it any different with the Lord? Yet, He is extremely patient with His people. He's always there waiting for a close relationship to begin, even while being ignored by millions of His children. What would happen if you ignored your natural father? You wouldn't hear the end of it. Yet the longsuffering Lord waits patiently for His children to come to Him.

When we learn to hear our Father speak, we will hear such wisdom that we'll wish we could take a tape recorder and plug it into our head so that everybody could hear. When He speaks, we'll often be in awe of the wisdom of the ages, and amazed at how much we have missed by not listening to Him before. There are few who can always be in the Lord's presence because of the distractions in their lives; however, we must try to seek times of refreshment with the Lord to sustain us for our days.

Comparison Between the "Secular" and "Lord's" Work-Worlds

Here's another way to look at it. Let's do a comparison of the work scene to the direction of the Lord. There might be a particularly long-term project our boss gives us for completion at some time in the distant future. There will also be short-term projects, projects which can often be completed in part of one day. So it is in the kingdom. We will know certain long-term assignments; however, we will not receive many short-term assignments from the Lord until the day the work has to be done. We can't get our assignments if we are not listening to the boss—in this case, the Holy Spirit.

If we aren't listening on particular days, the assignments that were to be ours may well be given to another more reliable listener. One day I was mildly ill, but the Lord wanted me to go to a certain prayer meeting and give a prophecy. I asked the Lord to send someone else since I wasn't feeling very well. He said He had no one else to send since no one was listening. I went in obedience and delivered the prophecy, and also received a healing from the Lord *after* I was obedient.

Let's continue on the work scene. What would happen if we showed up for work intermittently? At a minimum, our boss would consider us unreliable, and long term, couldn't trust us to be faithful, so the choice assignments would be given to the faithful workers (servants).

If we do our own thing and contact the Lord only at our convenience and when we desperately need Him, how can He trust us? He won't abandon us; but we've proven we aren't faithful in little things. How can we expect the greater ministries if after being tried by the Lord, we faithfully fail to show up for the work of the kingdom?

Let's look at it another way. What would happen if the boss gave us assignments and we didn't do them because of fear of failure, doubts about what the boss wanted us to do, or for fear of the people with whom we would have to interact? We probably would get several chances, and if we continued to not perform, we would get the axe.

We can also get the axe from the Lord. If we bury our talents, what we have is given to another. Remember the parable of the talents in Matthew, chapter 25. Three servants were given five, two and one talent respectively, according to their ability. The servants with the five and two talents earned an equivalent amount for their master. They were given those talents and were commended by the master. He said, ***"Well done, good and faithful servant,"*** to each of them. The Master was angry at the servant who had hidden his one talent. He took his talent and gave it to the one who had accumulated ten talents.

The two servants who had more talents used their talents, while the servant who only had one did not use even the little he had. So often this is true of those in the Kingdom. The busiest workers have greater and greater responsibilities and perform them well. There are many workers in the Kingdom who only have a few talents, but they fail to use even the little they have and they rarely progress in service to the Lord.

We should ask the questions: *"Where am I?"* and *"In which of the two categories do I now find myself?"* Even if you have hidden your talents in the past, let today be a new beginning—a decision to use that which God has entrusted to you.

151

In the world of work, the ones who perform well are expected to do more. The boss knows those workers who are faithful, reliable, who seldom complain, and who can successfully complete the job. Who gets the promotions, bonuses, and kudos? Again, it's those who do the job.

We know that promotion comes from the Lord, and that's true whether in the secular world or spiritual world. One of the fruit of the Spirit is faithfulness, which is translated into many areas of life. It includes faithfulness to our bosses and companies, to our friends and families, to our pastors and churches, and especially to God.

Let's look at our relationships to see where we are. If we are not faithful, recognize it and decide to start afresh. We may be faithful in one area and not another. We need to examine ourselves and choose to be faithful in all of them and start by being faithful in seeking the Lord on a daily basis. Ask His forgiveness for lack of faithfulness in the past and He is faithful to forgive us our sins and cleanse us from all unrighteousness (1 John 1:9). He's ready for us, let's be ready for Him each day.

Unreliable Christians

If you have been a believer for any length of time, you know there are Christians who hop from church to church and from one thing to another. They cannot be put into an area of responsibility in a church since the pastor cannot trust them to be reliable. Sometimes they have been truly led by the Lord to go from place to place for a season for various reasons.

Other times, it is merely that they are looking for the perfect church, which, of course, does not exist. Pastors and elders who look at these people come and go, know they can't be trusted with long term responsibilities in the church, since they may not be there long. Just as secular bosses look for responsibility and faithfulness in their employees, so do church leaders. It's the same with the Lord. Faithfulness and responsibility go hand-in-hand.

Faithfulness in daily communication with the Lord shows Him where our desires are. As we are faithful, He will see that we are responsible. He will know our heart's desire is to please Him and be a good servant.

Where is your heart? As you look at what you think about and what you do, you will know. Many of us are no different from the Pharisees. We have the outward appearance of being a strong Christian, but inwardly we are like a whitewashed sepulcher, full of dead men's bones. These are hard words, but as each of us examines ourselves, we will know if they apply to us. What we think and what we do each day demonstrates where we are in the kingdom. If you see yourself here, repent. Start by changing your thought patterns. Concentrate on the things of the Lord and seek Him today, for He forgives and is waiting for each of us.

Today, if you hear His voice, do not harden your heart. Go to Him daily for your assignments in the kingdom. The assignments may be simple, but it's important that we seek Him and do what He tells us to do. Decide today to be a faithful servant to the Lord.

PROBLEMS
IN LISTENING TO THE LORD

"See to it borhter that none of you have a sinful, unbelieving heart that turns away from the living God." (Heb. 3:12)

Chapter Thirteen

PROBLEMS IN LISTENING— MISUNDERSTANDING, TIMING, A WANDERING MIND, AND UNCONFESSED SIN

O ver the years, I have taught thousands of people to listen to the Lord. During these times I have found some of them have encountered problems in beginning to learn to listen. Others have experienced difficulties which hold them back in continuing to grow in listening. Still others stopped listening because of problems they encountered in their listening. If you have had difficulties in listening (and I believe most people do at times), you may well have had similar experiences and can relate to the problems and situations I will be describing in the next three chapters.

All too often we believe our experiences are unique and entirely different from those of others in the body of Christ. What you have experienced is common to all men. We know this intellectually and also because the Bible says so; but, it helps when we see experiences we can relate to. If you have been a listener, let's see if you can relate to these situations.

Misunderstanding

As we grow as Christians, we find we change our theology as we study the written Word and listen to many learned Bible teachers. We will frequently find we initially misunderstood the meaning of certain passages in the Bible. If we do it with the written Word, why isn't it likely that we will also do it with the spoken word? We do. John 11:47-53 discusses the word received by Caiaphas, the high priest, and his interpretation of it. It's one of the most dramatic misunderstandings of a word from the Lord. It states:

> *Then the chief priests and the Pharisees called a meeting of the Sanhedrin. "What are we accomplishing?" they asked. "Here is this man performing many miraculous signs. If we let him go on like this, everyone will believe in him, and then the Romans will come and take away both our place and our nation."*
>
> *Then one of them, named Caiaphas, who was high priest that year, spoke up, "You know nothing at all! You do not realize that it is better for you that one man die for the people than that the whole nation perish."*
>
> *He did not say this on his own, but as high priest that year he prophesied that Jesus* **would** *die for the Jewish nation, and not only for that nation but also for the scattered children of God, to bring them together and make them one. So from that day on they plotted to take his life.*

Now Caiaphas received a true prophesy from God, and, in fact, Jesus fulfilled that prophecy. The high priest spoke the word that God had given him, but he did not understand its meaning. He certainly thought he did. In fact, he had arrogantly said to the others at the council, *"You know nothing at all!"* The implication was that they knew nothing, but he had all the answers; after all, he was the *high priest.* He received the word from the Lord, and he, *of course,* understood its true meaning. But he blew it. Caiaphas assumed the Jews would have to kill Jesus in order to fulfill the prophecy. How tragic!

Another classic misinterpretation of the Scriptures was the belief the Messiah would come as a conquering king and not the suffering servant who showed up. The Bible clearly indicates the Messiah will certainly return in His Kingly glory, but it also shows Him coming as He, in fact, did, lowly and meek (Philippians 2:6-11). Remember, we too will reign with Him, but we will also suffer with Him (Romans 8:17). I wonder how many people believe the church will be reigning and conquering *before* experiencing the trials by fire necessary to purify us and refine us as gold. Are we looking for the glory *before* we endure the cross?

They missed the interpretation of the coming of the Lord the first time He came. I believe it is likely the church will misinterpret the coming of Jesus the second time as well. All you have to do is look at all the myriad end-times teachings and the confidence the teachers place on their interpretations. How many have come to pass? How many have even been close? Granted, some still remain to be tested in the future, but the track record of end-time teaching has been abysmal.

Another indicator is the variety of interpretations of the details of the end-time. Rarely is there agreement among the plethora of end-time teachers. Could it be that much of what we hear is merely an educated guess? Misinterpretations are rampant regarding the second coming. Do not disregard the teachings; however, take all of them with a grain of salt.

We can be assured of the certainty of Christ's second return and the fulfillment of the Scriptures; however, even Jesus doesn't know the day or the hour. Always be cautious of anyone who sets a date for the second coming. If Jesus doesn't know, then how can a mere mortal know?

Just as we misinterpret the written Word, we can also misinterpret the spoken word. The Lord told me to stay home one evening because I would have a prophecy for someone who would be calling me. I had no idea who would be calling and what the subject of the prophecy would be. I received a call from a woman who was a candidate for president of a new chapter of Women's Aglow. I was one of the advisors for the chapter being developed. The Lord told me I had a word for her and I gave it to her as directed by the Spirit. After I delivered the word, I was certain it was exactly the word she needed for her position at Women's Aglow. The Lord did not tell me that, but I assumed it by the content of the prophecy. She thanked me and said that was exactly what she needed for her position at the bank where she was working. She had just been discussing the situation at the bank with her father and was also seeking guidance from the Lord. The word answered her concerns point by point at the bank.

I had forgotten I was only a deliverer of the word; the word was not for me, but for her. My responsibility was to deliver the word just as a mailman delivers a letter. It was up to her to receive it and to understand its meaning. Just as Caiaphas misinterpreted the word, so did I.

Another time I was seeking the Lord regarding finances. I had two daughters in college and expenses were high. I asked the Lord what I should do regarding my finances. He said to get back to writing this book on listening. There was a lot of cleanup work on the manuscript and I had delayed getting back to it. I had gotten caught up in counseling, deliverance, the job, family, and especially, laziness. I assumed God meant I would write the book, it would be published and I would earn the money I needed. One day I finally got back to the book and spent quality time on some rewriting. That evening, my daughter Becky, who was a walk-on for the Clemson volleyball team, called me and said she had received a full ride for the spring semester, which amounted to about $6,000. Praise God. I was finally obedient, and He immediately came through in a way I had not expected. You look for this and He gives you that. He's always a God of surprises. The day I decided to be obedient, the Lord came through with the money. Don't expect immediate gratification all the time, but your obedience is important. It's often the trigger for answers to come forth.

Finally, misunderstanding of the spoken word will occur, often because we put our own interpretation or understanding on the words of the Lord. We have to be careful; however, when it happens, don't be discouraged. Know for a certainty that *God* is in control and not us. Praise the Lord!

Errors in Timing

This is one of the biggest problems we face in listening and understanding the spirit. I have heard it said (and I believe it) that *seventy-five percent* of the errors we make in listening are a matter of errors in our understanding of the timing of the fulfillment of a word God speaks to us. Why is that?

Here are two examples in the Bible regarding long delays before answers came. Abram was told by God He would make of him a great nation (Genesis 12:2). To the Eastern mind, that, of course, meant having many children. He was seventy-five years old at the time. The word was not immediately fulfilled and as years went by, Abram still had no children. How could he become a great nation without any children? God told him that his own son would be his heir and that his descendants would be as numerous as the stars in the heavens (Genesis 15:4-5). Abram thought he would help God out in fulfilling His promise, so when Sarai proposed that Abram get a child through Hagar, her servant, he agreed to it. Ishmael was born when Abram was eighty-six years old. Do you suppose that Abram believed Ishmael was the fulfillment of God's promise?

God changed Abram's name to Abraham when he was ninety-nine years old and Sarai to Sarah at the age of 89. He was now called the father of many even though he had only one thirteen year old son. God knew the child of promise would not come until Abraham was one hundred years old, twenty-five years after the original promise was made, but He didn't tell Abraham that. I wonder, during the long years of waiting for the child of promise, how many times Abram questioned God about the promises He had made to him?

God delights in fulfilling the impossible. When things look absolutely impossible, God will move. His timing for the child of promise came when Abraham was too old (according to man) for him to have a child with Sarah. God didn't need Abraham's help in bringing about His promises. If He said it, it would happen in His perfect timing.

Joseph is another example of timing. He was a lad of seventeen when God gave him the dreams that indicated his brothers, father and mother would bow down before him (Genesis 37:3-11). God made unilateral promises to Joseph, but they could not be fulfilled until Joseph went through the fire. He had to be put into humbling and humiliating situations so that he could learn to responsibly handle his elevation as Pharaoh's right hand. His dreams were fulfilled when Joseph was approximately thirty-eight years old, twenty-one years after he had received them. We know Joseph was thirty when he entered Pharaoh's service (Genesis 41:46). He had spent seven years accumulating the grain and at least one year before his brothers came down to Egypt. God's timing was not Joseph's timing.

Perhaps God has made promises to you that have not been answered in your life. Here are some reasons why.

First, God may have you in the crucible until you are ready to receive His promises and act on them in a responsible manner. He is working to remove the dross from all of our lives. Ask Him to show you if there are areas in your life that are hindering the fulfillment of the promises. He may be working on your pride to teach you humility, or He may have to create humility in you by humiliating you before He will fulfill His word.

Second, we have to look at our expectations. We expect the word to be fulfilled quickly. But remember, God is in no hurry; to Him a day is like a thousand years (2 Peter 3:8). We want things right now, but God has reasons for His decision to wait.

Third, He could very well be testing us to see if we will trust the word He speaks, notwithstanding the outward evidence that appears to be contrary to the fulfillment of the word. He wants to see if we have faith in Him rather than faith in our circumstances. Testing is always going to be part of our Christian walk. We are in the school of the Holy Spirit and the Lord wants to see if we have learned our lessons.

Fourth, we have to look beyond the word that was given. God may have multiple purposes in accomplishing the word. He, in all likelihood, will be working the fruit of patience in us while we wait for fulfillment of the word.

Fifth, He may be working on the obedience of another saint before the fruition of the word can be completed. Remember, most promises given by God are conditional and are often based on our obedience. If we walk in continual disobedience, the word will not be fulfilled in our lives. Don't forget, the Lord told the Israelites in Egypt that he would bring them into a land flowing with milk and honey. There were 600,000 men plus women and children in that group and only two men, Joshua and Caleb, made it into the Promised Land. The chief reason the others didn't was their disobedience, although other reasons included unbelief and sexual immorality. The disobedience of other Christians can cause us to wander in our deserts for a period of time.

Sixth, there may be spiritual warfare in the heavenlies that delays the answer. An excellent example of this is the twenty-one day delay Daniel experienced before an answer to his prayer came, due to spiritual warfare (Daniel 10:10-14). It states:

> *A hand touched me and set me trembling on my hands and knees. He said, "Daniel, you who are highly esteemed, consider carefully the words I am about to speak to you, and stand up, for I have now been sent to you." And when he said this to me, I stood up trembling.*
>
> *Then he continued, "Do not be afraid, Daniel. Since the first day that you set your mind to gain understanding and to humble yourself before your God, your words were heard, and I have come in response to them. But the Prince of the Persian Kingdom resisted me twenty-one days. Then Michael, one of the chief princes, came to help me, because I was detained*

*there with the king of Persia. Now I have come to explain to
you what will happen to your people in the future, for the
vision concerns a time yet to come.*"

Do not lose heart when you pray, but continue to seek God and, if you are praying in the will of God, do not stop praying. The answer will come, but not necessarily in the timeframe you might expect.

Seventh, sin in our lives may be delaying the answers. God has a plan for each of us; however, often we are not ready to fit into the Lord's plan because of areas in our lives the Lord has been trying to clean up and to which we have been resistant. Our sins may block fruition of the word from coming to pass. Ask the Lord if sin in your life is a hindrance to fulfillment of the word you are holding onto. If it is, then confess your sins and repent before the Lord.

God is in no hurry, and He will continue to work on us to get rid of the junk in our lives. If we yield, we will move ahead, and if we don't, we'll have to continue our walk without getting the answers we want until we overcome the sin that so easily besets us.

Notice I said *seventh* and not *last* or *finally.* There are other reasons God may have for withholding the answer. I cannot limit God, although I, as so many others, often try. If you have waited and waited regarding His promises, seek Him. Ask Him what lessons or hindrances are causing the delay in His answer. Ask Him what He's trying to teach you..

Ask if there is anything you can do to help the process along. In the final analysis, simply believe God and His faithfulness, for He is not a man that He should lie. Also, the Lord may give you such words as, "*patience,*" or "*trust me*" without giving anything more specific. Those answers may be frustrating, but the Lord is sovereign and we have only to wait on His timing.

My dear brother in the Lord Ed Wright was retiring from working at COMSAT and planning to move to New Hampshire at the direction of the Lord. He sought the Lord about putting his house on the market. He received one price from the Lord, but in January asked me to seek the Lord for him. The Lord gave me a price that was about $8,000 higher than the price he had received from the Lord. The Lord also told me to tell him to put the house on the market in February. Well, February came and went, and he didn't put it on the market. I was puzzled about the word, but dismissed it at the time. One year later in February, as he and his wife were praying early in the morning, the Lord said he should put the *For Sale* sign out that very day. He put the sign out at 6:00 pm, and in fifteen minutes someone drove by, saw the sign, came in, looked at the house, and immediately bought it at the higher price without any haggling. My friends Ed and Alice Wright didn't even have to finance the house, and this was at a time when most sellers had to help borrowers by providing innovative financing for them.

I correctly heard from the Lord regarding the amount of the sale and the month of the sale, *but I didn't ask Him about the year the house should be put on the market.* I assumed I knew the answer. Since I asked the Lord in January, and He said to put the house on the market in February, I assumed it certainly must be the very next month and not thirteen months later. I heard correctly, but the timing was way off.

What happens when we miss the correct timing is that when the time we believe something should be accomplished passes and the event does not occur, we lose confidence in the spoken word we heard, and doubts creep in about our listening. Be aware of this in your listening, and do not lose heart when the time passes. Check with the Lord to see what happened. He will resolve the confusion.

We always seek the Lord regarding our vacations. One year He told us to visit Suzie's sister, Judy, in Bath, New York, during a specific week. We were obedient, and during our visit we found out there was a Tuesday night prayer meeting at the church where we had been married. When we got there, we found that both individuals who led the music ministry were on vacations and the leader of the prayer meeting had been asking the Holy Spirit for help with the music. Because Suzie has a music ministry, she volunteered to do the music and the prayer group was pleasantly surprised how the Holy Spirit arranged for the music from a totally unknown and unexpected source since we had never been there before.

God directed us to take our vacation during that week primarily because He wanted to arrange for a surprise music leader for their prayer meeting. You will find that God is always full of pleasant surprises when you listen, and it's good to remember, God's timing is always perfect.

A Wandering Mind

One of the main problems we continue to have in trying to listen to the voice of the Lord is a wandering mind. By that I mean, starting to listen to the Lord and constantly losing our concentration. We may start well, but soon we are thinking about our jobs, the family, church activities, chores, sex, political events, our kids, etc. We soon realize the focus of our minds has changed, and we again try to get back into that conversation with the Lord. At first, we may succeed, but soon our minds are wandering all over the place again. Often, our attempts at conversations with the Lord wind up with only a fraction of the time actually communicating with Him.

How can we overcome this wandering mind problem? We have to analyze our times with the Lord in order to recognize whether this is a problem we have. If it is, we must realize God often is not first in our priorities, otherwise we would not be wandering from Him as frequently as we do. We have to take captive every thought that exalts itself above the living God (2 Corinthians 10:5). Then we must ask the Lord to help us in overcoming the problem of our wandering mind by giving us a more disciplined mind. We must be more aware of what we are doing and thinking during the times with the Lord, and fully concentrate on Him. Isaiah 26:3 states: *"You will keep in perfect peace him whose mind is steadfast, because he trusts in you."* Finally, we must develop a new habit pattern of concentration when we are talking to the Lord. If we call ourselves disciples of the living God, we have to learn to be disciplined in all areas of our lives. This is especially important in our attempts at conversing with the Lord. Let's discipline our thought patterns with the help of the Lord.

Unconfessed Sin

One of the biggest hindrances to hearing from God is sin in our lives. When we fail to confess our sins and repent of them because of the hardness of our hearts, we will have difficulty and confusion in hearing from God. We may not even be able to hear Him at all. One Scriptural example is Saul. He was disobedient when he failed to kill all of the Amalekites (1 Samuel 15). He was angry and jealous of David and tried to kill him (1 Samuel 18:8-11). He unjustly killed 85 priests at Nob, along with their wives and children (1 Samuel 22:18-19). 1 Samuel 28:6 states: *"He inquired of the Lord, but the Lord did not answer him by dreams or Urim or prophets."* God would not hear His anointed king because of his continuous sin against Him. He treats His children the same way today.

Isaiah 59:1-2 states: ***"Surely the arm of the Lord is not too short to save, nor his ear too dull to hear. But your iniquities have separated you from your God; your sins have hidden his face from you, so that he will not hear."*** God opposes the proud, but gives grace to the humble (1 Peter 5:5). Humble yourselves before the Lord, confess your sins and repent. Our God is longsuffering and quick to take you back.

1 Timothy 4:1 states: ***"The Spirit clearly says that in later times some will abandon the faith and follow deceiving spirits and things taught by demons."*** It is clear they had the faith to begin with, but followed deceiving spirits because of unconfessed sin in their lives. There will be some Christians who refuse to deal with longstanding sin in their lives and they'll be subject to attack by deceiving spirits. They'll believe they are hearing God, when in fact, they'll be hearing the evil one. We must strive for holiness. We cannot have one foot in the world and one foot in the kingdom. Continuous sin must be dealt with or we will open ourselves up to deceiving spirits.

Problems with listening *can* be overcome if we confess our sins and repent of them. Draw close to God and He will draw close to you. The best way to overcome problems with listening is to hide in the arms of the Lord. The closer you draw to God, the more the problems with listening will fade away.

Chapter Fourteen

CONFUSION, NOT HEARING ANYTHING, AND MISTAKES IN LISTENING

A long with the other areas which cause problems in listening described in chapters 13 and 15, the problems of confusion, not hearing anything , and mistakes in listening draw us away from the living God into a Christian walk which relies upon past experiences with the Lord and not into a walk of excitement, having the living God working actively in our everyday lives. As we learn about these problems and how to overcome them, we, too, can live the life of the saints as described in the Book of Acts.

Confusion

One of the many hindrances in listening to the Lord is confusion. Sometimes people hear more than one voice. They may ask a question of the Lord and they get a *"yes"* and a *"no,"* or they will hear a garbled message. They may also be hearing the voice of the enemy who is trying to confuse them. They are confused and stop listening, or worse, are led by the wrong voice. They may receive answers that are contrary to the answers others receive and confusion reigns. They ask, *"Is this me? Is this Satan? Is this the Lord?"* They don't know, and they back away from listening. Here are some areas of confusion.

One of the areas of confusion is getting different answers. Confusion in getting different answers may be a timing problem, a problem with a lack of dying to self, or an attempt to confuse by the enemy. One such example people encounter is to hear both a *"yes"* and a *"no."* What should you do when you get a *"yes"* and a *"no"* when asking the Lord a question? It may simply be a matter of timing, but God is not the God of confusion. He will clarify the confusion we are experiencing. As we seek the Lord more, He might be saying, *"Yes, I want you to do it, but no, not right now."* Ask Him to explain why there is both a yes and no.

I also recommend that if the problem of receiving both *"yes"* and *"no"* answers persists, then change the way you ask questions of the Lord. The questions should be such that they are answerable by other than a *"yes"* or a *"no."* For example, instead of saying *"Can I go to the prayer meeting tonight?"* say, *"What do you want me to do tonight?"* We will use this example later when we discuss asking the Lord neutral questions.

One of the causes for hearing different voices is a lack of dying to self. We want to hear from God, but we also want to do our own thing. We may sometimes hear what we want to hear. If we want our own way, God will not force His will upon us. He will give us the desires of our hearts, but we may have leanness of soul along with it. If our will is not submitted to God, we will hear what we desire while the Lord is trying to give us *His* desires. We will address death to self in much more detail in chapter nineteen.

A good way to avoid confusion in listening is to ask the Lord neutral questions, rather than leading questions. For example, do not say, *"Can I go to the prayer meeting tonight?"* Instead ask, *"What would you have me do tonight?"* In this way, self gets out of the way. You're not asking the Lord to give you an okay to do what you want to do; rather, you are simply asking for His will for that evening. Your questions to the Lord should not indicate a predetermined preference as to what you want to do. The questions should instead be geared toward seeking His desires, His will, and His way for our next steps in the Christian walk.

Dying to self is very important, but so is dealing with the enemy. Through my experiences in deliverance, I believe one of the main reasons for inner confusion when listening is the voice of the enemy. He is a deceiver and will attempt to speak to the mind of the believer in order to create confusion. The evil one spoke to Eve and led her astray. He spoke to Jesus in the wilderness, but Jesus responded to Satan's attacks by quoting the Bible.

I've seen confusion disappear when deliverance takes place. Numerous Christians have been set free from annoying, tormenting, distorting, deceiving, and lying attacks coming from the enemy, through deliverance. However, be aware that the enemy will continue to try to block believers from hearing from God, even after deliverance has taken place. The enemy will try to return and we must be on guard against his attacks.

God is not the author of confusion, and when there is confusion, the voice of the enemy is often present. Simply coming against the enemy will eliminate much of this form of confusion. If this is a continuous problem you have, find people in your area who are active in deliverance ministry to help you.

Sometimes there are numbers of spirits causing confusion when the believer is trying to listen. Several good deliverance sessions will eliminate most confusion when listening. I've found both deliverance and dying to self are the best ways to deal with continual problems with confusion.

Not Hearing Anything

At times, when I teach people to listen to the voice of the Lord, they won't hear anything. They see other Christians who hear the Lord readily and they wonder why they can't hear as easily. They become discouraged and feel like second-class citizens in the kingdom.

I sincerely believe all Christians have a right and a privilege to hear from God. Why do I say that? Let's look at the various relationships God tells us He has with us. First, he is our father. Would we ever expect to have a father who was silent and didn't communicate with his children? A good father always wants to guide, teach, and help his children. He has to talk to them to be able to do so.

Second, Jesus is our friend. Friends know each other mainly through conversations. They become intimate by frequent discussions regarding many subjects. I never knew any friends who didn't talk to one another.

Third, Jesus is the wonderful counselor, and one of the names of the Holy Spirit is Counselor. A counselor is an advisor and the counselee can discuss intimate details of problems with him that he/she would not discuss with anyone else. I've never heard of an effective counselor-counselee relationship without any conversation.

Fourth, Jesus is our brother. You always have ongoing conversations with your brothers and sisters. Can you imagine what your household would be like if your brothers and sisters didn't talk to one another?

Fifth, Jesus is our teacher, as is the Holy Spirit. A teacher uses a textbook as the basic text of the material to be covered, but also teaches verbally. Both written and oral material is necessary. We have the written text, the Bible, and also the spoken word.

These are only some of the relationships God has with us, but, I think you get the picture. Because of the relationship, oral communication is necessary. Therefore, be expecting to hear because God wants to speak to us.

Some of the reasons people do not hear include:

1) Unconfessed sin.
2) An unrepentant heart.
3) Doubt or unbelief that God will speak.
4) The need for deliverance.
5) You already know the answer.
6) The answer may be delayed because it depends on a future event happening.
7) The Lord may be testing you.
8) You may need prayers for spiritual hearing
9) Continued disobedience on previous direction from the Lord.
10) It may already be revealed in the written word.

If we don't hear, first, deal with unconfessed sin. One of the biggest hindrances to hearing from God is sin in our lives. We discussed sin and not hearing to some extent in the previous chapter and we will go into additional detail here. Saul could not hear from the Lord because of continuous sin. He had an unrepentant heart. Had he repented, God would have started the communication Saul so desperately sought.

We need to confess our sins, and repent. Our God is longsuffering, quick to forgive and eager to communicate with us. We may confess our sins but continue to commit them because we know God will forgive us over and over again. This shows we have an unrepentant heart. If we continue in that pattern and do nothing about our continuous sinning, we will block our conversational path with the Lord.

Once a man gave me a prophecy saying I would not hear from God for fifteen days because of my pride. I took the prophecy to the Lord to seek verification. The Lord said the prophecy was from Him and that, indeed, He would not speak to me for fifteen days. He had been dealing with me about pride, but I had been resisting. I continually asked for forgiveness, but would not change my ways. During that fifteen-day period, I received nothing but silence from the Lord even though I sought Him continuously. On the sixteenth day, the Lord resumed our conversations, but I remember feeling so lost without Him. I never want that to happen again.

After dealing with un-confessed sin, if we still can't hear, deliverance may be needed. I've found that, at times, there are specific demons of doubt, spiritual blindness, and spiritual deafness keeping us from hearing. We must bind these demons up and cast them out.

There was a pastor who had previously heard the voice of the Lord well; however, he began not hearing anything. As I was praying for him, the Lord said to come against the spirits of confusion, doubt and unbelief. I bound up those spirits and cast them out. Although there are many manifestations of deliverance, one of the most common is a yawn. He yawned, the spirits left him, and I easily led him into hearing from God again.

If we still do not hear, don't be discouraged. The problem may be a lack of faith that God will speak to you. I tell those who still can't hear to start studying the Bible about listening. I tell them to color-code the conversations between God and man, and they will find that much of the Bible consists of those conversations. When they see that so much of the Bible relates to listening, their faith will be built up and they'll be more expectant when they attempt to listen.

As I've said before, I've taught thousands of people to listen and in most of the instances, they clearly heard from God. *If we seek Him, we will find Him if we seek Him with all our hearts. (Jeremiah 29:13)* Hebrews 11:6 says: *"And without faith it is impossible to please God, because anyone who comes to him must believe that he exists and that he rewards those who earnestly seek him."*

Another major reason people don't hear is because the answer has already been given—either the Lord has spoken it to us, or it's revealed in the written Word. God will not contradict His written Word. He may not, therefore, speak to us about something we should already know. If we know the written Word and the answer is there, don't try to twist God's arm until you think you've heard an answer that pleases you.

One of the difficult areas is divorce. I and others have counseled men and women who "heard from the Lord" that they should get a divorce. The Bible clearly says that God hates divorce. Sometimes our desire or hardness of heart will get in the way and we want to hear from God that He wants them to get a divorce. There will be those times when we are in a horrendous marriage and God will release us, but often the listener is too close to the situation and is not objective. Be very cautious if you are hearing that you should get a divorce.

Sometimes God will not answer because circumstances have to unfold before the answer will be clear. The timing is not right. The answer may depend on the development of a future event or a certain response from another person. Wait on the Lord and trust Him.

Another reason for not hearing may be that God desires to test us. When we go to school, we learn the material and are tested on our knowledge of that material. When the testing takes place, the teacher won't talk to the students. There will be times when the Lord chooses to test us and not talk to us. This has happened to me and, I'm sure, to many of you. It's a dark night of the soul when the Lord seems far from you. When that happens, do not despair. Just continue your Christian walk, knowing that his *absence* is only temporary. Walk in the light you have.

You may need to be prayed for specifically for spiritual hearing. This happened to my wife. I had been teaching others to hear from the Lord, but my wife couldn't hear for three years. After we prayed for the Lord to give her spiritual hearing, she immediately began to hear.

Don't be disheartened if you don't hear about a certain issue. Ask the Lord the reason why you aren't hearing. Ask Him if the silence is due to unconfessed sin, an unrepentant heart, doubt or unbelief, the enemy, a testing of the Lord, the fact that the answer has already been revealed, or that the answer depends upon the actions of another. *Ask the Lord what He is trying to teach you in the situation. In fact, this last point should always be in the forefront in talking to the Lord. We are in the school of the Holy Spirit, and there will always be lessons He is trying to teach us. We need to be ever conscious of those lessons. Ask Him and He will tell you.*

Making Mistakes

We all make mistakes; no one is perfect, except the Lord Himself. And we will make mistakes more in the beginning of our learning to listen than we will as we become a more mature listener. I've certainly made my share.

There are some pitfalls we all have to avoid. There are those in the body of Christ who believe they never make a mistake in listening to the Lord and become indignant if you question the *word from the Lord* they've received. They believe their hearing is infallible. Be careful of these people, and be careful that you do not fall into that trap and become one of them. Satan wants us to think we are special, and he'll try to work on our pride to make us believe we are different, and more spiritual than the rest of the body. He'll make us think we have special knowledge others in the body do not possess. Be on guard that this doesn't happen to you.

All our direction from the Lord should be tested, first against the written Word, then against the other ways of testing as discussed in chapter nine. We should not be isolated from the rest of the body of Christ, but be willing to have all words from God tested by them. 1 Thessalonians 5:19-21 states: ***"Do not put out the Spirit's fire; do not treat prophecies with contempt. Test everything. Hold on to the good."***

The mere fact that the Bible says to hold on to the good indicates there is bad that sometimes comes along with the good. We need to test the words that come forth, and make a distinction between the good and the bad.

Don't throw out the baby with the bath water because of problems with individuals who give forth *words from God* which cause problems, are from self, or are not witnessed to by the body of believers. Test them, keep only what is good, and that takes discernment by the church leadership. There has been a tendency in many churches to stop prophecies and other gifts of the Spirit because of past problems with the words given or the lives of individuals who gave forth the words. It's sometimes easier for churches to simply stop the practice rather than work with the individuals who cause the problems. The Bible says to ***"despise not prophecies."***

I'm convinced problems lie primarily with the lack of care given to teaching about listening. People hear many voices, and they'll make mistakes. The key is to properly teach individuals who continually make mistakes. Give them fundamental teaching about listening, the need for deliverance when it's called for, and the ways of God in giving forth prophecies.

The difficulty comes with a lack of maturity of the one delivering the word. The wise man receives instruction. Often, feelings are hurt when a person is confronted with correction, but correction must be attempted, or the body will suffer.

Because of mistakes with prophecies in the body, churches are led away from allowing the Holy Spirit to speak. Because of errors in our own listening, individuals frequently stop listening. We shouldn't do this, but learn from our mistakes and go on with the added knowledge we've gained.

One time I thought I was led by the Lord to go and pray for a brother to be raised from the dead. The voice was urgent and insistent that I do it immediately. It said I didn't have time to get confirmation. I was young in the Lord and was *afraid* not to obey. I didn't have peace, but I obeyed the voice, went, and prayed for the man to be raised from the dead. Nothing happened except that I appeared very foolish. Later, as I learned more about testing the spirit, I realized it was the voice of the enemy speaking to me. I was a young Christian, very confused and hadn't had much training on the subject.

As a result of this, I stopped listening. I said I didn't want any part in it if it could cause such confusion. I continued to go to prayer meetings; however, I refused to give forth prophecies even though I believed I had them. God was very gentle with me and continued to speak. He would give me an anointing which would encourage me when I had a word to give and the fire burned within me to such an extent that I knew I had to come forth with it. I realized that once I started to listen to the Lord, I couldn't go back. I had learned an important lesson from my bad listening experience, yet knew I had to continue on. There was no way I could go back to the time before I was listening to the Lord. Once you've tasted and seen how good the Lord is, you won't want to return to the old ways either.

When you start listening to the Lord and hear His great wisdom, you dare not turn back. I tell people not to be a *chicken Christian*, one who wants to always be safe, afraid to make a mistake. You can do that, but you'll miss the many blessings for you and the church that come from being led by the Spirit.

I know a man in Christ who refuses to listen to the Spirit. He has been a Christian for decades and has seen many mistakes made by those who are hearing from God. He doesn't want to be deceived, nor does he want to deceive others in the Body. I understand his concerns, but oh, what he's missing.

Conversations with the Lord are a delight. To be in the presence of the Lord and hear the Master speak cannot be put into words. To miss out on that because of fear of making a mistake is a tragedy.

I don't want to be deceived either, and I clearly don't want to deceive others. I want to make sure the words I receive for me and words I receive to give to others are from the Lord. I don't want to cause any babes in Christ to be hurt by any deception I may unknowingly give. The best way to assure this is to lead a life pleasing to the Lord by reading and studying the Bible, listening and obeying the direction of the Lord. As I know the written Word more and know the voice of the Holy Spirit because of the many hours we have spent together, there will be fewer mistakes. I may never be perfect, but I will be better.

As we grow to love God with our entire mind (that is, studying and meditating on the Bible), when we hear the true God and His ways with us, we will know the truth. We'll be with the truth to such an extent that we'll recognize a counterfeit when we hear one. Those who try to ferret out counterfeit money do not begin by looking for counterfeit money. They intensely study the real thing and know it to such an extent that when they see a counterfeit, they know it instantly. That's how it is in the kingdom. We need to know the Bible and we need to know the Spirit. When we study both, and when a counterfeit (the devil or some false doctrine) comes by, we'll know it instantly because it's contrary to the Truth.

Come Back to the Lord

I want to encourage you to listen to God. Don't shy away from listening because of fear or whatever reason. Some of you reading this book now have already tried listening but have given up. You've been burned and have backed off, vowing never to listen again. God is calling you back to Him. *"Come back, my little ones,"* says the Lord. *"I am waiting for you. You have been hurt and I want to comfort you. I have so much for you. I will restore your confidence in me. The evil one has robbed you. Do not believe his lies. I have not abandoned you. Come back to me,"* **says the Lord.**

Chapter Fifteen

BELIEVING GOD
DOES NOT SPEAK TODAY,
DOUBT, UNBELIEF, FEAR,

Let's address several areas proven to be stumbling blocks throughout the history of man listening and obeying God. The importance of discussing these issues will lead to a better understanding of the reluctance some have in the area of listening.

First is the belief that God does not speak to us today. Second is the problem of doubting what we or others have heard from the Lord. Third is not trusting the Lord when He speaks about a subject and last is the problem with fear.

Does God Speak to Us Today?

I'll now discuss fears of listening to the Lord because the doctrine of certain denominations states that God does not speak to us today. There are many who believe God stopped speaking to His people when the Bible was complete. This is part of their doctrine, and many refuse to even listen about listening because of the doctrines of man. The verses they use for setting forth this doctrine are Revelation 22:18-19 which says:

> *I warn everyone who hears the words of the prophecy of this book: If anyone adds anything to them, God will add to him the plagues described in this book. And if anyone takes words away from this book of prophecy, God will take away from*

**him his share in the tree of life and in the holy city, which are
described in this book.**

There are a number of fallacies with this doctrine which has hindered
many Christians from really knowing their God. First, they believe that once
the Bible was written, God no longer had a need to communicate with man,
so that the Bible is all we need.

When the Book of Revelation was written, the Bible was not recognized
as such, so the words about adding to this book of prophecy cannot be
accurate, since there was no Bible until several hundreds of years later.
Further, many of the books of the Bible are not prophetic; therefore, the entire
Bible is not a book of prophecy although there are many books which contain
prophetic messages.

Second, the text of Revelation 22:18-19 is clearly referring to the events
described in the Book of Revelation. The plagues and the description of the
tree of life and the holy city are found there also. The context clearly refers
to the Book of Revelation. Certainly, there are descriptions elsewhere in the
Bible of the plagues in Exodus and the holy city in Ezekiel; however, they are
few in number.

Third, be careful of any doctrine based on only one verse, and especially
in this case when the verse is misapplied.

In another context about listening, God did not die and become a Bible.
The reason I say that is because some Christians believe God has stopped
speaking and believe the only revelation we have about God is in the Bible.
He is the same yesterday, today, and forever (Hebrews 13:8). He spoke in the
Old Testament and the New Testament. He never stopped speaking to man
during those thousands of years. Why would He decide to stop speaking
simply because the Bible was written? Taking the thought a step further, why
wouldn't God stop speaking during the time of the New Testament since the
Old Testament was written? It obviously does not follow logical reasoning.

Furthermore, if God stopped speaking when the Bible was written, what
version of the Bible did God use to make the decision not to speak anymore?
At what point did God stop speaking? The books of the Bible were written
many years after the events took place. Was God speaking during that time?
What about the time it took to complete various versions. In some cases it was

hundreds and hundreds of years later. Do they refer to the early manuscripts or the King James Version, or some other translation as the point in time when God chose not to speak? I could go on, but I think you can see all the fallacies in the reasoning.

God spoke in the beginning and He continues to speak even now. He desires to speak to His children, and wants to have that close intimate relationship He had with Moses. We want to be a friend of God and we can be. If you have been reluctant to even believe the Lord can and does want to talk to you, put away your doctrine that keeps you from knowing God more intimately. Look at the Word of God rather than the doctrine of man. Don't let man's doctrine hinder you from having friendship with your Lord.

What Is Doubt and Unbelief, and How Do We Overcome It?

Let's look at what doubt and unbelief are according to Webster's Dictionary. Doubt is *to waver in opinion, to be uncertain in opinion or belief, to be undecided, to be inclined to disbelieve, to be skeptical of.* Unbelief is *a withholding or lack of belief, as because of insufficient evidence, especially in matters of religion or faith.* As you can see, doubt is a wavering, which, if fostered, can lead to unbelief.

James says it very succinctly in James 1:5-8 when he said:

> *If any of you lacks wisdom, he should ask God, who gives generously to all without finding fault, and it will be given to him. But when he asks, he must believe and not doubt, because he who doubts is like a wave of the sea, blown and tossed by the wind. That man should not think he will receive anything from the Lord; he is a double-minded man, unstable in all he does.*

James writes sharp and to the point. We ask, we believe, and if we don't, we don't receive. By wavering, we continually fail in our walk of faith. Doubts are part of the lives of most of us Christians, no matter where we are in our walk. However, we can learn to overcome doubts, but it doesn't happen overnight.

The word says: *"Trust in the Lord with all your heart and lean not on your own understanding...." (Proverbs 3:5)* Often this is easier said than done. We want to be doers of the Word and not hearers only; but there's a reluctance to put ourselves out on a limb, fearing the limb may be cut off.

Let's remember the faithfulness of God. He won't let us down. Though man may fail us, God never will. We need to trust and obey, but it doesn't come easy for most Christians. There is an uncertainty regarding the word we or others hear from the Lord. We frequently ask the questions, *"Was it really the Lord speaking?"* or *"Can I rely on what I heard?"*

God wants us to trust what He says to us, and we'll learn to as we see His faithfulness. Moses didn't trust God right away, and was doubtful about the assignment God had for him. As Moses learned about God's faithfulness, his attitude changed. God brought him additional and more difficult tests, but Moses had learned to listen and obey, and he saw God's faithfulness.

The method God used with Moses is the same one He uses with us. We, at the beginning, are nervous, fearful, and doubtful. However, we must continue to listen and obey. Our doubts, which are many, will dissipate. Just as Moses did, we too, will grow in trusting the word God gives to us. The first steps are difficult and we are like the double-minded man of James; but we can change.

The way to overcome doubt is to first read the accounts of the men and women of God who overcame their doubts and fears. The list includes Moses, Abraham, Gideon, Peter, and the early Christians who experienced fear initially and then boldness that followed when they saw the faithfulness of God.

Second, we must keep listening and obeying the Lord. We should not let our doubts stop us from serving the living God. Even if we have reservations, let's obey the Lord. We'll see positive results and our faith will increase.

We must not shrink back because of our doubt. If we let doubt prevail, an attitude may develop which causes our doubt to grow and grow. We'll put ourselves in a position where doubt will lead to unbelief. If we doubt that a word came from the Lord and we'll doubt our hearing and some of us may even get to the point where we believe the Lord doesn't speak. Doubt feeds on itself and we find ourselves doubting more than we believe. Satan will help our doubt along and attempt to get us totally away from the living God by having us doubt to such an extent that we stop listening.

Here are some examples of doubt I've experienced that demonstrate what goes through our mind as we're walking out obedience to the Lord's direction.

One day the Lord told our family to go to King's Dominion, an amusement park two hours from our house. It was raining heavily that morning He told us to go, and we had doubts about going. However, the Lord continued to say *go* as we got in the car and headed for the amusement park. As we drove, the rain increased and it seemed we were going on a futile trip. However, the Lord didn't change His direction to us and though every sign we saw seemed to go against what He was saying, and in spite of our doubts, we were obedient. The rain stopped about five minutes before we got to King's Dominion and didn't resume the rest of the day.

Because of the rain, the number of people at the park was greatly reduced, resulting in *no waiting* at any of the rides. If you've ever been to an amusement park, you know how long the lines can be and on this day there were none at all.

The family was tested by the Lord. Then, only because of our obedience did we pass the test. There were doubts as we were going through the test; however, after we saw the results of the day, we realized what the Lord was trying to accomplish in our family. We were instructed to go, we were tested on the way and passed the test, even though we had doubts. Then, and only then, did we see the results. God could have said to us that there would be no rain at the park; however, where would the test be if He had told us the results beforehand? It also shows that God is not an old stick-in-the-mud, but wants us to have fun.

Doubt, Unbelief, and Then the Wilderness

The examples God gives us in the Old Testament are there for our benefit. They are there to teach us the mistakes of the past so we will avoid them in the present. Let's look at the Bible on this critical area of doubt and unbelief. Hebrews 3:12-15 states:

> *See to it, brothers, that none of you has a sinful, unbelieving heart that turns away from the living God. But encourage one another daily, as long as it is called Today, so that none of you may be hardened by sin's deceitfulness. We have come to share in Christ if we hold firmly till the end the confidence we had at first. As has just been said:*
>
> *"Today, if you hear his voice, do not harden your hearts as you did in the rebellion."*

Those with Moses were not able to enter the rest of God because of unbelief. Their hearts were hardened by the deceitfulness of sin. They had started out well, but did not continue on. Those in the wilderness had a sinful, unbelieving heart that fell away from the living God.

God warns us not to do that today. We must not let unbelief cause us to fall away from the living God. We should not live in the past, the way the Israelites did in recalling the past in Egypt, because of refusing to listen, and heed the calling of God each day.

The Israelites were tested by God in the desert to see if they would obey (e.g. instructions regarding manna in the desert). God provided miraculously time after time, and yet there was doubt which led to unbelief, murmuring and complaining. Because of their initial unbelief due to the bad report of the spies, they were in the desert for forty years. However, even though they didn't enter into the Promised Land during that time, God was still providing for them. He led them with a cloud by day and fire by night. When the cloud moved, they moved. When it remained, they camped. The desert is exceedingly hot, and yet they were protected from the scorching sun by the cloud during the day. The desert gets cold at night, but the fire warmed and protected them from the cold. God fed the people with manna, quail, and water provided supernaturally by Him. Their clothes didn't wear out for forty years, and yet they complained. (Deuteronomy 8:4) During this time, God didn't lead them into the land flowing with milk and honey, but He certainly provided all their needs. But needs aren't enough for some people. They wanted their wants, not just their needs. Murmuring and complaining were rampant.

They didn't want to hear from God. They told Moses to do it for them. They tested God, and even though they told Moses to do the listening for them, they didn't follow the direction from the Lord through His servant Moses.

They had unbelieving hearts even though they were continually, miraculously provided for by God. They didn't believe the living word of God through Moses.

What about us? Do we put God to the test? We see His miracles time after time, and yet we are often no different from those in the wilderness. Because of our doubt and unbelief, we wander around in our own wilderness, a wilderness of our own choosing. We know how to get out, but we don't put into use the principles we have learned. We wander aimlessly in our Christian walk and never get into the Promised Land. We witness the miracles of God and believe they are for today; however, they are not being manifested in our lives or the lives of our church. Why not?

Doubt and unbelief are two of the main culprits. They cause us individually, and our churches corporately, to shrink back from the living God. We don't deny the power of God, we simply don't see it. We look at the pages of the Bible and ask ourselves, since we believe the miracles, healings, and deliverances are for today, why we don't see them? I'm convinced the miracles recorded in the Bible are for today. I expect to see healings and deliverances, and I do. I will not let the doubts and unbelief of the past rob me from walking in victory today. Today, if I hear His voice, I will not have the doubts of yesterday. I've learned to trust in Him, because He has been faithful time and time again.

Trust and Believe

As we walk in the truth, and the truth is Jesus, we will overcome. Instead of doubting what we are hearing, we should start to believe the word we hear. The God who created the universe is speaking to us. *If we have done all we can to make sure the voice we are hearing is the Lord's, (chapter ten), then we should walk in the knowledge that the Lord is speaking to us and act accordingly.*

If He tells us to do something—we should do it. If He gives us a promise—believe He will fulfill it. But also know there will generally be a time of testing. God will invariably test us to see whether we'll believe the word we heard and are willing to act upon it.

The tests will vary in frequency and intensity. God is seeing what we are made of. Will we pass the tests or shrink back as those in wilderness did? He wants us to continue to listen and do what He says even though the tests will be different and, at times, difficult. He wants us to trust Him, believing He will fulfill that which He promises. He's waiting for us to move along with Him. Our growth depends on us, not on the Lord.

May we be as little children, trusting completely in our Father. Little children believe their fathers can do anything. Let's develop that same type of faith in our heavenly Father.

Fear

Fear is another big hindrance in listening to the Lord. As we grow as Christians, we have all kinds of fears to contend with. At times we have fear of man. *"What will people say if I'm wrong and it wasn't the Lord leading me or speaking to me?"* We have fear of the future. *"What if God doesn't provide for me the way He said He would?"* We have fear of making mistakes and deceiving others. *"What if the word I give to another is not from the Lord?"* We are fearful of what will happen if we obey Him and fearful of what will happen if we don't obey Him.

Fear is trusting in the promises of Satan, believing the worst case scenario will happen. Walking in fear means a Christian is looking for negative things to happen in the future. If we have fear, the Lord will help us overcome by proving who He is in our lives.

I used to be very fearful, constantly afraid of what would happen next. I was afraid to listen to the voice of the Lord and afraid not to listen. The Lord patiently helped me overcome my fears.

Approximately 35 years ago, there was talk on the newscasts about droughts on the farms and possible water and food shortages. Since I was a relatively young Christian, I hadn't learned to trust the Lord as much as I do now. At that time, I had four young children, so I was concerned as to how I would provide for them in the event of food shortages. I knew intellectually that I should trust the Lord, but I was caught up in the events of the day and I feared for the future.

One day, a friend asked my wife Suzie if she would like some chicken left over from a party. Suzie said yes, so the friend brought over a huge platter of chicken, more than we could eat in half a week. I asked the Lord why He provided so much chicken. He said He wanted to show me His provision, and that I should not fear for the future. He would always provide for us in abundance. He knew I needed reassurance at the time.

Also, our friends Greg and Carol Loss were short of food at that time and we shared the chicken with them. In addition, we found out later that the man who ordered the chicken got the order wrong and ordered more chicken than he should have, so he bought more chicken than he needed to and we and our friends reaped the benefits.

However, He didn't stop at that one incident to show His provision. One day I bought a swing set and slide and was putting it up in the backyard. When I had finished assembling the slide, the instructions directed me to apply a film of wax to the slide. I realized I didn't have any wax in the house and was thinking I might have to run out and buy some.

Just at that time, my son came running over with a can of car wax that was almost empty, and, since he couldn't read, asked me to tell him what it was. I told him what it said and asked him where he got it. He said the neighbor next door used it on his car and had thrown the can away. (This neighbor had never waxed his car before, I later learned.) Steven picked up the can and brought it to me. The can contained the exact amount of wax I needed to apply to the slide.

I thought of what God had done. He caused a neighbor to decide to wax his car for the first time, at the very same time I was putting up the swing set. He had my son pick up the can of wax and bring it to me as I was reading the instructions to put wax on the swing. I pondered the situation and was amazed at how the Lord orchestrated all the events just to get me a little wax at the time I needed it. I asked Him why He bothered to do all of that for a little wax. He said He wanted to show me He was in control, and that I need not worry about the future.

Satan is defeated by the words of our testimony. When we hear how the Lord works in the lives of the saints, our faith is built up. Even more so as we realize He does the same in our own lives. Don't fear about the future, God is in charge. Even with the little things.

I would be fearful when my wife or daughters went out at night. We live in a close-in suburb of Washington, DC and crime is common in the Metropolitan area. The Lord helped me overcome these fears as the result of several incidents when I sought the Lord while my loved ones were out at night.

One night my wife was late and I asked the Lord about her. He said, *"Don't worry; she'll be home at 10:00 pm."* I went back to what I was doing and after awhile I heard the clock start chiming. It was 10:00 pm and immediately I heard the car pull into the driveway.

Another time Suzie was late and after I sought the Lord He told me to count to twenty. When I got to sixteen, the car pulled into the driveway.

One night several of my nieces, nephews, and our children went to see the Washington Monument. I gave them specific directions about how to get there and get back home. After many hours, I was concerned when they were late in coming home. The Lord said, *"Don't worry, they got lost and will be home shortly."* I told the Lord they couldn't get lost because of the directions I gave them. They came home around 10:45 and they indeed had gotten lost. Instead of heading back to Cheverly, Maryland, they took a wrong turn and wound up in Virginia. As always, the Lord was right again.

My fears were overcome by the continual faithfulness of the Lord. After the last incident, the Lord reminded me that He loved my family more than I did and that He would take care of them. Psalms 34:4 says:

"I sought the LORD, and he answered me; he delivered me from all my fears." Notice that it says *all* my fears. He will do it. Yield to Him and trust Him for your deliverance.

Prayer to Overcome Doubt, Unbelief and Fear

We all want to grow in the Lord and get out of the wilderness we've been walking in these many years. God will help us through it. Pray this prayer with me:

> *O Lord, I have been fearful and have doubted that you have been speaking to me. Lord, I ask you to forgive me for my doubt and unbelief. I want to learn to be stronger in you. Lead me to the place where I will have much greater faith in listening to your voice. Help me to overcome my unbelief. I want to trust you more each day. Help me by giving me circumstances that will enable my faith in you to grow. Thank you Lord.*

Now believe the Lord heard your prayer and that He will answer. God will provide the way if you have a willing and open heart. He is there waiting for you. He will now create the necessary circumstances each day to make you into the strong Christian you are yearning to be in the Lord.

Chapter Sixteen

DRAWN AWAY
BY THE CARES OF THE WORLD,
PERSECUTIONS,
THE DECEITFULNESS OF RICHES,
AND THE DEVIL

Distractions abound in our attempts at leading the life of a godly person. We generally have good intentions; however, we often don't accomplish what we set out to do. We want to draw closer to the Lord, but we find time after time, our attempts fall short of the mark. We know this, we continually try, frequently failing, and like the spider going up the waterfall, we try again. We are frustrated by our failures and try to understand what went wrong. Often our failures are due to the cares of the world, persecutions, the deceitfulness of riches, or the attempts of Satan to thwart our Christian growth. In order to overcome, we need to be aware of the distractions and learn to conquer them. Here's a parable Jesus spoke on the subject, Luke 8:5-8:

> *A farmer went out to sow his seed. As he was scattering the seed, some fell along the path; it was trampled on, and the birds of the air ate it up. Some fell on rock, and when it came up, the plants withered because they had no moisture. Other seed fell among thorns, which grew up with it and choked the plants. Still other seed fell on good soil. It came up and yielded a crop, a hundred times more than was sown.*

Jesus provided an interpretation of the parable for us in Luke 8:11-15. He said:

This is the meaning of the parable: The seed is the word of God. Those along the path are the ones who hear, and then the devil comes and takes away the word from their hearts, so that they cannot believe and be saved. Those on the rock are the ones who receive the word with joy when they hear it, but they have no root. They believe for a while, but in the time of testing they fall away. The seed that fell among thorns stands for those who hear, but as they go on their way they are choked by life's worries, riches and pleasures, and they do not mature. But the seed on good soil stands for those with a noble and good heart, who hear the word, retain it, and by persevering produce a crop.

The Cares of the World

Of the many distractions that draw us away from the Lord, preoccupation with the cares of the world is probably the biggest culprit. It can hinder our being the kind of Christian we need to be. What are the cares of the world? They are the everyday, ordinary kinds of activities all of us have. A list which is by no means complete includes eating, sleeping, washing the dishes and the clothes, cleaning the house, leisure activities, brushing our teeth, bathing, dressing, commuting, working, cooking, watching television, reading the newspaper, participation in children's activities (including their sporting events, plays, time with them, homework, etc.), developing relationships with relatives, church activities, and dealing with cars and their problems, etc. There are always things or activities that take our time. Often these are put before our time with God. He may get what's left over if we have the time or energy.

We know this ought not to be; however, this is reality in the lives of many Christians. Now that we know we have a problem, what can we do to correct it? We should realize, first of all, that these activities are part of our lives and will continue to be. But we have to make time for our Bible study, our prayer time, and listening to the Lord.

Here are some helpful hints. Even while we participate in some of our activities, we can also be involved in the things of the Lord. We can listen to teaching tapes, Christian music tapes, Christian radio, or tapes of the Bible while driving the car, cooking, or cleaning. We'd be amazed at how much we can absorb during those times.

If we're disciplined enough to carry out the secular activities each day, we must start to discipline ourselves to do the things of the Lord. We can find time if we want to. Often, we don't want to because dullness has crept into our Christian walk. Why? One important reason is we really don't know the Lord the way we should. If we really knew Him the way we should, we would have a greater desire to draw closer to Him. The way around a dull Christian walk is to get to know the Lord.

We must remember, He is a perfect gentleman and will not force Himself on us. We have to initiate a relationship with the Lord. He is there waiting for us but it is up to us to decide to choose to seek Him. Anyone seeking Him will find Him if he seeks Him with all of his heart. That's one of the reasons I'm in the habit of asking questions in my approach to God. He will not force Himself on us, and He often wants us to be the initiator of the conversation. The use of questions helps in developing that relationship.

Cultivating a relationship with Him in our private prayer closet is important. This is our best place; however, we can have a conversation with Him at any time, any place. We can start talking to Him as we are walking down the street. Frequently, I would take walks at lunchtime while working to talk to the Lord. My lunchtimes became great conversation times with Him.

We can pray in the spirit as we are walking down the halls during our jobs. It's a matter of choosing to discipline ourselves into a new way of relating to the Lord.

We must remember that we can't cultivate a new relationship unless we begin to develop good habit patterns that lead to Christian growth. Some of our habit patterns are presently detrimental to us. Needless to say, many of us watch too much television. One day the Lord told me the television had become an idol to me, and He wanted me to spend as much time with Him as I did before television. He said I didn't have to watch all those newscasts and news programs. One was enough. He was right. Choose Jesus over the boob tube.

Do you know what the biggest idol is in our lives? I know what it is in your life. Would you like me to tell you what it is? It is whatever you spend the most time on. We must analyze what that idol is and change our approach to it. It could be sports, our children, our house, the internet, watching television, our sexual thoughts, etc. God is a jealous God who wants us to love Him with all our heart, mind, soul, and strength. He will not force us; we must choose Him. Let's put Him as a number one priority in our everyday activities.

God will guide us in the decisions we have to make each day if we choose to consult Him. He's ready, but usually won't interfere with our decisions unless and until we choose to seek Him and ask Him what to do.

One experience regarding the cares of the world relates to my mother who was living with us when her health deteriorated rapidly. She had great difficulty walking, was incontinent, and was rapidly losing her memory. We were having great difficulty caring for her at home. She was having mini-strokes which were affecting her abilities. We sought the Lord as to what He would have us do. One day the Lord told us to put her into a nursing home. Although reluctant to do so, we obeyed the Lord, knowing He knew what was best for the situation. We put her in the home in September, and she continued to rapidly deteriorate. She didn't recognize my children when they came to visit, and the time came when she didn't even recognize Suzie or me.

Suzie and a friend were told by the Lord that He would take her home by the end of the year. The Lord wanted our daughter Laura to see her grandmother during Christmas break before He took her home. My mother died on Christmas Eve. I remember in the past when I asked her what she wanted for Christmas, she would always say she wanted a new pair of legs. After she died, the Lord said He took her home and now she had a new pair of heavenly legs for Christmas. She is now walking with the Lord, without pain in her legs, with her new heavenly body.

Even though I knew it was the will of the Lord, it was difficult putting her in the nursing home. I had a great deal of anguish and soul searching about the decision. I used to say I would never put my mother in a nursing home, and I used to be judgmental toward those who did. I now have compassion for those who have to put their parents in a nursing home. I didn't understand what happens until I myself had to go through it.

This type of situation is one that many of us have to face. We sought the Lord and obeyed in the midst of trying circumstances. Let God be the director of all the *cares of the world* that you face. He will be if you let Him. We will always have *cares of the world* in our Christian walk; however, do not let those cares separate you from our wonderful Lord. Let the Lord be a major part of the solution to those cares. He knows the best thing that needs to be done in each circumstance.

Persecution Because of the Word

The above parable also talks about those who hear the word, receive it with joy, but fall away in times of testing. This is another part of the *cares of the world.* When we hear from God and move out and act on the word, there will be persecution and testing. We often talk about believing the promises of Scripture. There is one verse which is a scriptural promise, but I don't know anyone who wants to claim that Scripture. John 15:20 in part states: ***"Remember the words I spoke to you: 'No servant is greater than his master.' If they persecuted me, they will persecute you also..."*** We don't want to hear that, but it's true. Further, 2 Timothy 3:12 says: ***"In fact, everyone who wants to live a godly life in Christ Jesus will be persecuted."***

I myself, and other sincere Christians I've talked to about persecutions after obeying the Lord, have backed away from listening because of the persecution. Some are hurt so badly that they decide to stop listening. I did that for a short season, but I knew I had to return to listening and obeying the Lord.

If you've been burnt, know that persecution is part of our walk in the Lord. If we haven't been persecuted, can we say we are living godly in Christ Jesus? I ask you to put away your hurt feelings and return to listening and obeying our Lord. He is waiting with open arms to receive you.

The Deceitfulness of Riches

Another menacing stumbling block in developing into the kind of Christian we need to be is the deceitfulness of riches. We live in a fast paced society, one in which wealth unfortunately can be a large measure of our success. It shouldn't be that way; however, it is now and it was at the time the books of the Bible were written. Luke 12:16-21 is a prime example of the deceitfulness of riches. It states:

And he told them this parable: "The ground of a certain rich man produced a good crop. He thought to himself, 'What shall I do? I have no place to store my crops.'

Then he said, 'This is what I'll do. I will tear down my barns and build bigger ones, and there I will store all my grain and my goods. And I'll say to myself, "You have plenty of good things laid up for many years. Take life easy; eat, drink and be merry."'

"But God said to him, 'You fool! This very night your life will be demanded from you. Then who will get what you have prepared for yourself?'

"This is how it will be with anyone who stores up things for himself but is not rich toward God."

This is a sobering parable. We can spend much time in pursuit of riches and comfort while ignoring the things of God. We sometimes use the excuse that if I have more, I will be able to give more to the work of the Lord. While this is true and cannot be ignored, it is often an excuse so that we can enjoy the abundance of the ninety percent after we give ten percent.

We have a tendency to worry too much about the things we need. Our thoughts are often concentrated on the needs of our families and ourselves to the detriment of the needs of the body of Christ and the Lord. Matthew 6:31-33 addresses these concerns of ours and instructs us as to what our main priority should be. It states:

So do not worry, saying, 'What shall we eat?' or 'What shall we drink?' or 'What shall we wear?' For the pagans run after all these things, and your heavenly Father knows that you need them. But seek first his kingdom and his righteousness, and all these things will be given to you as well.

We have a tendency to want the luxuries of life. God never promised those to us, although they may come as they did with the abundance that God gave Abraham, David and Solomon. God promises He will provide the basics, food and clothing. We have to learn to be content in whatever state of life God places us and not be envious of others because of the material possessions in their life. We should be aware that their material possessions may actually possess them since they will spend too much of their time on this earth working to pay their creditors because of the abundance of debt they have accumulated. The *American dream* they worked so hard for has become the *American nightmare,* for that's what it winds up to be in the lives of too many people.

We'll also find many people believe they will be happy if they can only have *that car,* or *that house, that man or woman,* or *that whatever.* We find that once we have the thing or the person we so long for, our attitude doesn't change. Happiness doesn't come with possessions. Neither can happiness be found in another human being. Possessions were never meant to bring happiness. True satisfaction in life can only come from the love of the Lord and service to Him and the saints.

One example of God's direction being more important than financial gain comes to mind. One evening, my family was sitting together at home, when the Lord said to call Domino's Pizza. The delivery man came after the thirty minute time period for delivery, and I was ready to pay him $3.00 less than the bill. At that time, Domino's reduced the price of the pizza if it was delivered later than 30 minutes after the telephone order. The Lord, however, told me to pay him the full amount for the pizza and to also tell him the Lord told me to pay the full amount, which I promptly did. The Lord also told me to witness to him, and he was most receptive. He readily accepted the Lord as I led him in a sinner's prayer. The moral of the story is to order pizza when the Lord directs you since He might be providing you with an opportunity to lead someone to Him.

Seriously, when we wind up with an opportunity to get three dollars off the price, we think we have a bargain. I could have argued with the Lord about the three dollars, but I've learned that God knows what He's doing. If He said to pay three dollars, He has a good reason. In this case, it was a small price to pay for the salvation of a man's soul. Don't worry about money. God owns everything anyway, and He can easily replace any amount you use in obedience to the Lord.

Another Perspective on Working

We have looked at the perspective of working too much and not giving the Lord the time He deserves. Now we will look at the other extreme; that is, not working at all or waiting until the perfect direction about a job comes from above.

We all have to work at something. The Bible says that if we don't work, we don't eat (2 Thessalonians 3:10). The key is proper balance. It's important to get direction from the Lord regarding our vocations and the amount of time we spend in our pursuit of riches.

On the other hand, there are Christians who sit around waiting for the Lord to lead them to a job. They say that unless the Lord leads them, they will not seek a job. They may be sincere, but they're often lazy. If we don't have a specific word from the Lord, we need to act on what we have. The written word is very clear. If we don't work, we don't eat (2 Thessalonians 3:10). If we don't have a job, our number one job is to get a job. This is called *sanctified common sense.*

Those who are sitting around waiting for a specific revelation from on high need to get out and pound the pavement. At times the Lord will provide the specific direction after we have pounded the pavement and several opportunities have presented themselves. Sometimes jobs may seem to be too *unspiritual* for some. Remember, Jesus was a carpenter; Paul, a tent maker; Lydia, a dealer in dyed purple cloth; Simon, a tanner; and many were fishermen. Although these jobs are not very spiritual, they provided a living for those willing to work. In fact, some jobs are downright dirty and not highly regarded. So what! Don't be so spiritually-minded that you're no earthly good.

Also remember to seek the Lord about a job. Let Him direct your steps in your job assignments. He will help you perform if you let him.

Examples of Being Led by the Lord in Work Situations

Here are several examples, one good and one bad, of how the Lord worked on my job. We'll start with the good example. I was working as a procurement analyst with the U.S. Office of Education before it became the Department of Education. I sought the Lord for several years about seeking a job with another Federal agency since the morale in the office where I was working was terrible. He didn't give me permission to do so until January of 1980. Finally, He told me to submit my SF 171, an application for a Federal job, when several promotion possibilities arose.

One Thursday afternoon, I received a call for a job interview the next morning. As I sought the Lord, He told me, *"If they offer you the job, accept it."* That evening, I called another brother in the Lord who was a listener. The Lord told him, *"If they offer you the job, take it."* I went into the interview knowing the will of the Lord. The job was primarily for writing procurement regulations. I had no experience in that area, and I honestly informed the interviewer of that fact. There were fifty-four applications and I thought I wouldn't have a chance. How wrong could I be!

After the interview, I was immediately offered the job, a promotion to a GS-14 position. Since I already knew it was the Lord's will for me to take the job if it was offered, I immediately accepted. That afternoon, my office received a call from the personnel office for a release date. *Now, anyone who knows the Federal government knows you don't get a call for a job interview, have the interview, get a job offer, and get a release by the personnel office in less than 24 hours. Usually the process drags on for months and months. It just doesn't happen, unless the Lord is in it.*

To top it off, the last day on my old job was Good Friday and I started my new job on Easter Monday. How appropriate. It was death to the old job and resurrection with the new one.

On the other hand, I'll share an incident of my failure to obey the Lord regarding work. About seven years later, one day the Lord told me to take off Friday from work to update my SF-171. I was a GS-14 at the time. I delayed and delayed, and by Sunday night I had not obeyed the Lord. I asked Him if I could update the SF-171 at a later date; however, He said it was too late. The next day when I went into work there were job announcements for two GS-15 jobs in our immediate offices for which I would be qualified; however, the jobs closed that very day. I didn't have time to update my SF-171 that Monday.

The jobs were apparently wired for two other people, and one was filled immediately; however, the other job was not filled for six months for various reasons. Had I been obedient to the Lord, I sincerely believe the second job would have been mine. I learned a valuable lesson about being obedient in the time frame called for by the Lord. Another lesson is that when you know how to hear from God and have been experienced at it for years, He expects you to obey. If you don't obey, you will pay the consequences. I never received a promotion to GS-15.

Moses' disobedience in striking the rock instead of speaking to it in Numbers 20:9-12 is an excellent example of this. He was not able to enter the Promised Land because of one instance of disobedience. Let us soberly look at this example and learn from it.

Wiles of the Devil

The tricks of the devil to draw us away from the Lord are many and varied. He is the deceiver of the brethren and will attempt to deceive us every way he can. He is the father of lies (John 8:44) and will speak lies to us as we seek the Lord. He knows our weaknesses and will attempt to have us fall so we will try to hide from the Lord as Adam did. He will criticize and question the promises of the Lord and try to make us believe they'll not come to pass. He will try to make us fall and then accuse us before God and ourselves. He'll say things to condemn us such as *"You're a Christian and see what you've done."*

He won't come to us directly and say he is Satan, but will plant thoughts in our mind we believe to be our own. He will place critical thoughts about the Lord, our church, our family, other Christians, our bosses and co-workers into our minds. Negative thoughts are one of his specialties. He will try to get us discouraged and hopeless, all the time trying to lead us to eventually think about suicide. His mission is to steal, kill, and destroy (John 10:10). He'll try to rob us of our peace, kill our body, and destroy relationships including those within the Body of Christ, outside the Body, and with our spouses and other family members.

He is subtle, sneaky and wily. Most people aren't aware that they're being spoken to by the evil one. They believe the thoughts they're hearing are their own. He will have his demons speak thoughts of fear, depression, rebellion, lust, inferiority, worry, pride, etc. He wants us to dwell on these things.

He'll put doubt in our minds about the voice of the Lord. He did it right at the beginning with Eve. The first question in the Bible was asked by the devil trying to put doubt in the mind of a human being about the goodness of God. This is something he continues to do even to this day. Typically, what will happen is that God will give us a word, we'll receive it, and then Satan will come to steal that word. He'll distort the spoken word, cause us to believe God didn't say it, and try to make us believe it wasn't God at all, or try to cause us to believe God deceived us when fulfillment doesn't come about in our time frame.

When doubts creep into our lives about words the Lord has spoken to us, we must, above all, doubt the doubts. Realize this is one of the prime ways the devil tries to destroy our faith. We must come against those doubts and trust in the word of the Lord.

The Bible gives the prescription for us to follow. James 4:7 states: ***"Submit yourselves, then, to God. Resist the devil, and he will flee from you."*** It's clear that we first have to submit ourselves to the word, whether written or spoken, and believe *it* rather than the circumstances. The Word is true, even if all men are liars and we need to hold fast to it, even when (I say *when* and not *if*) Satan tries to steal the word from our hearts.

Resist the devil and come against those negative thoughts causing us to doubt. Command him to go, plead the blood of Jesus, and tell him that Jesus said it, you believe it, and that's good enough for you! Resist, and the Bible promises he'll flee. However, he'll try to come back and tempt us again. If we have a weak point, he'll continue to work on that weak point to bring us down. We need to recognize the areas of attack and fortify ourselves with relevant scriptural verses. We're in a struggle, a wrestling match with Satan (Ephesians 6:12) and we must know his tactics and fight against them by strengthening ourselves with knowledge of the Bible and of the Lord.

We are in Christ Jesus and have the right to fight the enemy. Don't give in to his ways and wiles because he's a defeated foe, and we are more than conquerors. We don't need to fear him, but rather take the offensive and attack. We have the victory, let's walk in it.

Christians Dabbling in the Occult

Recently I've noticed an increase in Christians becoming involved in occult activities. Sometimes it's just dabbling; other times it becomes deep involvement *after* they've become Christians. Television is increasingly being used by Satan to bring his direct influence into the lives of all people. Psychic television programs are becoming endemic. Satan is becoming bolder and is using the medium of television and the movie industry to draw people into his clutches.

Too many people do not have a strong enough Christian foundation and are easily sucked into the demonic realm. I'm finding more Christians are involved now than even a few years ago. We must warn our brothers and sisters in the Lord, together with those who do not know Christ, of the dangers of the occult. We must tell them of the evil they are getting themselves into, and lead them into the everlasting goodness, kindness, and love of the Father, Son and Holy Spirit. Only in the Holy Trinity can we find the truth. I call you to help draw them back from the edge of the abyss.

Conclusion

We need to know that preoccupation with the cares of the world, the deceitfulness of riches, and the devil are three areas that defeat us. Let's analyze our own Christian walk and determine what area defeats us most. Perhaps we have problems in all three; however, we should work on the biggest problem first. We cannot let the world, the flesh and the devil rob us of our place in Christ. Don't be discouraged, hold fast to the Scripture that says, *"...he who began a good work in you will carry it on to completion until the day of Christ Jesus." (Philippians 1:6)*

MORE LESSONS
IN PUTTING LISTENING
INTO PRACTICE

3/29/14

"As a result, he does not live the rest of his life for evil human desires, but rather for the will of God." (Heb. 4:2)

Chapter Seventeen

GIFTS OF THE SPIRIT
AND LISTENING

Developing a relationship with the Lord and being in a conversation with the Lord on a continual basis are critical if we want to be used to the maximum by the Lord. This is especially true in using the gifts of the Spirit. In this chapter, we will look at the gifts of the Spirit and see how listening plays a part in their use. 1 Corinthians 12:7-11 addresses the gifts, and states:

> *Now to each one the manifestation of the Spirit is given for the common good. To one there is given through the spirit the message of wisdom, to another the message of knowledge by means of the same Spirit, to another faith by the same spirit, to another gifts of healing by that one spirit, to another miraculous powers, to another prophecy, to another the ability to distinguish between spirits, to another the ability to speak in different kinds of tongues, and to still another the interpretation of tongues. All these are the work of one and the same spirit, and he gives them to each one, just as he determines.*

First and foremost, we must see that the gifts are given for the common good. If the Lord chooses to give us any gift, it's not for our benefit, but for the benefit of others. The gifts are not given to us so that we might lord it over other people, boasting that we have certain gifts and they don't. Our attitude must be one of humility, always being available to help the body.

Second, these are gifts, and gifts are not earned. Gifts are freely given by the Spirit to those who are willing to use them for the benefit of the body. The gifts are part of God's grace through yielded individuals to the church.

Third, understand it is the Spirit of God who decides who gets what gift. We cannot conjure up gifts on our own. What we need to do is get to know the Lord intimately and get into constant communication with Him so that He is our close friend. When He speaks, we'll know it is the Lord, and we'll be obedient to His call.

God is looking for availability in His people. He'll use those individuals who are open to being used. That will come with time and practice. When He wants us to say or do something, we can't be the reluctant servant and balk because we're unsure of ourselves and fear the consequences of doing what He told us to do.

When we're available for use by the Lord, since He is the Lord and we are His servants, He will be able to use us in many ways. He may start us off with one gift and if we use that gift wisely and according to His will, He'll see that He can trust us and give us other gifts as well in order to benefit the body.

The Lord is trying to use us to the maximum of our potential. If we are faithful in little things, He will entrust greater responsibilities to us (Matthew 25:21). But first, we have to be faithful with what we have. We shouldn't envy others for the ministry they have, nor should we compare ministries, for the Lord chooses the gifts. The Body is made up of many parts, and we need to function well in the part that has been given us at the time. We shouldn't complain if we're a belly button. Do whatever a belly button has to do, and the Lord, when He sees we're ready for more, may well expand or change our function in the body.

Listening and the Gifts

Let's see what part listening plays in using the gifts of the Spirit. We'll take them in the same order as set forth in 1 Corinthians 12. A word of wisdom may or may not be a word from God. It could be an impression, an example, or something else; however, since God is wisdom, He often will speak a little wisdom to the hearer for the edification of the body. When Jesus walked the earth, He heard the Father and the Holy Spirit and did what they said. He used all the gifts of the Spirit in His ministry. How did He know what responses to give to the Pharisees and Sadducees? The Spirit probably gave Him the words of wisdom at the necessary times.

I would like to say that you don't always have to be listening to God for Him to give you a little bit of His wisdom. There have been times when I've been teaching or preaching and some wisdom or profound idea would come forth that I didn't even know I had. I knew it was God giving forth His wisdom through me without my listening for it. I know others have also experienced this phenomenon.

Wisdom is also the application of knowledge, the ability to put together that knowledge of God that you have accumulated. God is a God of variety, and even within each gift, there may be a variety of applications.

The word of knowledge is simply a little bit of knowledge God imparts for a specific situation. I have experienced numerous examples in my counseling ministry. One example is when I was ministering to a man and the Lord said "dead deer." He laughed. There was a neighbor who shot a dead and the dead died on the counselee's land. The neighbor wanted the deer and he allowed him to take it, but he had resentment against him. He forgave the neighbor.

We go on many mission trips with Global Awakening and the word of knowledge is used extensively in healing. Because of the accuracy of the words of knowledge, and the fact that many are healed after receiving the word of knowledge causes many to see the power of the Lord and subsequently come forward when the salvation message is preached. Randy Clark of Global uses the ministry teams extensively in using words of knowledge with continuous results.

Before I get into deliverance with an individual, the Lord almost invariably has me teach individuals about the need to forgive. The Lord brings many examples of unforgiveness through a word of knowledge in the past lives of individuals so they can forgive and be cleansed by the Lord.

I had to overcome reluctance, and, at times, fear of man, in doing what the Lord wanted me to do. There is fear of getting egg on your face, and having someone say you don't know what you're talking about, or worse yet, calling you a false prophet. This is something we all need to understand. God will tell us to do something; we'll pit our intelligence against His and question Him as to whether He really wants us to do that thing. Of course, He'll say *yes*. We then decide to do His will, though reluctantly. We'll see the results only after we obey and will then understand why He had us do whatever it was He wanted us to do.

The reason for this is the Lord is testing us. He wants to see whether we'll obey, whether or not we understand. We'll find that once we obey and see the results, we'll have more confidence in the word He gives the next time. Our confidence in Him will grow as we see the continued fulfillment of His word in our lives, and we'll lose that earlier reluctance we had in obeying His word.

The next gift of the Spirit is faith. Sometimes faith is imparted through listening, for faith comes by hearing and hearing by the word of God. That is the rhema word, the spoken word. However, it could also be a supernatural impartation of a greater measure of faith for a particular time. Only faith is both a gift and a fruit of the Spirit. The supernatural impartation of the gift of faith is different from seeing the Lord come through time and time again, and growing in faith because of our growing in closeness to God.

The gift of healing is another gift that may or may not be imparted by listening to God. Some individuals have a special healing anointing. Healing takes place in many ways in the Bible including the following: when the elders anointed with oil, hands were laid on an individual, mud was put in the eyes of a blind man, the word of healing was spoken from a distance, demons were cast out, Peter's shadow passed over the sick, anointed handkerchiefs were applied to a sick person, sins were forgiven, and two or more believers prayed a prayer of agreement.

However, listening plays an important part in healing. For example, when Naaman, the Syrian, obeyed the word of God through Elisha and dipped in the river seven times, he was healed (2 Kings 5:14). Elisha listened and did what the Lord told Him to do. So He heard what to do, obeyed, and the healing of leprosy took place in the life of an unbeliever, Naaman.

A woman came to our prayer meeting at the Blood of the Lamb prayer group in downtown Washington and requested prayers for the healing of arthritis. As we were praying, the Spirit said to me that He would not heal her unless she forgave the doctors and lawyers. She had been involved in an accident and had deep resentment against them because of the small settlement she received. I was about to tell her what the Spirit said to me when she said she could not forgive the doctors and lawyers. I told her the Spirit had just said the same thing to me.

I taught her about the need to forgive; however, she wouldn't. I told her I couldn't pray for healing unless she forgave, since that would be contrary to the direction of the Holy Spirit. So I prayed in the Spirit. She continued to attend the prayer meetings and continued to ask others to pray for her rather than to ask me, because every time she came to me for prayer, the Holy Spirit would repeat the same statement: *"I won't heal her until she forgives."* She became more and more arthritic and eventually could no longer get to the meetings. As far as I know, she never forgave the doctors and lawyers, and the Lord never healed her.

While we are on the subject of arthritis, I have continually found that one of the main causes of arthritis is unforgiveness. When unforgiveness is dealt with, and prayers for healing and deliverance take place, remarkable results generally occur. I have seen dozens of arthritic saints have all their pain leave. But the key is dealing with unforgiveness.

The demons of arthritis often leave through the extremities (the arms, hands, legs, and feet), and the saints can-feel the demons as they proceed to the ends of the extremities through the fingers and toes. However, as with any deliverance, there has to be a renewing of the mind. If unforgiveness was a problem before deliverance, it will continue to be so after deliverance takes place unless it is dealt with biblically. If the mind does not change afterward, and resentment still has a stronghold in the life of the believer, then the arthritis demons will come back in and the pains will return. However, once the saints are conscious of the need to forgive and continue in that realm, the enemy has no right to come back in and torment the believer.

I've seen countless examples of healing when other saints and I merely listened to the voice of the Lord and prayed what He said to pray. Again, listen and do what the Great Physician says.

The gifts of miracles are in the same league as healing. Miracles are instantaneous, while many healings may take some time. They can be accomplished with or without listening, but I keep going back to Jesus. He was a constant listener and the miracles flowed. Let's follow the Master's example.

Here are several illustrations showing how the Lord is in charge of the weather and how we can exercise authority over it if He directs us to pray about it. One day in the mid 1980s, there was in the Gulf of Mexico, a hurricane that was headed on a path toward Washington, DC. During our time of intercession that evening, the Lord told me to pray that the hurricane would go around Washington. I prayed according to the direction of the Lord.

Another brother was told we were to pray that prayer, not only for us but for our children also. Again, we prayed the prayer as directed by the Lord. The hurricane did, in fact, go around Washington; however, a more exciting thing happened. The next day we found out the daughter of someone in the prayer group had an experience the night we were praying. A tornado, spawned by the hurricane, was headed straight for her house; however, it went around her house and then went back to its original path. *Now, tornadoes just don't do that unless the Lord's hand is in it.* How's that for a miracle directed by the Lord?!

At the end of February, 1991, as we were interceding in our prayer meeting, the Lord said to pray for the end of the drought on the west coast. The west had had a devastating five years of little rain and snow. We started to pray as He led us and rain came in abundance in the month of March.

Every time we gathered during the month of March the Lord had us pray for rain in California. Boy, did it ever rain. Parts of Southern California received over twenty inches of rain in one month. The Sierra Nevada Mountains had a tremendous amount of snowfall. At the beginning of the month, there was no snow on the ground in some places in the mountains and at the end of the month, one newscast related there were fifteen feet of snow in parts of the Sierra Nevada. The news called it *Miracle March.*

On April 1st, the Lord then forbade me to pray for more rain. The rain stopped in Southern California when I stopped praying. I asked Him why He had me stop and He said, *'I want to show you the power of prayer as led by Me.'* I'm sure many saints throughout the nation were praying for rain in California, but it certainly had an impact on my prayer life as I saw the Lord work the way He did.

In the late eighties, the southeastern part of the United States had a period of drought. One particular reservoir near Washington, DC was dry, and the ground in the reservoir was cracked, indicating severe dryness. The Lord told me to pray that the river and the reservoirs be filled. Within two weeks the Lord brought rain, and His prayer through me (and I'm sure others) was fulfilled. There was rain in abundance, and the drought was broken.

The next gift is prophecy. We already discussed prophecy in chapter six. We've seen that in order to prophesy, we have to hear from God. When this gift is in use, we can't give forth the words of God accurately without hearing from Him.

I would like to relate one incident when I was reluctant to do the will of the Lord regarding prophecy. One evening, both my wife Suzie and son Steven were sick with high fevers and the flu. The Lord directed me to go to a certain prayer meeting to deliver a prophecy which He had given me previously. I asked the Lord for permission to stay home instead since Suzie and Steven were sick. The Lord continued to direct me to go without saying anything else. I was not a happy camper, but went at the direction of the Lord.

As I delivered the prophecy, which *just so happened* to fit into the teaching which came later, and went home after the meeting. I had been gone about four hours. When I walked through the door, both Suzie and Steven were well. *The Lord healed them as I walked in obedience to Him.* He didn't tell me before I went that the healing would take place. He said he wanted to see if I loved Him more than my family. John 14:21 says: ***"Whoever has my commands and obeys them, he is the one who loves me."*** I was tested on Matthew 10:37-38 and passed the test. It states:

> ***"Anyone who loves his father or mother more than me is not worthy of me; anyone who loves his son or daughter more than me is not worthy of me; and anyone who does not take his cross and follow me is not worthy of me."***

Distinguishing between spirits (or discerning of spirits) can often be done by listening. There is discernment when we can sense the evil or good in a situation, place or circumstance. However, the more frequent manifestation of discerning of spirits is in deliverance when God will specifically name the evil spirits which must be dealt with. It's the Holy Spirit who relates to us the names of the evil spirits that have to be bound and cast out.

Speaking in tongues can be done without listening to God; however, in order to have an interpretation of those tongues, the person must hear the interpretation from God. Therefore, if one interprets, one must be a listener of the Lord.

We can see that listening plays a vital part in the operation of the gifts of the Spirit. If we want the gifts to be manifest in our lives, the first thing we must do is become listeners. As we cultivate that close relationship through conversation with the Lord, He will use us to aid the body, and we'll be ready.

Use of the Gifts in the Church

Most churches have structured services. God is a God of order, and that order is often translated into structure. Usually, this standard service is done simply because we are creatures of habit. We say: *"This is always how we've had our church services."* Sometimes because of past abuses, this is a way of controlling the use of the gifts. More often, it's simply that we are creatures of habit, and what has worked well in the past is expected to in the present. We don't like change.

This structure (or stricture) can have the effect of stifling the Holy Spirit. We have to ask ourselves whether our agenda is more important than the Lord's agenda. However, God is an accommodating God. Because He is a God of order, He will speak through His people at a certain point in the service set apart for the Lord to speak to His people. In many services, that is often the time right after praise and worship. The people of God want to hear from their God. It's important to know what is on the heart of the Lord for the people at that particular time.

The Scriptures in 1 Corinthians 14:26 says in part: ***"…When you come together, everyone has a hymn, or a word of instruction, a revelation, a tongue or an interpretation. All of these must be done for the strengthening of the church."***

I encourage all to seek the Lord before a service and ask if they have anything to bring to the service. Now I know this may be difficult to do in a large church. However, as I said before, God is very accommodating. He will give messages to whom He so chooses and, if given an opportunity, the word of the Lord will come forth.

There will be times when individuals are given words by the Lord, and the opportunity to give them will not present itself. What do you do then? This happened to me a number of times, and I developed resentment since I believed the church was interested more in accomplishing its own agenda than in hearing the word of the Lord. However, when I became a leader, I found that, although I had no intention of stifling the Spirit, I did so at times.

Leaders are human and they will not always hear from the Lord. If you have been unable to deliver a word from the Lord, don't let a root of bitterness rise up in you. First, seek the Lord to see what He wants you to do. God is much more patient than we are and may simply have you pray more for the leadership. If He instructs you to go to the pastor, elder, or leader, then do so; but go in a spirit of humility, not in condemnation or judgment. He may also have you deliver the prophecy at a later date. Be obedient to the Lord's direction.

The Gifts Working Together

When you listen to the Lord and do what He says, you don't need to make a distinction between the various gifts of the Spirit. They will flow in unison. You don't have to say, *"This is a word of knowledge," "This is the distinguishing of spirits,"* or some other gift. You merely listen and obey.

I'll give you an example of how the gifts work together. When I counsel individuals, the Lord usually has me work in one session on teaching and dealing with unforgiveness, renouncing the occult, breaking curses which have been passed down from generation to generation, praying for the lengthening of arms and legs, counseling, deliverance, healing, and teaching the saints how to listen to the voice of the Lord. During those sessions, which often last between two and three hours, the gifts of the spirit flow. In most sessions, healings, words of knowledge, words of wisdom in counseling, distinguishing of spirits, sometimes miracles, and prophecy come forth. I do not try to make a distinction between the gifts. I merely say whatever the Lord says to say and do what He says to do.

Most saints leave completely changed. When they come, they are depressed, hurting, or fearful; as they see how God works on their behalf, they leave joyful and full of praise for the work the Lord has done. I cannot take credit for what is done because for a good part of the session, I merely listen to the Lord and do what He says. The results are the Lord's work in their lives. Isn't He a remarkable God?

The Fruit of the Spirit

Although the gifts of the Spirit are important, we must never neglect the prime purpose of God's work in our lives. He wants to change us into His image. He wants to develop the fruit of the Spirit so the character of Jesus will shine through. In all our listening, the Lord will always be working to mold our character. We must not concentrate so much on the gifts, that the fruit becomes secondary, but keep 1 Corinthians, chapter 13, the great love chapter, in the forefront.

Keep in mind that the love chapter is between 1 Corinthians, chapters 12 and 14, are the two main bible sections on the gifts of the Spirit. Love always has to be in the forefront when we use the gifts God gives us. Where do we stand in relation to these great chapters? If fruit is developing along with the proper use of the gifts, praise God! If not, let's take stock and concentrate on our character flaws. That's what God primarily works on in our relationship with Him. *You shall know them by their fruits, not by their gifts. (Matthew 7:16).* And as the fruit of the Spirit becomes more and more manifest in our lives, we are made more and more into His image and likeness. The fruit inspectors, the church, will see the change, and isn't that what we're all about in the first place? Being changed into His image? Don't neglect the gifts for they are important for building up the body, but constantly look for the continuing manifestation of the fruit, which is the development of the character of Jesus in us.

Chapter Eighteen

KNOWING THE WILL OF GOD

If there is one question that is predominately on the hearts and minds of Christians, the one question for which they earnestly seek answers concerning their lives, and the many decisions they have to make, it is, *"What is the will of the Lord for me?"* I believe most Christians truly want to follow the Lord but are frequently unsure how to do that. We can, however, know part of his will, the part He chooses to reveal. I sincerely believe we'll never completely know His will for us since He'll never reveal everything, but just those things He knows we need to know at a particular time. However, we'll make it much easier to know His will if we listen to His voice.

First, I will again start with the Bible since that is the primary revelation of the Lord and His will for everyone. He will also reveal His will through listening to Him for direction, circumstances, and authorities in our lives, prophecy, finances, and other ways.

The Bible

The Bible is the revelation of God's unchanging universal will for our lives. The reading of the Word of God, the Bible, should be first and foremost in knowing the will of God. God has revealed Himself in the written Word, and many of the answers we're seeking are already contained in the Bible. That's why we have to immerse ourselves in the Word and know the Word. His written Word must be the foundation to show us how to live. It's a standard for godly living. God reveals His will in the Bible in order to develop Christian character in the saints. We have to be obedient to His instructions in the Bible to aid us in our growth.

What are some of the examples of His will in the written Word? I won't go into everything, but here are some examples.

Mat: 6:10 states,

> *Your kingdom come, your will be done...*

It is God's will that we bring heaven to earth. There is no sickness in heaven and there are no demons in heaven. He wants us to pray for healing and deliverance for the sick so we can bring heaven to earth.

Ephesians 5:17-21 says:

> *...but understand what the Lord's will is. Do not get drunk on wine, which leads to debauchery. Instead, be filled with the Spirit. Speak to one another with psalms, hymns and spiritual songs. Sing, and make music in your heart to the Lord, and always give thanks to god the Father for everything, in the name of our Lord, Jesus Christ. Submit to one another out of reverence to Christ.*

This is only part of understanding what the will of the Lord is in Ephesians. The end of chapter four through Ephesians 6:18 provide instructions on how we are to live. Read it and put it into practice. Another example is in 1 Thessalonians 4:3-6 which states:

> *It is God's will that you should be sanctified: that you should avoid sexual immorality; that each of you should learn to control his own body in a way that is holy and honorable, not in passionate lust like the heathen, who do not know God; and that in this matter no one should wrong his brother or take advantage of him...*

Again, in 1 Thessalonians 5:16-18 the Bible says:

> *Be joyful always; pray continuously; give thanks in all circumstances, for this is God's will for you in Christ Jesus.*

Also, Eph. 5:17-20 states,

> *Therefore, do not be foolish, but understand what the Lord's will is. Do not get drunk on wine, which leads to debauchery. Instead, be filled with the Spirit. Speak to one another with*

psalms, hymns and spiritual songs. Sing and make music in your heart to the Lord, always giving thanks to God the Father for everything, in the name of the Lord Jesus Christ.

Finally, for this book, let's look at Romans 12:2 which states:

Do not conform anymore to the pattern of this world, but be transformed by the renewing of your mind. Then you will be able to test and approve what God's will is—his good, pleasing and perfect will.

God has revealed His will for us in the Bible, and we need to read, study, meditate, memorize, and especially, put into practice His will for us as revealed in the Bible. We need to hide His Word in us that we may not sin against Him (Psalms 119:11).

Another way the Lord reveals His will in the Bible is when we have a question, He will quicken a particular verse to us. We will know that a particular Scripture has been enlightened to us for a particular situation.

I can't tell you how many times I, and numbers of Christians whom I've discussed this with, have discovered the will of the Lord for a particular situation through reading the Bible and having a particular verse quickened by the Holy Spirit. It could be that, in our regular reading of the word, we will see a particular scripture meant for the situation. Or we may have an impression to read a certain book of the Bible or a specific chapter or verse. Often, He will lead us without our knowing it. We must not limit God in how He will lead through the Scripture, for He is a God of infinite variety.

The Spoken Word

One of the most practical and consistent ways to know the will of the Lord is to ask Him in order to know His desire, will, and mind. A most profound portion of 1 Corinthians, chapter 2 illustrates how we have the mind of Christ. 1 Corinthians 2:6-16 states:

We do, however, speak a message of wisdom among the mature, but not the wisdom of this age or of the rulers of this age, who are coming to nothing. No, we speak of God's secret wisdom, a wisdom that has been hidden and that God destined for our glory before time began. None of the rulers of this age understood it, for if they had, they would not have crucified the Lord of glory. However, as it is written: "No eye has seen, nor ear has heard, no mind has conceived what God has prepared for those who love him" but God has revealed it to us by his Spirit.

The Spirit searches all things, even the deep things of God. For who among men know the thoughts of a man except the man's spirit within him? In the same way no one knows the thoughts of God except the Spirit of God. We have not received the spirit of the world but the Spirit who is from God, that we may understand what God has freely given us. This is what we speak, not in words taught us by human wisdom but in words taught by the Spirit, expressing spiritual truths in spiritual words. The man without the Spirit does not accept the things that come from the Spirit of God, for they are foolishness to him, and he cannot understand them, because they are spiritually discerned. The spiritual man makes judgments about all things, but he himself is not subject to any man's judgment: "For who can know the mind of the Lord that he may instruct him? But we have the mind of Christ."

This speaks of a mature man, a man who knows his God and receives direction from the Spirit of God, the Holy Spirit. We will receive the mind of the Lord as we listen to Him reveal His will for us at that particular time. We hear the words of God and then, and only then, know the next steps we have to take. We, as His servants, receive the charge of our Lord, Jesus Christ, and do what He tells us.

As I've said before, God will not force Himself on us. If we ask Him questions, He'll respond and He'll reveal His will for us at that time. Once we've learned to listen to the voice of the Lord, when we ask Him a question, He'll usually tell us the answer because He wants to lead us in the way we should go. He wants to light our way, for He is the Light of the world. If we ask our natural fathers to guide us in our decisions, shouldn't we expect the Lord to do even more than our natural fathers? If we ask a guidance counselor at school for guidance, wouldn't we expect to receive it? Wouldn't the Wonderful Counselor be more concerned about us than the school's guidance counselor? If we ask a teacher for an answer to a question puzzling us, shouldn't we expect to get an answer from that teacher? Jesus is the Teacher of teachers and the same applies to Him.

If we don't get an answer right away, ask and keep asking, seek and keep seeking, knock and keep knocking, for the Lord will not turn us away. There will be times when we'll have to be prepared to wait, however, for we may not get the answer in our timeframe.

We talk about developing a personal relationship with the Father and we can do it if we choose to listen to the Lord. Listening and immersing ourselves in the Bible are the best ways to get it.

Questions on the hearts of so many Christians center around things as, *"Where should I go to school?"* *"What job or career should I go into?"* *"Who should I marry?"* or *"What is my ministry?"* The Lord will tell us, but we need to ask, expect answers, and be patient if the answer doesn't come immediately. God is in no hurry, and the answer will be made clear when the right time (God's time) comes. He directed each of my children in different ways regarding school. He generally will not do it the same way for everyone because He will not be put into a box, lest we expect Him to work only one way and think we have no need of him.

Circumstances

God will work through circumstances much more than we give Him credit for. ***The steps of a good man are ordered by the Lord. (Psalms 37:23)*** He will direct by His voice at times, and also by visions, dreams, and prophecy; but He will also direct by orchestrating events in our lives which we will simply fall into as we follow our everyday, ordinary business. God is extremely creative and uses a myriad of methods to have His will fulfilled in our lives.

If the heart of the king is in the hand of the Lord, and the Lord does direct the thoughts of unbelieving kings, He will and certainly does direct the thoughts of believers and unbelievers alike for His glory. He will cause individuals to cross our paths when needed at a particular time in our lives.

Even as I'm typing this, the Lord reminded me of an incident of how He leads by circumstances. Frequently, I have counseling and deliverance sessions with saints coming to the house for ministry. One day a man took the Metro to Cheverly. The Metro is the subway system in the Washington, D.C.

area. He intended to call me when he got off the Metro and I would pick him up since I live less than a mile from the station. However, he left my name and telephone number at home and was at a loss as to how to reach me since he didn't even remember my name.

He went over to the escalator at the Cheverly Metro station and asked the first person coming down the escalator for assistance. He said he had a counseling session with someone in Cheverly, but couldn't remember his name. The man just *happened* to live four doors away from us and asked if he was looking for Norman Audi. The man was shocked that the first person leaving the station happened to know me. Our neighbor brought him to our house for ministry.

I always like to analyze situations to see what the Lord had done. What are the chances that the first person leaving a Metro station would happen to know me and my ministry? That person could have been one of several thousand other people. It should be noted that few people in Cheverly are aware of my ministry since I had been led by the Lord to a church twenty-five miles away. God, in His wonderful wisdom set that whole thing up. He created the circumstances, or should I say *God incidence.*

It helps when we listen, but even if we don't, the Lord has many varied ways for His will to be performed in the lives of those Christians who seek to do His will. Often, when I teach people to listen to the Lord, they receive answers and direction to do things they are already doing. Why is that? It is simply because they have been led by the Lord without their knowing it.

So we shouldn't get uptight and paranoid because of failure to obtain specific answers. Let's continue in the walk we are walking, seeking the will of the Lord, reading His Word, and being renewed in the spirit of our minds. May His will be done in our lives. Philippians 1:6 says: ***"Being confident of this, that he who began a good work in you will carry it on to completion until the day of Christ Jesus."*** What God started, He will complete. Even if we fail to do what we are supposed to do at times, if our hearts are toward the Lord and our desire is to follow Him, He will work in our behalf.

The following example is dear to my heart and shows the wonderful provision of the Lord, and how He creates circumstances for His people. Years ago, when I was baptized in the Spirit, I didn't *feel anything,* so I decided to have another group pray for me. Again, nothing happened and I thought I was a second class citizen in the kingdom of God. So many others whom I knew had been zapped by the Lord. They felt an anointing, starting to cry when the Lord touched them, started to speak in tongues, among other manifestations. I received nothing, or so I thought.

The day after hands were laid on me for the baptism of the Spirit, I was sitting at work when the wife of a co-worker called and wanted to talk to him. He wasn't there and she said she wanted to talk to him about giving away a Pin-the-Tail-on-the-Donkey game, a chaise lounge for a child, and training wheels for a bike.

The next Saturday was my son's birthday and I intended to get him a Pin-the-Tail-on-the-Donkey game for his birthday party and training wheels for his bike. I told her I would like to have the training wheels and the game if I could, and my co-worker brought them in.

Now no one had ever offered or even discussed training wheels or a Pin-the-Tail-on-the-Donkey game. *Imagine the timing of the Lord.* The day after I was baptized in the Holy Spirit and received no manifestation, He arranged for me to freely acquire two seemingly insignificant items, but not insignificant to me. God was so interested in the smallest details that He arranged for the offer to be made. I wanted two things and He threw in a third. *He's an amazing God!*

He also informed me that nothing in my life is insignificant in His eyes. This incident was more meaningful to me than feeling an anointing. The reality of God in my life became clearer as a result of what He did. He knows the intimate details of what we are and what we need. He even numbers the hairs on our heads, each one has a number. There's a lot of subtracting going on in my head, but the remaining hairs each have a number! He knows us and what we need far better than we know ourselves.

He also knows what each of us needs at the time. What is meaningful to one person is not to another. It's different strokes for different folks. Talk about a personal relationship with God!

Authorities

We addressed the issue of authorities in chapters one and nine, when we discussed the issue of testing the Spirit. Therefore we will not go into detail here. However, we need to recognize that God will use authorities over us to show us His will. God respects the authorities He has placed over us, and we should recognize that all authority is from Him. He will, at times, manifest His will through the various authorities over us and we must recognize that truth and respond favorably. The tendency for humanity is to resist authority, but God wants us to learn to submit, since all authority is given by Him.

Prophecy

God will use the prophetic word through another individual to tell us the will of the Lord. Prophecy will often be confirmatory to something we already know from the Lord, but it also may be a new word. When someone gives us a prophecy, we should always take it to the Lord and seek Him as to whether the prophetic word is meant for us. If it is, we should ask the Lord if He has any more information on the subject of the prophecy that He wants to tell us at this time. If not, then put it on the back burner and wait for the Lord to work it out.

Another reason for us to listen to the voice of the Lord is that we need to confirm the word when prophecies are given to us. Too many people have been put into bondage by a supposed word from the Lord and have been living in bondage for years.

Finances

How do finances come into play in knowing the will of the Lord? Many saints are *led* by the Lord to quit their jobs and go into full time ministry. Some are truly led by Him, while others are not. Even if you know that you know you're to quit your job and go into full time ministry, timing is extremely important; the *when* to quit your job must be known. One of the best ways to know if you are being led by the Lord is if the finances come in to meet the needs of yourself, your family and your ministry. If the Lord leads, He will provide.

Think twice and pray long and hard about quitting a job that provides for your family because you believe the Lord is leading you into full time ministry. A number of years ago, I was given a *word from the Lord* from a brother who said the Lord told him I was to quit my job and go into full time ministry. Whenever I receive a *word from the Lord* from anyone, I go before the Lord to seek confirmation and any further direction the Lord might have for me. The Lord told me I already was in full time ministry even though I was working in a full time secular job. He didn't want me to quit my job at that time. That was over 25 years ago. Had I followed that false word, I would not have been able to provide for my family.

I have known a number of saints who quit their jobs prematurely, and wound up in failed ministries and poverty because they either misinterpreted the word or moved out prematurely. They may often wind up confused and take jobs which frequently pay less than their original jobs since their original jobs are no longer available.

Another reason for wanting to leave a secular job is because of the ungodly things that might take place there. Christians may not believe they're making a difference where they are and they want to be around the saints more. Often God wants us to be lights in the midst of darkness. I suggest you stay put unless and until you know the Lord is telling you to go, the finances are there, and you have the Lord's timing about leaving.

Now that I've said that, also know the Lord will and constantly does lead His people to work full time for Him and provides for their basic needs, but may not provide in the manner to which they are accustomed. Part of the work of the Lord is to bring us to a point where we rely strictly on the Lord and not on the luxuries of our past lives. He may be testing us to see if we believe He will meet our needs. He is an eleventh hour God, and will often bring us to the brink before He supplies our needs.

As I mentioned before, the Lord directed our daughter Laura to go to Oral Roberts University. Of course, I was concerned about the cost and how I would be able to provide. But the Lord told me not to worry, He would provide. Well, He certainly did over the years.

Laura was in her senior year when one Thursday in May, 1991, I had just finished paying a number of bills and had no money left in our checking or savings accounts. The tuition and room and board for Laura's senior year at ORU would be about $8,400 and I had no idea how the money would be paid. I even told the Lord I had no rich relatives who would leave me any money. Then I told Him it was His idea to send her there and reminded Him of His promise to provide. He didn't say anything to me at that time and I have to admit, my attitude wasn't the best while reminding the Lord of His promise to provide.

When I got home from work on Friday, the next day, there was a letter from a law firm containing a will. An uncle by marriage, whom I had seen no more than five times in twenty years, had died in March and left me $8,333. I was amazed. The Lord provided almost exactly the amount I need the day after I had raised the issue with Him. *As usual, the Lord was faithful to His promises!*

I asked the Lord why He had done it in this way and He said, ***"Just as you like to surprise your children, I like to surprise mine. And I also have many other lessons for you to learn in this. First, the provision for each of the years was different. Learn to expect the unexpected. Second, I often wait until the last moment. I am always trying to build the faith of my people, and that cannot be done unless they are tested. Third, everything is in my hands, and I am in control. Learn to trust me more, for I will not let you down. Fourth, you know that Satan is defeated by the word of your testimony. When you testify about my provision and how I did it, the faith of many Christians will be increased and they will be stronger."***

You never know what to expect from the Lord, but know for a certainty that the unexpected will be the routine, and He'll always fulfill His promises. He will never let us down. *It's a joy to serve the living God!*

Various Other Ways God Leads

In our quest to find and do the will of the Lord, we sometimes look for the Lord to work in a certain way and He'll not always lead us in that way. Look at Paul. He was told not to go into Asia. He was stopped from proceeding into a certain area and God, at times, will stop us in a way similar to Paul's. However, we cannot put God into a box and say, *"Lord, I will begin this project, and will stop only when you direct me to stop."* First, before doing anything, we should attempt to get specific direction from the Lord. If we don't have it, then we should act based on our common sense, the circumstances that arise, the counsel of others, our knowledge of the situation, the inward peace or check from the Holy Spirit, guidance from authorities, and certainly the written Word of God which may be quickened for the situation.

God can lead us in dreams and visions. Paul received a vision from a man from Macedonia who begged Paul to come journey there (Acts 16:9).

He may also lead in general ways, but not give specifics. There are a number of reasons for this. The direction may be for a future time and the specifics are not important now. Another reason is the specifics of the direction will get clearer as we walk in the light we have. If we know a certain area is directed by the Lord, then by all means we should walk in it. As we get closer to the goal, the specific direction will be clearer.

Look at the Example of the Family

God teaches us so many things through looking at the family structure. He teaches us submission to authority, loving our brothers and sisters, unselfishness, patience with one another, and many other truths. Look at the family as a mini-church. God is the head of the church, while the father is the head of the family. If we study relationships in our family, we will better understand relationships in the Body of Christ.

Let's hone in on the aspect of knowing the will of our father in a family. Our earthly father lays ground rules for us to follow and expects certain behavior. He gives us principles by which we can guide our lives. He teaches the family members through examples and through the many situations that occur in the family. He should be giving us his expectations for the family and each family member, but he doesn't direct all our steps. There will be direction, but often he'll expect us to walk uprightly within the general parameters he has given us. We shouldn't get paranoid and keep asking him what He wants us to do next. We know his expectations, and if we are obedient, selfless, loving family members, we will walk within those expectations. It should be a relaxed, easy relationship. His direction is there when we need it, and he will give it when we ask him.

So it is with the Lord. He will not give us direction for every step we take. Being led by the Spirit should be similar to the relationship at home. God is always there for guidance and direction if we ask Him, but He doesn't tell us to do everything. At one time, I was asking Him everything. He told me that He gave me a mind and that He wanted me to use it. We are not mindless robots in the family; neither are we robots in God's plan.

While our parents are fallible and make mistakes, that is not true of the Lord. His direction is perfect and we would be foolish to ignore it when He gives it. But relax. Don't get hyper when we don't have it. He will not give us everything.

God's Will Regarding a Mate

In regards to marriage, for years my wife and I have been praying for God's choice for our children and for specifics about them, as the Lord directed. The Lord told me Laura would find a husband at ORU. She also received a prophecy from another brother that she would not meet her husband her freshman year. She did indeed meet Rob, her husband, at ORU, and during her sophomore year. She knew that Rob was God's choice for her, since a number of very specific items the Lord told her had already come to pass. Further, the first time Rob saw Laura, the Lord told him Laura was to be his wife.

In addition, both Rob and Laura, his parents and Suzie and I had the most wonderful assurance since God told all of us that this marriage was absolutely from Him. We can all now rest in God's assurance for their marriage. He did the same thing for our son Steve and his wife, Trish, and our daughter, Becky, and her husband, Lance.

We must learn to yield to the Lord regarding a mate. Put it in the Lord's hands and let Him do His work. An experience I had with a woman who came for counseling is significant. Her long-term boy friend would not bring up the issue of marriage. Led by the Spirit, I told her one Saturday to give up the right to marriage and yield it to the Lord, letting Him decide whether she should be married and who that individual should be if the Lord decides she should be married. She reluctantly did so. She yielded up to the Lord her right to be married, and said she wanted whatever would glorify the Lord the most, whether it be the single or married life. On the following Wednesday evening, she came back to the prayer meeting beaming. She said her boy friend asked her to marry him. When God is given permission in our lives to direct our choices, he will do so. He won't, however, unless we yield to the Master.

If you are concerned about a mate, constantly asking the Lord if that's the one for you, stop and rest in the Lord. If you are walking in the light you have, God will create circumstances to bring the right person into your life.

Relax in the Lord

We shouldn't get paranoid about getting direction from the Lord. If He gives us specific direction, then we should by all means be obedient and walk in that specific direction. However, if He doesn't, then we should do what we believe is good and right in the situation. When God doesn't give us answers regarding questions we have, we must walk in the light we have, and not sit around waiting for a thunderbolt from heaven.

Waiting on the Lord does not mean we are inactive. There are certain things we must continue doing, whether we have heard from the Lord or not. For example, the everyday, sometimes mundane activities need to be continued. We don't have to ask the Lord whether we should brush our teeth or get dressed in the morning. We should be constantly in the Bible, whether we hear from the Lord or not. If a student, then we must go to the school we believe would be in our best interests if God has not already directed us to a specific school.

If we are without a job, then by all means we must get one. God may, and often will, tell us the specific job for us. However, He may not. The fact that He did not specify the job should not cause us to sit home and wait. There are too many Christians who are ill-advised and sit and do nothing, waiting, waiting, and waiting. Our job is to go and look for a job we know we can do. God gives us sanctified common sense, and He wants us to use it. Finally, if we have done all we know how to do, then stand. God will do the rest. Count on Him.

Chapter Nineteen

DEATH TO SELF

We hear we must die to ourselves and live for the Lord, but what does that mean? How do we do it? How will it affect our lives? If we have been unable to do it, how do we start now? In this chapter we will be discussing death to self. The necessity of dying to ourselves is found in the parable of the seed falling to the ground in John 12:23-26. It states:

> *Jesus replied, "The hour has come for the Son of Man to be glorified. I tell you the truth, unless a kernel of wheat falls to the ground and dies, it remains only a single seed. But if it dies, it produces many seeds. The man who loves his life will lose it, while the man who hates his life in this world will keep it for eternal life. Whoever serves me must follow me; and where I am, my servant also will be. My Father will honor the one who serves me."*

Jesus is speaking here of several things. First, He is addressing His need to die so that many will be raised up. Second, in the thrust of this chapter, He is pointing out our need to follow Him, to learn to die to self, to learn to love His direction for our lives instead of our own desires for our life. Jesus wants us to decide to follow Him notwithstanding the cost to our personal desires or happiness. He wants us to abandon our direction for our life and take up His direction. We do not know what that will mean in our lives; however, Jesus wants us to freely choose Him and the direction He has for us.

We must decide to hate our choices for our lives and decide on the Lord's choices. We must get direction from Him daily, just as a servant gets direction from his master. That means we must learn to love His choices for our life, whatever they may be. We must learn to say *no* to our desires and plans and *yes*, a willing *yes* to our Lord's plans and desires.

Think what this literally means. Once we know how to be led by the Spirit, we voluntarily give up our life choices. We are the servants of the living God. If we are a servant, that means the Master decides what the servant will do, where he will go, and what he will say. In the days of the Bible, when a servant was set free, but freely decided to remain with and serve His Master, his ear was pierced. The piercing of the ears meant he was free, but freely chose to be a servant of his master. We have been set free by God, but we freely choose to serve the Lord. We are all slaves of someone, either of Satan or the Lord. We freely choose His direction for us for our lives. Our ears are spiritually pierced so we can hear from our Master and forever freely choose Him on a daily basis.

One day I was leaving a supermarket and rushing to make a prayer meeting. I noticed a car with a man changing a flat tire. The Holy Spirit told me to go over and help. I told the Lord I would be late for the prayer meeting, and besides, there was already someone changing the tire. The Lord continued to direct me to go over and help without telling me why. I walked over and volunteered my help. The man who was changing the tire for the owner of the car, a woman about sixty years old, asked me to take over since he was in a hurry. She had her granddaughter with her. As I changed the tire, the woman told me that the tire I was changing was a recent acquisition. I said, *"Praise the Lord anyway."* She was joyful since she, a believer, found another believer to help her. After I was through and on my way again, the Lord reminded me of the parable of the Good Samaritan. He wanted to make the scriptures come alive in my life. In addition, the Lord said it was a witness to her granddaughter since I was white and they were black, but there is no difference in races in the Lord. We are all one in Him. I could have been religious and gone on to the prayer meeting since it was the *right* thing to do. However, God always wants us to do His will. That truly is the right thing to do.

Submit Your Life Decisions to God

We have to choose to submit to the Master concerning a place to live, work, go to church, and in every service of the King.

We put an addition onto our house at the Lord's direction. We didn't want to do it because of the cost, but the Lord said it was His will and He would provide the funds to pay off the loan. The money has been coming in, just as the Lord said. As it turned out, He had other plans for the addition. We have a house church and could not have done so if we hadn't had the addition.

At His direction, we took a trip around the country for five and a half weeks. Again, we were reluctant to go because of the funds; however, the Lord provided abundantly. We drove 12,000 miles across the states from Washington, DC into Mexico, to California, and into Canada. During the trip, we drew closer to each other as a family, and we all drew closer to the Lord. He directed our paths, and we witnessed to those the Lord led us to. It was the best vacation we ever took as a family.

We also live where the Lord wants us to live, not choosing to live somewhere else because it is no longer our choice. We sent our children to the schools He directs them to go to, even if we, in our finite wisdom, would choose something else for them.

We go to the church He wants us to attend. It's no longer our decision. We've chosen not to make these decisions, for they are the Lord's to make. This has not always been easy. Some of the churches the Lord had us involved in for a season were dead spiritually, but the Lord had specific reasons for us to be there at the time.

He directs our paths and we, as a family of eight, have chosen to submit to the Lord. That limits our family choices. We have chosen to have only one choice. Whatever He says to do, we do. We have been protected by the Lord and He always supplies our needs, although not necessarily all our wants. We have never been without. The Master is responsible for His servants, and He provides well in that responsibility. The Lord is literally the head of our family

Witnessing

We also have to learn to die to ourselves in the way we witness. We should go where the Lord leads us, and to those pointed out by Him. He prepares hearts ahead of time. Let's be like Philip in Acts, chapter eight, Ananias in chapter nine, and Peter in chapter ten. The Lord led each one in a different way. We don't want to get into a witnessing pattern, but die to our own pattern and be tuned in to the Lord.

One year we had a New Year's party at our house for the members of our prayer meeting. One of the women brought her husband, an unbeliever. I was about to start witnessing to him when the Lord told me to talk about the Washington Redskins. After a while, we had exhausted that subject and the Lord told me to talk about basketball. We spend over a half hour talking only about sports. Then the Lord told me not to witness to him that night. He started to come regularly to prayer meetings and in less than two months, he was saved, baptized in the Spirit and immediately began prophesying.

In one of the conversations I had with him, he said his wife dragged him to many Christian events and he was sick of Christians always witnessing to him. He was surprised and delighted that I talked about football and basketball and didn't try, as so many others had, to shove the gospel down his throat.

Be attentive to the Holy Spirit and do what He tells you to do. The Lord knows where individuals are in their lives. He knows what they need. All too often, if we aren't listening, we become a hindrance to them rather than a help. Be a friend at first, rather than trying to get another notch on your Christian belt. Meet people where they are, and not where you want them to be. People want to know you care for them and are not just interested in making a convert. Love them into the Kingdom.

Prayer

We also need to die to ourselves in prayer. Seek the Lord as to how to pray. When we pray according to His will, He will bring it about.

One day a woman asked me to pray for her husband Leon for salvation. The Lord told me to pray that Leon see the neon. I simply prayed that Leon see the neon. He accepted Jesus as Lord and Savior within two weeks. How's that for God's humor?

Death to Idolatry

Death to self especially includes our idols. I, like so many Americans, tend to go overboard as a sports fan. I've learned it can be an idol in my life. The

Lord knew it, too, when one day He told me as I was about to watch the Washington Redskins, *"Do you love me more than these?"* I told the Lord I loved Him more than the Redskins. He again said, *"Do you love me more than these?"* I again said I loved Him more than I loved the Redskins. He asked me the same thing a third time and again I answered Him in the same way. He then asked me if I was willing to give up watching the Redskins ever again. I reluctantly told Him, if it was His will, I wouldn't watch them ever again. So that Sunday I didn't watch them, and I figured I wouldn't be watching them for the rest of my life.

The next Sunday I was reluctantly seeking the Lord, asking Him what He wanted me to do during the time I ordinarily watched football. He told me to watch the Redskins. I asked Him why, since He had told me to give them up. He told me He was testing me to see if I was willing to yield to Him the thing I loved and when He saw I was willing, He gave it back to me. He saw that football was not more important to me than He was; therefore, He was willing to restore it to my life. That means, in the future, God has first priority on my time, not the Redskins.

Avoiding Death

We know we have to die to self, but often we rebel. When we are submitted to the Lord that means *I can't do what I want to do.* There will be times in the lives of all Christians when we will want our way notwithstanding what the Lord wants us to do. That's nothing more than rebelliousness. And we need to see it for what it is.

Know for a certainty that the Lord only wants the best for us. We may not see it by what He's leading us to do now, but we will see it if we are obedient. We must rest in the plan of God even though we may not like His specifics at the moment. Father knows best.

There may well be times we will choose not to listen to the voice of the Lord simply because we don't want to hear what He may be telling us. If we don't listen, we rationalize we won't be responsible for not obeying, since we haven't heard specific direction from Him. Having taught numbers of Christians to listen, I know this frequently happens in the lives of believers. Some purposely choose not to listen so they won't have to be obedient or disobedient. If there's no direction, there's no responsibility.

We know how to listen; however, we aren't always willing to die to self. Our plans and ideas are sometimes more important than the Lord's. We remain Christians, go to church, and read our Bibles, but have chosen not to follow the daily leadings of the Lord. If any of us are in that boat, we must choose this day to start again. God will forgive us if we repent. We must go to Him and start getting direction for our lives. Whatever He chooses for us will be much better than what we would choose for ourselves.

The Rubber Meets the Road

Daily dying to self as a Christian is where the rubber meets the road. Are we playing at being Christians or are we living the lives of Christians? The word *Christian* literally means *to be a follower of Christ.* It's very simple. If our life-decisions are ours and not the Lord's, we are not dying to self and we are not following Him. We are all servants of someone: the devil, ourselves, or the Lord. We cannot be a servant of the Lord and ignore the directions of the Lord. We cannot call Him Lord and fail to do what He says. It's a contradiction in terms. *I die daily* has to be the theme of the dedicated Christian. It's not a death of convenience, whenever I feel like it. Rather, it's a daily decision to follow the Master's lead.

The Lord's Plans for You Are Good

I want to turn things around. Don't look at the dying and be forlorn. Look at the results. We'll bear much fruit; we'll be more productive in the Kingdom of the Lord. His plans are good for us and not evil, because a father always wants the best for his children and will work toward that end. God is much mightier than any earthly father and His plans for us are greater than we could ever imagine. We all know Romans 8:28. It states: ***"And we all know that in all things God works for the good of those who love him, who have been called according to his purpose."*** All things work for the good of the Kingdom, but also our good when we have been called and are obedient to God's purpose.

Some of the things we go through, even when we are obedient, may not seem to be good at the time, but the Word of God is true. Goodness is in the eyes of the beholder. God says it's good, how can we say otherwise? He knows every detail of our being. He knew us while we were still in our mother's womb. He has plans for us, and they're for good (Jeremiah 29:11). In His kingdom about which we can only speculate, He is working those good plans in our lives. When we continually yield to the Master, become clay in the hands of the potter, and readily, as part of the Body, submit to the Head, we can be assured the best is yet to come. He's molding and fashioning us for His purpose, and His purpose is only for good.

My brothers and sisters, yield to the Master, for it's to your own benefit to do so. Lay down your life and live in Him for it is in Christ that we live and move and have our being (Acts 17:28).

Pray this prayer with me: *"Lord, I'm willing to die to myself, my plans, my ideas, and my life. I want to live for You. Lead me each day by Your Spirit. Show me what You want me to do. I'm ready to be Your willing servant. Direct my paths. I want to follow You every day in every way. I want You to be my Lord each day—receiving Your direction to fulfill Your will in my life."*

EPILOGUE

Now that most of you have learned to listen to the voice of the Lord, you can now begin a new walk. Jesus is your Lord and Savior, and as such, wants to lead His servants into the plan He has for them. You can now cooperate more fully in that plan, since the Lord will direct your paths in ways you could only imagine before you learned how to listen to the Master.

Now begins the testing and growing since the school of the Holy Spirit has begun. Your progress depends on your cooperation with your teacher, the Lord. He's ready to lead and guide you each day, and numbers of times within a day. As you practice listening and become more proficient in learning His ways, you will speed your progress toward the goal the Lord has for you.

I ask you to begin and not shrink back. Don't let the cares and worries of the day, persecutions, the deceitfulness of riches, the evil one, confusion, mistakes, sin, doubt and unbelief stop you from daily being led by the Spirit. He wants to do it. The extent of your submission to His directions will determine whether or not you really want it. Only time will tell. Learn to overcome and learn from the problems I've discussed in this book. Learn to continually come to the Lord. The Lord is calling His children.

The Lord says to you:

"My children, I am ready and waiting for you to come unto Me. I have been waiting a long time for you to draw near. My yoke is easy and My burden is light. Do not back away from My directions for you. I have only good for you, and not evil.

My heart yearns for a close, intimate relationship with you. You are My sons and daughters, and I want you to learn of Me. I am here waiting, waiting patiently for more of My children to draw close. Hear Me, My little ones. I am waiting for you. Come to Me continually. 'Come,' I say, 'come.'"